Death of a Miser

A Sophie Parker Coupon Mystery

Jenna Harte

Kenmore, WA

A Camel Press book published by Epicenter Press

Epicenter Press
6524 NE 181st St.
Suite 2
Kenmore, WA 98028

For more information go to:
www.Camelpress.com
www.Coffeetownpress.com
www.Epicenterpress.com
www.jennaharte.com

This is a work of fiction. Names, characters, places, brands, media, and incidents are either the product of the author's imagination or are used fictitiously.

Cover design by Scott Book
Design by Melissa Vail Coffman

Printed in the United States of America

Praise for the Sophie Parker Coupon Mystery series

"Jenna Harte pulls you in and holds you captive with a cast of quirky personalities in a fast-paced story. You'll worry, laugh and cheer with your favorite murder suspect, the wacky, irresistibly funny Sophie Parker as she tries to untangle a plot that put a target on her back. A fun and exciting read that will warm the cockles of your heart."

—*Diane Fanning, Edgar-nominated Crime Writer*

"Watch out, Stephanie Plum. Sophie Parker has arrived! And she's a force of nature. Watching Sophie get herself in and out of trouble is a roller coaster ride with a most satisfactory ending."

—*Betsy Ashton, Author of the Max Max Mysteries*

"*Death of a Debtor* is a funny, fast paced mystery. Jenna Harte has given us another sleuth to love!"

—*Mollie Cox Bryan, Agatha Nominated Author of the Cora Crafts Series*

To Jay
After a year of lockdown, we're still laughing
and enjoying each other's company.

Acknowledgments

There are many people I need to thank for bringing Sophie Parker to the world. A big thanks to the Writers Group of Fluvanna who laughed in all the right places and gave me good feedback to improve Sophie's story. Thank you to the Roanoke Medical Examiner's office for answering questions about autopsies in Virginia and not calling the cops when I asked about poisoning someone. Also, thank you Jennifer McCord, my editor at Camel Press, for helping whip Sophie Parker and the coupon crew into shape, and to Phil Garrett at Epicenter Press for putting Sophie Parker out into the world. Sophie's story wouldn't exist without the support of my family. Thank you to my mom, Patricia, for giving Sophie a quick beta read to find the holes and mistakes before I sent it off to my editor. A big hug and thank you to my husband, Jay, who listens to me talk about my characters as if they're real people I visit each day. Finally, thank you to all the readers who enjoy the Sophie Parker Coupon Mysteries, and my other books. I'm humbled and grateful for your support.

Chapter One

I checked myself in the mirror of the bathroom. My thick dark curls were tamed into a cute doo. My makeup was festive without overdoing it, and the red dress adequately showed off my assets without being too sexy. All was perfect for the Jefferson Grove Winter Holiday Jamboree—not that a certain airplane repo man would notice.

I frowned. This was the fourth time in two months that AJ cancelled on me because of a last-minute job. I'd known his work in airplane repo often took him out of town, but over the last several weeks, I'd hardly seen him as he not only took jobs he was assigned to, but also volunteered to help the other repo people in his company. What did that mean? Was he tired of me? Did he think if he just faded away, I'd forget about him and our relationship?

"Sophie, I'm sure you look fine enough. If we don't get going soon, I won't get my pie entered into the contest." My great Aunt Rose's love was making pie and fussing. She did both extremely well.

"Yes, ma'am." I shook off my disappointment at missing another date with AJ and exited the bathroom. "Let me get my coat."

When I was ready, I met Aunt Rose in the living room. I'd never seen her done up more than church clothes before. Tonight, she wore a black dress with her usual pearls and sensible black pumps.

It might have looked a bit plain, except she'd gotten her hair done that morning in her usual tinted purple.

"You pining over AJ again?" Her eyes narrowed as she studied me. She had a way of making me feel like she could see into my soul.

"Yes." I figured I might as well tell the truth. She'd suss it out if I tried to hide it.

"I told you before, men aren't worth the effort."

I nodded. I might have argued, but at the moment, I wondered if she wasn't speaking the truth. She knew better than I did, if the rumor I'd heard about Carl Jackson leaving her with an engagement ring when he joined the military and coming back a few years later with a wife were true. That sort of thing would put anyone off of the idea of love ever after. As a die-hard fan of fairy tales, I hadn't given up on love yet, but if AJ came home with a wife, I'd learn to bake pies and fuss too.

I'd been looking forward to the community holiday event, but now, not so much. The problem with living in a small town was that everyone knew everyone else. Even if you didn't know someone in person, you knew their business. For example, if someone who didn't know me was asked, "Do you know Sophie Parker?" that person would most surely respond, "She's the one who's dad and brother are in prison for running a Ponzi scheme, and her mother ran off with her personal trainer." They might even throw in, "She lives with crazy old Rose Parker and she's dating a Devlin, isn't she? My how the mighty have fallen."

While most people had the facts right, their attitudes were often off. Rose wasn't crazy. She was old enough to do and say what she wanted, so she did. AJ was a Devlin, which meant he was considered to be on the lowest rung of the social ladder with the rest of the Devlins and people of Cooters Hollow. But like many social hierarchies, historical prejudices prevailed despite the facts. Everyone knew AJ and his siblings got out of the hollow and had successful lives, but that didn't matter; being a Devlin from Cooters Hollow did.

Because everyone knew my business, I'd be asked where AJ was at tonight's holiday festivities. Especially by the members of my coupon group, who not only knew I was dating him, but also that he'd cancelled a lot on me lately. I could see it already; Lani's expression of pity and Vivie's smirk and some comment about Devlins being white trash. I wasn't interested in any of that. But I was Aunt Rose's ride, so we climbed into my old Volvo and headed to the community center.

It had snowed the other day, but the roads now were clear. Thankfully, Bull had put new tires on my car a month ago. Bull fit his name; large and scary, but underneath he was all cream puff. He worked with AJ in the repo business. He also seemed to know a lot of criminals, so I had to ask if the tires were stolen.

"Why Miss Sophie, you cut me. I didn't steal them. A guy owed me."

That sounded ominous too, but I didn't ask. New tires weren't cheap, and while my financial situation wasn't as dire as it had been when I first returned home six months ago, I couldn't afford to waste money either.

As we drove, Aunt Rose prattled on about Carl Jackson and whether he would be a judge in the pie contest again. It was the same comments she'd always make about him, so I didn't have to pay too much attention. Every now and then I'd nod or say, "Uh huh," and then she'd be off again complaining that he was a liar and cheat, and shouldn't judge pie contests.

I pulled into the community center parking lot, which was an old elementary school that my dad had attended. It was converted to a community center about twenty years ago when the new elementary school was built. Because Rose was entering a pie into the holiday pie contest, we were early and therefore I was able to get parking in the lot near the door.

"If I'm lucky, Carl will have slipped on ice and broke his neck and won't be judging tonight," Aunt Rose said when I turned the car off.

I rolled my eyes. "You always win, Aunt Rose. Even Mr. Jackson gives you high marks."

"Well of course he does. There's nothing wrong with my pies. But then he adds a note fussing about one thing or another. Like he knows about pies. I know more about astrophysics than he knows about pies."

I got out of the car and then held the pie as she got out on the passenger side.

"I see Mrs. Bealton," I said as I walked with Aunt Rose to the sidewalk.

"I think she has a thing for Carl." Aunt Rose took the pie back from me.

"Really?" I had a hard time imagining people in their eighties getting crushes, then again, I recently read that there was a dramatic rise in STDs among the elderly.

"I try to warn her, but no, she gets all googly-eyed when he looks her way. Ffftttt."

"Hello Rose, Sophie," Betty said as we approached her.

"Betty." Aunt Rose nodded at her.

"I hate to tell you, Rose, but Carl is judging tonight."

Aunt Rose grumbled under her breath.

"Alice Filmore entered a pie too. But I'm sure yours will win."

Aunt Rose frowned. "Whose side are you on, Betty?"

"Why yours of course. I just thought you'd want to know what's going on."

"I'm two minutes from turning my pie in where I'll know what's going on. How does your telling me now help when I'm already here?"

Betty inhaled sharply. Everyone did that when they were on the end of Aunt Rose's sharp tongue. I called it the Aunt Rose Sniff.

Betty mustered a smile. "Carl brought his grandson too."

"He's probably a lie and cheat too. Come on Sophie, I need to get my pie in."

I gave Betty a sympathetic look. It was a wonder Rose had friends. Betty and the rest of Aunt Rose's friends at the senior center seemed to put up with it. Then again, I knew firsthand how difficult she could be, but when it counted, she was there with good advice and support

- - - - - - - -

The community event was held primarily in the large room that once was used as a combination cafeteria, theater, and basketball court in the elementary school. Tables and benches were folded into the walls, except for a few that were pulled out for event activities. Faded red and blue strips of paint on the floor marked the basketball key and free-throw line. A stage anchored one end of the room. Currently the fading maroon curtains hung shut, but when Santa arrived tomorrow, they'd open and that was where he'd take orders for Christmas. Rumor was that Lawson Davis, who I not so affectionately referred to as Sergeant Scowl, would be Santa this year. I couldn't imagine him pulling off jolly.

On the opposite side of the room from the stage was the kitchen, blocked off by a wall with a pass-thru window where the kids would get their hot meals served to them, and a door on each side where staff could enter the kitchen area.

I walked with Aunt Rose to the window.

"Oh Rose, there you are." Mrs. Conner hurried toward her side of the window looking harried and older than her sixty-something years. "Come in through the door over there." Her hands flailed around.

"I wonder what's got her all riled up?" Aunt Rose muttered to me as we moved to the door. I opened it and let Aunt Rose go in.

"You can set your pie here." Mrs. Conner patted the large island in the middle of kitchen. On the other side, Carl Jackson stood looking spiffy in his dark suit and signature fedora.

Aunt Rose set her box down, but kept her hands around it. "Carl, how is it you always end up being a judge?"

He smiled with his usual twinkle in his eye. "Ah Rose, I'd never miss judging one of your pies. They're to die for."

She scowled. "If you say my pie kills people, I'll throttle you myself."

"I think he meant that as a compliment," I murmured to her.

"No, he didn't. You've got to be careful with sly foxes like Carl. Don't let their charm fool you."

He grinned. "I look forward to your pie. What did you bring?" He reached toward her box, but she pulled it back.

"Just you never mind until the contest."

He laughed, and walked away.

"Don't you worry about it, Rose." Mrs. Conner scribbled on her clipboard. "Carl just likes to poke at you sometimes."

"Let him go poke someone else," Aunt Rose said.

"You can leave the pie. I'll take care of it." Mrs. Connor reached for Aunt Rose's pie box.

Aunt Rose's eyes narrowed. "Where are the other pies?"

"They're on the counter over there. I'll put yours there too." Mrs. Conner taped a slip of paper with some sort of code on Aunt Rose's box. I guess that was to identify who owned the pie after the blind taste test.

Aunt Rose finally relinquished her pie.

"Why don't we go find Betty?" I said.

"When is the contest?" Aunt Rose asked.

"Eight o'clock." Mrs. Conner picked up the pie box and brought it to the counter at the back of the kitchen.

Aunt Rose nodded and we turned to leave but were stopped when Alice Filmore entered. Alice was my father's age, in her mid-fifties, but she looked older. She'd always reminded me of the woman in the American Gothic painting. She had the long narrow face and her graying hair pulled back in a low bun. She never smiled, although she wasn't necessarily dour. She'd married old man Filmore, who everyone called Tubby, when she was forty and he was in his mid-sixties. Tubby lived up to his name weighing over three hundred pounds when he died. Interesting, it wasn't an obesity-related heart attack that took him. He was incinerated when he lit his cigarette while distilling moonshine in the woods in the back of their house. Apparently, moonshine fumes were flammable.

"Rose," Alice said with a curt nod to my aunt.

"Alice," Aunt Rose responded with the same tone. Alice and Aunt Rose normally got along, except during a pie contest. They were both fierce competitors when it came to pie. According to my dad, Aunt Rose had been the one to encourage Alice to submit a pie years ago at the county fair. When Alice won that year, Aunt Rose wasn't happy about it. Since then, they've had a rivalry. Aunt Rose said that one year, Alice paid the judges to help her win. Even so, Aunt Rose still won more often than not, but she believed so deeply in her pies that in her mind, she should always win.

It was strange; when they weren't competing, they seemed to be friendly, which was odd for Aunt Rose. She wasn't one to change how she treated someone. She either liked or didn't like a person. There wasn't much in-between or indifference. Maybe Alice was treated different because Tubby had been Aunt Rose's cousin. Or maybe it was because Alice thought Carl Jackson was a lying cheat too because apparently, he'd swindled Tubby out of some sort of business or real estate deal.

"How are you, Sophie?" Alice asked me.

"I'm very good, and you Ms. Filmore?"

"I'm alive. I have to thank the good Lord for that."

Aunt Rose rolled her eyes. "Come on Sophie, let's go find the eggnog."

We left the kitchen and entered the main festivities area. While there were other rooms in the building hosting activities, most were in the large hall. More people were arriving, and kids were running around looking for Santa.

"Ms. Parker, Sophie, Merry Christmas." Aggie Parnell from my coupon group stepped up to us with her husband Earl.

"Merry Christmas," I said. "Aunt Rose, you remember Mr. and Mrs. Parnell."

"Sophie, I'm old but not forgetful. I've known Aggie and Earl since before your daddy was born. How are you?"

"We can't complain, can we Aggie?" Earl said with a grin to his wife.

"Well, we could but who'd want to listen?" Aggie responded. Aggie and Earl were in their seventies and retired. They both had cocoa skin, white hair and twinkle in their eyes, although Aggie's always looked mischievous while Earl's was charming.

"We're looking for the adult eggnog," Earl said giving me a wink.

"You know they're not allowed to serve alcohol here," Aggie said.

"This is the south, honey. Since when do we follow the rules, especially when alcohol is involved?" Earl smiled, showing a full set of white teeth one would expect from a man that had once been a dentist.

"I'd like some of that adult eggnog myself," Aunt Rose said. "Do they use bourbon or whisky?"

"Does it really matter?" Earl asked.

"I suppose not."

"Sophie." I heard my name called from across the room. I turned and saw my best friend since high school, Lani, with her husband Dwayne. Since he wasn't in his deputy uniform, I guessed he was off duty.

"I'm going to say hello to Lani and Dwayne." I looked at Aunt Rose to make sure she was alright with that. I'd just turned twenty-eight, but felt I needed permission to do some things when it came to Aunt Rose.

"Yes, yes, go." Aunt Rose shooed me away. I had to hope Aggie would keep her from drinking too much adult eggnog that was certainly flowing somewhere in the building. During the fall, I'd woken to Aunt Rose sleep walking. It took a little investigating, but I finally figured out that it happened on days when she hadn't watered down her bourbon.

I made my way over to Lani. Unlike me, Lani had never left Jefferson Grove after graduation. She'd stayed home and married her high school sweetheart, Dwayne Lafferty. She and I had kept in touch when I went off to college and then attempted to live on my own. She'd been the only friend I had when I first returned home, broke and carrying the burden of my father's sins.

"Hey, you off tonight?" I asked Dwayne.

"Yep. Taking my gal out for a night on the town." He leaned over and gave Lani a kiss on the cheek. They'd been a married ten years and were still really sweet together. I wondered if AJ and I would make it ten years—not if he kept cancelling on me, we wouldn't.

"Is AJ here?" Lani asked.

"He had to work."

She frowned. "Again? What's up with that?"

I shrugged. In the past I'd come up with an excuse, but I was tired of trying to justify his behavior.

"What sort of plane is he getting?" Dwayne asked.

Lani pursed her lips. "Who cares? No repo is worth standing Sophie up."

As if he'd just caught on, Dwayne shook his head with disapproval. "Nah man, that's not cool."

"Hey girls." Vivie's voice cut through the din of voices around us. Vivie was in the coupon group with Lani, Aggie and me. She was the classic soccer mom with her blonde hair, an hour-a-day at the gym—her toned body, and fake tan. She'd hated me from high school on until a few months ago when I helped clear her of a murder she was accused of committing. While we got along at the moment, I wasn't convinced she wouldn't someday turn on me again. Vivie could be a fair-weathered friend, and living in the south, I was aware that storms could come out of nowhere.

"Hey Viv," Lani said.

"I'm getting some punch." Dwayne rushed off. I didn't blame him. Vivie could be hard to take.

"Where's AJ?" Vivie scanned the room.

"He had to work."

Her gaze swung to me, her blonde hair whipping around like a shampoo commercial. "Again?"

I shrugged and waited for whatever snarky retort she'd give.

"You know, Carl Jackson's grandson is visiting and he's a looker, Sophie. You should find him before Gwen gets her talons in him." Vivie nodded to the other side of the room, where another member of our coupon group, Gwen, stood talking to a man I didn't know, but based on what Vivie said, I suspected was Carl Jackson's grandson.

Gwen stood out not so much because she died the tips of her page boy haircut interesting colors, green this week, but because no other woman in Jefferson Grove was six feet tall. Carl Jackson's grandson, unfortunately, didn't quite reach six feet, which made Gwen stand out more next to him.

"Gwen, bless her heart, should move to a place with a basketball team," Vivie said with a shake of her head. "What man wants to walk around being shorter than his wife?"

"Tom Cruise did it," Lani quipped.

"He's not married now, though, is he?" Vivie snapped back. She turned to me. "Really Sophie, AJ doesn't appreciate you. You should move on and Tyler Jackson could be the guy. He's going to inherit Carl's estate. You'll be rich again."

"Carl Jackson isn't rich," I said. Not that he was poor, but Vivie's definition of rich involved a large house in Monticello Heights or a horse estate, a fifty-thousand-dollar car, and named brand clothes. Carl lived in a brick rancher just outside of the downtown limits, drove a mid-2000s Buick, and as far as I could tell, owned only two suits; a white one in summer that made him look like Colonel Sanders, and a dark one like he wore tonight.

"Sure, he is. He just doesn't spend it or share it. My mama calls him Scrooge Jackson," Vivie said.

"I've heard that too." Lani nodded. "That he's tight with a nickel."

My Aunt Rose often said things about his miserly ways, but I figured that was just her complaining about him.

"Even so, I can't date his grandson. Aunt Rose despises Carl. I couldn't put her through that."

Vivie rolled her eyes. "Your aunt despises everyone. Besides, Carl will be dead and y'all would be rich. Surely that would be worth it even to Rose."

In Vivie's world, money trumped just about everything.

"Where's Randy?" Lani asked of Vivie's husband, changing the subject. I mouthed thank you to let her know I appreciated it.

"I don't know." Vivie's gaze scanned the room again and her expression was impassive, but I didn't buy it.

I looked at Lani, who's eyes widened for an instant giving me the impression that she was thinking the same thing I was; the honeymoon for Vivie and Randy must be over. It was bound to happen, much like eventually Vivie would change her tune about me. Vivie and Randy were high school sweethearts, except for the one week I'd dated him, and caused Vivie's original dislike of me. They got pregnant and married, had a few more kids, and lived in the affluent Monticello Heights neighborhood although I knew money was tight. Both had cheated on the other, but after Vivie's and my ordeal a few months back when she and I were locked in the trunk of a car by a murderer who was planning to add us to the list, she and Randy had a reconciliation. It appeared those sunny days were waning.

Since I no longer worked at the Booty Burgo, the pirate-themed sports bar Randy owned where I'd once bartended, I didn't know if Randy was back trolling for women as he used to do there.

"I see Amy. I'm going to say hi. Don't forget what I said, Sophie. Go talk to Tyler. He's much better for you than any Devlin." Vivie walked off toward another group of women.

"Where do you think her kids are?" I asked Lani. I scanned the area and saw the usual people. After being gone ten years, it was strange to see people I'd known in high school, now as adults—especially when they had kids running about.

"Probably at home with her mother. I think the majority of kids activities are tomorrow."

I nodded in agreement. "Dwayne is sure taking a long time with that punch." I looked toward the refreshment area and saw him chatting with Mrs. Willoughby. I didn't know her well, but had gone to high school with her son.

"Now that Vivie has sauntered off, he'll be back." Lani frowned. "I know you said you weren't interested in Tyler Jackson, but what I didn't hear is you stick up for AJ. What's going on Sophie?"

"You know what's going on." Hurry up Dwayne. This was another conversation I didn't want to have.

"He's working at lot. You used to work a lot too at the Booty Burgo and the library. Remember how he'd meet you at two in the morning at closing."

I did. It felt like forever ago, even though it was only a few months. "It's different. I can't go meet him after work. He's usually out of state."

Her expression was sad, like how fans look when they learn their favorite celebrity couple has called it quits. "You're not thinking it's going to end, do you?"

My nose burned, the telltale sign that tears were close by. "I don't know. I just feel like maybe he's not that into me anymore."

"Girl, you need to fight." Lani's exotic green eyes turned fierce.

"If you want him, fight. Or at least find out what's going on. You can't live in love limbo."

I swallowed back my tears. "You're right."

"Of course, I'm right."

"Who's right?" Dwayne said as he rejoined us.

"I am." Lani's expression dared him to disagree.

He grinned. "Well of course you are honey." He kissed her temple again. "I got us cider instead of punch. It's Mrs. Fillmore's."

"Oh, she makes good cider." Lani took the cup he offered. Then she looked at me again. "Think about what I said. You need to talk to AJ about how you're feeling."

I took my cup of warm cider from Dwayne and nodded. Even if she was right, I had no choice but to stay in love limbo until I saw AJ again, and who knew when that would be?

Chapter Two

When I first moved back to Jefferson Grove six months ago, I'd resigned myself to being a hermit. I'd grown up in the small Blue Ridge town, so I knew firsthand that everyone knew everyone else's business and gossip was a commodity. Coming home after my father and brother went to prison, while my mother escaped arrest by running off with her personal trainer, there was a lot of business and gossip surrounding me. So, my goal was to hide and not have to suffer the looks and whispers, and in some cases outright confrontation from townsfolk.

But within a couple of months of coming home, I had friends in a coupon group and a boyfriend, albeit he was from Cooters Hollow, the mountain version of the other side of the tracks. I'd even helped solve a murder, which elevated my status, although not to the heights it had been when I grew up here. That was okay. I didn't need to be rich and popular.

Now six months later, I felt acclimated back into the community. People probably still talked, but with good friends like Lani, and A.J., when he was around, I wasn't alone. Even Aunt Rose was on my side when I really needed it.

With their support, spending the evening with people of the community wasn't scary for me anymore, and along with Lani and

Dwayne, I mingled and circulated to catch up on . . . yep . . . gossip. When Dwayne saw Sergeant Scowl arrive, he wandered off to talk to him. Men just didn't have the stamina for gossip.

Lani and I saw Gwen with Tyler Jackson and decided it was time to meet Aunt Rose's nemesis' grandson.

"He is cute," Lani said as we drew closer.

Gwen saw us, her eyes narrowed slightly, but then she smiled.

Lani leaned toward me and whispered. "I think that quick glare was a message that Tyler is hers."

"Why would she be worried about us?"

Lani gave me that pity look. "Because you know . . . you and A.J . . ."

"I'm not interested in Tyler Jackson." We reached Gwen. "Happy Holidays."

"This is much more of an old fogies' event," Gwen said. "I was trying to talk Tyler into heading up to the Booty Burgo."

I shivered. If I ever walked into the Booty Burgo again, it would be too soon. I was done with the wench waitress uniform, even if A.J. found it alluring.

"Hi, I'm Lani and this is Sophie."

"Oh, I'm sorry, where are my manners?" Gwen said with a slight slackness in her words. I got the feeling she'd found the adult eggnog. "This is Tyler Jackson, he's Carl Jackson's grandson." Gwen looked over at me. "You might not want your aunt to know you're hanging out with the enemy."

"Enemy?" Tyler looked to Lani and then me. Lani was right in that he was handsome in a polished sort of way. I could tell by looking at him he was a city boy so Jefferson Grove had to feel like the end of the earth to him.

"My great aunt is Rose Parker." I watched his expression to see if there was any indication that he knew her. Did Carl talk about my aunt?

"Who?" His ignorance appeared genuine.

"Well, that's a first." Gwen laughed. "Everyone in Jefferson Grove knows Rose Parker and her disdain for your grandfather."

Tyler smiled but his eyes narrowed in confusion. "Why?"

"I'm not sure." I shrugged. Of course, I had an inkling, but I wasn't about to spread gossip about my aunt. She was just ornery enough to retaliate if she found I'd been talking about her.

"Rumor is that he dumped her," Gwen said with a mischievous glint in her eye. Gwen was normally nice, so I suspect booze and wanting to keep Tyler to herself were the cause of her snippy tongue toward me.

Tyler sighed. "There are a lot of rumors about his loving and leaving women."

All three of us went wide-eyed.

"Really?" Now I was curious.

"Do spill the tea, Tyler." Gwen leaned closer to him.

"I don't know the details so much as he's known to use his charm to get what he wants."

I laughed. "His charm doesn't work on Aunt Rose. At least not now."

"Once bitten twice shy." Lani nodded in agreement.

"You're saying my grandfather likes your aunt?" Tyler asked.

"I don't know about like in a romantic way. He enjoys poking at her. You know, like a schoolboy pulling the pigtail of a schoolgirl." At least that was the way I saw it.

"He never gives up, though. Must be the challenge of the chase," Gwen said. "Maybe that's why Aunt Rose always wins the pie contests."

"Oh lordy, don't say that anywhere around her." I quickly scanned the area to make sure she wasn't close by. I saw her over by Alice Filmore, Carolyn Jenkinson, and the other pie contestants as the pies were being brought out for the taste testing.

"You do like to live on the edge, don't you, Gwen." Lani laughed.

"She doesn't scare me." Gwen flicked back her green-tipped hair with a red, glittery fingernail.

"You're not from around here," Lani said.

"Why are people afraid of her?" Tyler asked.

"She's got a sharp tongue and isn't afraid to skewer you with it." Lani looked to me as if she wanted verification or for me to expound.

"She doesn't put up with nonsense and will call you out on it. She doesn't have a filter. And, she can hold a grudge," I expounded.

Tyler shrugged. I supposed in the scheme of scary things, Aunt Rose would be low on the list. She wasn't deadly like a snake. Still, most people in town tried to avoid her except her card buddies, who she'd been friends with forever and were likely acclimated to her temperament.

"Are you here to visit your grandfather for the holidays?" Lani asked him.

He nodded. "My parents decided we should spend the holidays with him. They've got this idea that he doesn't have many more years ahead of him so we should spend more time with him."

"You don't agree?" I asked.

"He seems spry to me. Personally, I think they just want to make sure my dad is in the will."

"Harsh." Gwen winced.

"Especially since there's nowhere else it would go unless he left it to charity or something. My dad is an only child."

"So, you're not enjoying this visit?" Gwen asked.

Tyler shook his head. "Don't take offense. Your town is charming, but it's not Chicago."

"Is that where you're from?" Lani asked.

"Yes. I work for a financial firm there. What do you ladies do?"

"I work in finance too. Assistant manager at the bank." Gwen smiled at Tyler like she was eager to go over numbers with him.

"I'm a secretary at the sheriff's department," Lani said.

"Children's programmer at the library."

"Librarian?" Tyler quirked a brow as his eyes took tour along my body. I sneaked a look at Gwen, whose cutting glare threatened to slice me into shreds.

"Children's programming. My boyfriend repos airplanes." There! That should put his attention back on Gwen.

"Is that a thing?" Tyler stepped closer to me with too much interest in his expression.

"Even rich people can be deadbeats." I stepped back, wanting Gwen to know I wasn't after her conquest.

He laughed. "Careful, that's my grandfather you're talking about."

Once again, he had his audience wide-eyed.

Tyler shrugged. "Maybe not a deadbeat. But he's stingy and not always true to his word."

"Yes." I quipped thinking about how Carl had made promises to Aunt Rose that he didn't keep.

"So maybe your dad has cause to worry about his inheritance, after all." Gwen shifted, forcing me to move to the side as she put herself in front of Tyler again.

He laughed. "Maybe."

I worked to come up with a reason to leave the conversation. I had no interest in getting between Gwen's attempts to attract Tyler.

A sharp screech came through the loudspeaker, causing all of us to grimace and cover our ears.

"We have the winners of the pie contest. I third place, we have Carolyn Jenkinson. In second place is Alice Filmore."

"Oh, that's a good sign." Lani elbowed me. I hoped it was. If Aunt Rose didn't place at all, she would be impossible to live with.

"And, in first place. Rose Parker."

Whew! There was some clapping, but for the most part, people continued to do whatever they'd been doing.

"I should go find Aunt Rose," I said.

"Why? She won," Lani said.

"Because they always get notes from the judges and no doubt, Carl will have said something she doesn't like." I glanced at Tyler to see how he'd take my comment.

"You'd think old people would be more mature." He grinned and shook his head.

"You'd think. Excuse me." I made my way over to where the pie contest had been held.

Aunt Rose stood with one hand on her hip, the other wagging a finger at Carl Jackson on the other side of the table. "You take that back, Carl Jackson."

"Now Rose, your pie was perfectly fine." He spoke in a soft southern drawl. His eyes twinkling in success at riling up my great aunt.

"You said it's too sweet." She turned to me as I came to stand with her. "Too sweet!" I wasn't sure how to respond to that. Fortunately, she turned her ire on Carl again. "It's a pie, Carl. Dessert. It supposed to be sweet."

"Yes, of course, Rose," he said with a smile.

I looked to the others around the table. Mrs. Conner was putting the pies on a tray. Alice Filmore was rolling her eyes at Aunt Rose. Carolyn Jenkinson pursed her lips and had a disapproving glare toward my aunt.

"You won, Aunt Rose. Congratulations."

"Of course, I did Sophie, no help to that no-good Carl." She shook her head. "Too sweet? I've told you before he shouldn't be a judge."

Mrs. Conner picked up the tray. "Many times, Rose. I'm going to take these back and pack them up for y'all." She headed to the kitchen with Alice and Carolyn in tow.

"I'll see if they need any help," Carl said.

"You stay away from my pie, Carl. I mean it." Rose shook her fist at him.

"Yes Rose."

"Do you want to go home?" I asked, shifting my body to draw her attention away from Carl and the group heading into the kitchen.

"Yes, I do, but I told Betty I'd look at her piece for the art contest."

"I think the art contest is in one of the other rooms." I was glad for that because it seemed like a good idea to get Aunt Rose away from Carl and the pies. We exited the large room and made our way up the hall along what used to be classrooms.

"Here it is," I said pointing to the sign on the open door that said Art Exhibit.

"I hope it's good because I don't think I have it in me to lie tonight."

"I'm sure you can think of something nice to say." I crossed my fingers hoping that was true.

"Oh Rose, look. I got fifth place." Betty stood by a painting of some sort of animal. I couldn't decide if it was a cow or a dog. "I know it's last place because . . . well . . . only five people entered, but still. I got a ribbon. I've never won anything before."

I held my breath as Aunt Rose studied the painting. "Well, that's a mighty fine painting of Charley, Betty. Those classes at the senior center paid off."

Charley. It was Betty's beagle.

"And I heard you won the pie contest. Well of course you did. No one makes better pies than you."

"Do you think they're too sweet?" Aunt Rose asked Betty.

Betty looked at me like she wasn't sure if it was a trick question.

"Carl Jackson's note said it was too sweet," I explained.

"Ah, well, it's a dessert, Rose. It's supposed to be sweet."

"That's what I said," Aunt Rose exclaimed. "Sometimes I wish Carl would choke on his pie. Put us all out of the misery of having to deal with him."

"We were getting ready to leave," I said to Betty, hoping Aunt Rose would take the cue and we could go home.

"I have to get my pie first, before Carl Jackson sullies it more." Aunt Rose started walking to the door.

"You two enjoy the rest of your evening," Betty said.

Aunt Rose and I made our way back to the long corridor. As we came up to the ladies' room, I excused myself to use it.

"I'll meet you in the kitchen," Aunt Rose said. I vacillated on whether I should just hold it and go with her. But some things weren't worth risking. I went into the bathroom, did my business, and then washed my hands, looking at myself in the mirror. I wondered if in fifty years I'd be cranky like Aunt Rose. I hoped not, although I didn't get the idea that she was unhappy per se. Mostly I got the feeling that she felt her life was too short to deal with nonsense and so she was going to call it out and put an end to it whenever it crossed her path.

I made my way back to the large room and toward the kitchen. Everything seemed calm and I crossed my fingers that Rose hadn't gotten herself worked up again over Carl.

I walked to the door.

"Are you taking Rose home?" Alice asked. She was standing with Carolyn Jenkinson near the table where the contest had been held. I didn't know for sure, but I suspected they'd been talking about my aunt being an ungracious winner. While on the one hand, it had to be annoying that she fussed after winning, on the other hand, Carl didn't have to always find something to criticize about her pie, especially since it seemed like he did it only to watch her get all riled up.

I smiled. "Yes. She just wanted to get her pie."

"She's laying into Mrs. Conner, you might want to wait," Carolyn said.

"It's probably better if I intervene." I pushed open the door, wondering why she was picking on poor Mrs. Conner unless it was for allowing Carl to be a judge again for the pie contest.

"Are you ready to go home?" I asked Aunt Rose.

She whirled one me, her sharp eyes cutting right through me. "Carl Jackson stole my pie!"

Male comedians often joked at how difficult it was for men to understand women, but I swear I couldn't figure out what the heck was up with Carl Jackson. It was one thing to poke at Aunt Rose to watch her go off, but taking her prize-winning pie?

"You know how Carl likes to rile you up, Rose. You might consider it a badge of honor. He didn't want to take any of the other pies," Mrs. Conner said.

Chances were, he didn't take the others because it wouldn't make Alice or Carolyn crazy, but I went along with Mrs. Conner's thinking. "He does love your pies."

"He's a thief," she snarled. "Where's Lawson? I want to report my pie stolen."

Mrs. Conner looked at me with eyes that said, *please take Rose home.*

"Let's just go home, Aunt Rose. It's late. We can talk to Sergeant Sco . . . Davis tomorrow."

"Yes." Mrs. Conner perked up. "He'll be here to play Santa for the kids."

"Oh alright."

I put an arm around Aunt Rose to escort her out.

"I hope there isn't a statute of limitations on stolen pie," she muttered.

"I'm sure there isn't."

I got us both home and she headed off to bed. I went through my nightly routine and then checked my phone for a message from A.J. There wasn't one. I considered waiting up late to see if one would come through. I didn't have to work at the library tomorrow since most of the kids would likely be at the holiday jamboree. The library did have a small exhibit there that I agreed to man for a short time, but I didn't need to be there until noon. I decided that managing Aunt Rose as well as the library exhibit would require a full night's sleep, so I went to bed.

The next day, I dressed in jeans and a festive red sweater, and then met Aunt Rose out in the kitchen.

"When are we going to the community center?" Aunt Rose snapped at me before I'd gotten my morning coffee.

"I don't need to be there until noon." Then I remembered that she wanted to talk to Sergeant Scowl. "I can talk to Sergeant Davis for you, if you like."

"No, I'll do it. If Carl is there, I'll enjoy watching Lawson put him in handcuffs. It's long overdue if you ask me. He's a liar and cheat, and now a thief."

I sighed. "We'll leave here about quarter till twelve."

"Good."

"Have you ever thought about just ignoring Mr. Jackson," I asked as I filled the coffee carafe with water for the coffee maker. "I mean, he seems to enjoy getting a rise out of you. If you ignored him, the fun of it would stop for him."

I wasn't brave enough to look at her response to my suggestion, so I poured the water into the coffee maker and then pulled the bag of grounds from the cupboard.

"There's no ignoring him. He's like a gnat. The only way to make it stop is to squash it. Too bad there's no fly swatter big enough to squash him."

- - - - - - - -

At noon, Aunt Rose and I walked into the community center again. This time it was filled with kids and vendors selling a variety of arts and crafts, home baked goods, and holiday décor.

"Do you want to come to the library booth with me?" I asked Aunt Rose. "I have a holiday book I was going to read to the kids and an art project related to it."

"Nah. I'm going to find Betty and Tilly. I think Tilly is selling her nuts. When will Lawson be here?"

"I think he's on at one."

"Good." She moved off into the crowd and all I could do was cross my fingers that Carl wasn't here.

"Hey Sophie." Vivie pulled up to the library table with her brood of kids. "This is Miss Sophie. You remember her from the library, right?"

I sure remembered them. As kids went, they weren't the worst, but they definitely could use a firmer hand than what either Vivie or Randy gave them. Immediately, two of the three were getting into the craft supplies.

"I can leave them here, right?" Vivie smiled sweetly at me. I considered telling her that only worked on men.

"I'm not a babysitter, Vivie."

She huffed a breath at me. "RJ," she snapped at the older boy who was doing something on his phone. "You're in charge of your brother and sister."

He shrugged.

"Did you hear me?"

"Yeah, sure." He didn't look up from his game.

"I'm going to find your father. He better not be with Santa's helper."

I arched a brow. "Who is Santa's helper?"

"Shelby Conner. She just turned twenty-one and now works at the Booty Burgo. I blame you for this, Sophie."

"Me?"

"If you still worked there, he wouldn't have hired her."

"Speaking of Shelby Conner, is her grandmother here?" I wanted to warn Mrs. Conner that Aunt Rose was on the warpath.

"Ah, I think I saw her with Carl Jackson. He didn't look so good."

"What do you mean?"

Aunt Rose was small, but she was feisty, and I think all that rolling of pie dough made her strong. I wouldn't be surprised if she punched him.

Vivie gave me an annoyed glare. "I don't know. Like he had the flu or something. I think she was getting him some water and trying to find Tyler. One guess who's got her claws in him. Really, Sophie, you shouldn't have let Gwen get to him before you."

I resisted rolling my eyes.

"I'll be back for you rug rats in a little bit."

Along with the help of one of the library assistants, I was able to keep Vivie's kids as well as the other children occupied. There were many folktales and stories about monsters and witches around Christmas, but I decided that I'd avoid upsetting the good folks of Jefferson Grove, Virginia by sticking to traditional stories. I read a story about how St. Nick became Santa Claus and then had an activity in which the kids could make their own paper stocking.

When my shift was done, I thought I'd do some holiday shopping at the various venders, but worried about what Aunt Rose was up to. I hadn't heard any fussing, and no one had come by the library booth to tell me Aunt Rose was riled up, but that didn't mean she wasn't causing trouble.

Over near a booth selling scarves, I saw Betty.

"Hi Mrs. Bealton. Have you seen Aunt Rose?" I asked.

"Oh Sophie, isn't this lovely?" Betty held up a red and green striped scarf.

"It's very nice. Do you know where Aunt Rose is?"

Betty untwirled the scarf from around her neck. "I think I saw her over by the kitchen."

"Thank you." I pushed my way through the crowds of people toward the kitchen. An announcement was made that Santa was there, which sent a rush of children flowing against me as they made their way to the stage.

Finally, I reached the edge of the kitchen area. Tyler Jackson was leaning against the wall outside the kitchen looking at his phone.

"Bored already?" I asked.

"Just waiting for my grandfather."

Oh dear. I looked inside the kitchen through large pass-through window but didn't see Carl. I only saw Rose, shaking her finger at the ground.

I walked to the door.

"Thank goodness you're here, Sophie," Mrs. Conner said. She and Alice Filmore were managing a baked goods table outside of the kitchen area.

"She's giving Carl a piece of her mind. Why she bothers, I don't know," Alice said.

I pushed open the door, wondering how Aunt Rose was giving Carl a piece of her mind when he wasn't in there.

"Stop being stupid, Carl." Aunt Rose said. "Get up!"

I approached her standing at the side of the large island.

"What's going on?" I looked to where her attention was directed and saw Carl laying on the floor. "Oh . . . what happened?"

"He's being a fool as usual," she said to me. "I hope you're choking, Carl because you aren't funny!" She snapped at him.

I looked at him again and didn't get the vibe that he was playing around. Carl always had a sly smile and a twinkle in his eye when he was poking at Aunt Rose. He had neither of those now. His eyes were unfocused and drool was dripping from his mouth. His face was red, like one might get from heat exhaustion.

"I think something might be wrong." I bent down next to him.

"Everything about him is wrong, Sophie." Rose huffed.

"Mr. Jackson?" I pushed against his chest. "If you're playing around, now is the time to stop."

His body moved only from the force of my pushing him. The rest of him remained still. His eyes didn't flutter. In fact, it didn't appear that he was breathing.

I wasn't a medical professional, so the only thing I could think of was that he was choking or maybe had a heart attack.

I worked to remember the CPR training I'd had years ago, but it was fuzzy. "I think I just do compressions," I said. Except if he was choking, maybe I needed to do the Heimlich. Crap. What to do?

"I'll compress him."

I looked up at Aunt Rose. "I think he's really in trouble." I handed her my cell phone. "Call 911 and then see who's here that knows how to give emergency medical attention."

"He's just fooling with us, Sophie."

I took the phone back. "I don't think he is." I dialed 9-1-1 with one hand, while I tried to push on his chest with my other hand. When the dispatch answered, I told her where I was and what I thought had happened. Once help was on the way, I set the phone down to use both hands.

Aunt Rose leaned over me. "Is he dead?"

I thought he might be, but didn't want to say that. "I don't know. Maybe you can go get help."

"You just called for help."

"Someone here would be able to help faster. Like a doctor or something." My arms were getting tired already as I hummed the *Stayin' Alive* song in my head, the one thing I did remember from CPR.

Aunt Rose walked off, but I was too focused on Carl to know where she was going or what she was doing. The screech of the PA system threw me off my rhythm for a moment. Then Aunt Rose's voice echoed through the building.

"Is there a doctor in the house? I think Carl Jackson done died."

Chapter Three

Santa Claus, aka Sergeant Scowl, aka Sergeant Lawson Davis, stood over Carl Jackson's body. He yanked off the white polyester beard.

"Sir, there are kids right outside," Dwayne said, glancing toward the room full of families.

Sergeant Scowl glanced at him.

"They think you're Santa, sir." Dwayne's face scrunched up like he knew his boss thought it was a strange thing to worry about with a dead man in the room, and at the same time, felt it was important for the kids not to be disillusioned.

"Oh, for Pete's sake. There's a dead man here, and you're worried about them seeing me take off my beard?" Sergeant Scowl confirmed my theory.

Dwayne shrugged. "They can't see Mr. Jackson behind the island."

"How about I shut the passthrough window?" Mrs. Conner pointed toward the open space where a crowd was beginning to form.

"Yes, please," Sergeant scowl said. Then he turned to Aunt Rose and me. He had that look he always had when he saw me that said, "You again? I should have known." He took off his hat and began to remove his coat.

"Don't go stripping in here, Lawson," Mrs. Conner said to him when she finished closing the window. While the gawkers couldn't see in, there were still quite a few of us in the kitchen, including Alice Filmore, Carolyn Jenkinson, and Tyler Jackson.

"I assure you; I have clothes on under here."

I couldn't blame him for wanting out of the Santa costume. To be honest, it was creepy to have Santa looking over Carl's dead body.

"What happened?" he asked when he was before us in jeans and a t-shirt, but still in big bulky Santa boots.

"Carl died," Aunt Rose said.

He put his hands on his hips. "Walk me through what he did before he died."

"Last night, he stole my pie and I came in here to give him a piece of mind about it. Then I was going to find you to arrest him." Aunt Rose looked down at Carl's body. "I guess I won't be pressing charges after all."

Inwardly I winced at her insensitivity, although for Aunt Rose, perhaps it wasn't insensitive. At least she hadn't said something about meeting his maker and having to atone for his sins.

"How was he when you were talking to him?" he asked, taking a notepad from his back pocket.

Rose huffed out a breath. "He tried to sweet-talk me like he always does."

"Was his demeanor different? Did he seem ill?"

I hoped to God that she didn't make a remark that he was always ill.

She shrugged. "He didn't seem to have his usual pep, if that's what you're asking."

"He was under the weather," Mrs. Conner said from back by the closed pass-through window. It appeared that she was trying to stay as far away from Carl as possible. "I brought him in here and got him some water and then sent someone to find Tyler."

"Who's Tyler?" Sergeant Scowl looked around the kitchen.

"I am." Tyler stepped forward. He kept his eyes on Sergeant Scowl. When he first came running in after Aunt Rose's announcement, he skidded to a stop over Carl's body. Then he staggered back and until this moment, had been in shock.

"Was Carl sick?" Sergeant Scowl asked him.

Tyler shrugged. "He said he wasn't feeling well. I thought it was because he'd had too much to drink last night. You know, a hangover."

"Since when does Carl drink?" Aunt Rose demanded.

"What do mean?" Sergeant Scowl turned his attention to her.

"Carl was never much of a drinker even when he was younger," she said.

Everyone in the room's brows arched as Aunt Rose shared details about Carl that didn't involve him being a liar and cheat and stealing her pie.

"But he gave the stuff up when Dot died. It was part of his plan to get healthy so he could carouse again," Aunt Rose finished explaining.

"Carouse?" Sergeant Scowl asked.

"He's a womanizer, along with being a liar, a cheat and a thief."

Sergeant Scowl scanned the room, but there didn't seem to be any confirmation of that. Finally, he turned back to Aunt Rose. "What did he say or do before he fell?"

Aunt Rose scrunched up her face in thought. "He asked if it was snowing."

We all looked out the window. The sun was bright and there wasn't a cloud in the sky.

Sergeant Scowl lifted his head from writing notes. "Snowing? Why?"

"How would I know? He just said it seemed like it was snowing. I figured he was just being Carl." Aunt Rose leaned toward Sergeant Scowl. "He had a crush on me, you know."

"Anything else?" Sergeant Scowl asked.

"He was a bit off," Mrs. Conner said. "He seemed confused. I wondered if maybe he'd had a stroke or something. Or maybe just a bad fever."

Sergeant Scowl nodded and scribbled on his notepad. Then he asked Aunt Rose, "What happened when he fell?"

"He started breathing funny, and I told him to stop being a pervert and then he just sort of fell over."

"Breathing funny?" Sergeant Scowl asked.

"That sounds like how my uncle Hoyt died," Carolyn said from the corner of the room.

"What do you mean?" I asked.

Sergeant Scowl glared at me in a "I ask the questions" type of signal, which I of course ignored. It was a game we played whenever I happen to be around somebody who had died.

"It seemed like he had the flu, and then he acted all confused for a while and then he dropped dead. That thing about seeing the snow. That's what stands out to me. He kept walking around saying he was in a snowstorm but it was the middle of July," Carolyn explained.

I looked over at Sergeant Scowl to see if he was going to follow up on that, but with his jaw tight he kept his attention on Aunt Rose. It was clear he didn't have any interest in what Carolyn was saying.

"So, what did he end up dying of?" I asked, recognizing that it was insensitive, but at the same time she brought it up.

"Bad moonshine."

That statement had all of us turning to look at her, but I think it was more out of not expecting that answer, than actually being intrigued by it. Ultimately, Sergeant Scowl rolled his eyes and turned back to Aunt Rose.

"And you didn't think to get help?" Sergeant Scowl asked.

"I thought he was being a jerk like he always is." She was still talking about him in the present.

"Mr. Jackson liked to poke Aunt Rose's buttons," I explained, hoping to make her seem less callous.

"And then what?" Sergeant Scowl asked.

"He just lay there, playing dead. Then Sophie came in and decided he really was dead. And now you're here. What are you going to do about it?" Aunt Rose looked at Sergeant Scowl like she expected him to fix this issue.

The kitchen door opened, and Dwayne went to stop whoever was coming in until he saw it was other sheriff's deputies and EMS.

We all moved to let the medical people check out Carl, although it was clear there was nothing they could do for him.

One paramedic stopped to talk to Sergeant Scowl, while the other confirmed the death and they made arrangements to take him to the local hospital.

"Let the hospital know that we need an autopsy so he'll need to be transported to Roanoke to the Medical Examiner," Sergeant Scowl told the paramedic.

She nodded and went to help her partner while we all moved to the other side of the room.

"Did Mr. Jackson have any health problems?" Sergeant Scowl asked the group of us.

"He was missing his heart," Aunt Rose murmured.

"His grandson is here," I said, giving Aunt Rose a look that said *watch what you say.* "He might know."

Sergeant Scowl looked over at Tyler who was standing near Mrs. Conner.

"Did your grandfather have any health conditions?" Sergeant Scowl asked.

Tyler shook his head. "I don't know. He seemed alright to me."

"What about last night? You just thought he'd had too much to drink?" Sergeant Scowl asked.

"Yeah. We got home and he was going to bed, but then I found him in the kitchen eating the pie."

"See! He stole my pie."

I put my arm around Aunt Rose hoping it would calm her down.

"That was unusual too," Mrs. Conner said. "Carl usually only stole a piece of her pie. Enough that she'd notice. This was the first time he'd taken it all."

"Is it possible there was something in the pie?" Sergeant Scowl asked.

The entire room erupted with a collective gasp at his question.

I couldn't hold Aunt Rose back. "Are you saying there was something wrong with my pie and it killed Carl?"

As if he only realized what his question suggested, Sergeant Scowl waved a hand. "I'm not saying you did anything wrong, Ms.

Parker. But if Mr. Jackson didn't drink, but was acting drunk last night and confused today, leading to his death, I need to consider he ingested something."

She sniffed. "There's no booze in my pie." She narrowed her eyes over at Mrs. Conner. "It's against the contest rules."

To be honest, I'm not sure that was true. At least the part about no booze in the pie. I was pretty sure Aunt Rose had a bottle of bourbon handy while she made her famous pecan pie.

"You know, bad moonshine is a thing. Wood alcohol," Dwayne said to Sergeant Scowl.

Sergeant Scowl reluctantly looked at Dwayne. "We determined he doesn't drink."

"Maybe he didn't know it was in the drink," Dwayne offered. I wondered if he was trying to ingratiate himself to Sergeant Scowl as I knew he was working towards becoming a detective.

Sergeant Scowl's expression suggested he was patronizing Dwayne when he asked, "Where would he have gotten bad moonshine at the Winter Jamboree?"

Dwayne shifted uncomfortably but stood his ground. "Well, if it was bad moonshine or wood alcohol, then he probably would've ingested it yesterday. It takes twenty-four hours or so depending on how much is ingested."

Sergeant Scowl looked over at Mrs. Conner, who was one of the organizers of the holiday event. "Drinking at the jamboree? Where would somebody be serving alcohol here?"

"Now Lawson, everyone knows that adult eggnog is served at the Winter Jamboree. If you know where to look for it," Rose said.

"But if it was this wood alcohol or moonshine, where would he have gotten that? Is that what they're putting in eggnog?"

"The stuff I drank last night had bourbon," Aunt Rose said.

Alice and Carolyn gave Aunt Rose a look. The adult eggnog was supposed to be a secret, I guess.

"It's a possibility," Dwayne said.

"And how do you know so much about this?" he asked Dwayne.

"I did a paper on prohibition in high school that talked about all the people dying from the homemade moonshine."

Sergeant Scowl thought for a moment. "Does this bad moonshine taste like bourbon because the regular stuff tastes like paint stripper."

Alice Fillmore laughed. "Moonshine is like drinking gasoline. I don't think somebody would drink it in eggnog and not notice."

"Maybe it wasn't wood alcohol. Maybe it was ethanol glycol," Dwayne said.

Sergeant Scowl studied him for a minute.

Dwayne shrugged. "I took a course on poisons through the justice training academy that was offered last year. Ethanol glycol is similar to methanol, the wood alcohol, except of course you don't have to make it in a still. Most people have it around their house."

"They have it around the house?" I asked shocked. It was a wonder more people weren't poisoned.

"Yes, it's an anti-freeze. And it is said to have a sweet taste, so maybe that's how they got past the taste."

Sergeant Scowl frowned and shook his head. "We're getting ahead of ourselves here. Chances are Carl died of natural causes. I doubt Carl accidentally or with the help of some nefarious person drank antifreeze."

Having been involved in a couple of murder cases, I knew I didn't want to be involved in the third one, so I nodded in agreement. At the same time, I remembered Carl's critique of Aunt Rose's pie; it was too sweet. I got a sick feeling in my stomach.

"I wouldn't put it past someone to poison Carl," Aunt Rose quipped.

I winced at her comment.

"Why would you say that, Ms. Parker?" Sergeant Scowl asked.

I really needed to teach her about the fifth Amendment.

"Because Carl was a liar and a cheat. I don't know how many times I have to say it, but he was a liar and a cheat and thief. He stole my pie last night." She set her hands on her hips and glared at Sergeant Scowl. "And before you start accusing me, Lawson Davis, I would never sully one of my pies with poison."

He stepped back and for once I saw an amused smirk on his face. "Well, this is all very interesting, but until we have an autopsy, we don't really know what happened to Mr. Jackson except for the fact that he left here last night acting inebriated, and he showed up here today not feeling well and died. There could be a perfectly logical explanation. In fact, I suspect the death will be from natural causes. We'll just wait to see what the medical examiner says."

Dwayne stepped over and leaned closer to him. "We should probably ask them for toxicology specifically checking for poison, if we think it's a possibility."

Sergeant Scowl sighed. "I appreciate your tenacity, Deputy Lafferty. I know you're eager to become a detective, and I'd be happy to have you help me with this case, but I'm certain that Mr. Jackson wasn't murdered."

I got the sense that he didn't want to work over the holidays and just wanted this to be a sad case of Carl Jackson dying of natural causes. To be honest, I did too.

Dwayne nodded. "Maybe we can wait and see what they do find, and if it's uncertain or unclear, at that point they can do it toxicology."

Sergeant Scowl shrugged. "Okay. But, I'm sure there's no one here who wanted Carl Jackson dead, despite what Ms. Parker says."

Everyone looked at Aunt Rose.

"Or is there, Ms. Parker?" Sergeant Scowl asked.

"There's a difference between wanting someone dead and wanting to murder them, Lawson."

Needless to say, the festivities ended sooner than usual. Fortunately, Aunt Rose and I were allowed to leave, although Sergeant Scowl said he might have more questions for us at another time. That sounded ominous to me. I mean, why would he need to talk to us further if Carl died of natural causes or an accident?

Chapter Four

Sunday was a regular day in terms of how Aunt Rose and I spent our time, but the death of Carl Jackson hung over us. At Church, the pastor said a few words about Carl but there was no word on a funeral yet. The ladies at the potluck cried as they all shared their memories of Carl. Everyone was acting as expected considering a long-time member of the community had died.

Aunt Rose's behavior, on the other hand, was slightly off. She seemed subdued, but I was too afraid to ask if she was sad that her long-time sparring partner was gone or maybe feeling guilty that she'd often wished bad things to happen to him and it finally did. The only Aunt Rose-like thing I heard from her was when she grumbled about how the ladies at the potluck had a terrible memory when it came to Carl.

"How so?" I dared to ask.

"Well, I can't speak ill of the dead, but he wasn't the saint they made him out to be," she said clutching her handbag as I drove us home.

"I think it's normal after someone dies to not fuss over their character flaws."

She didn't say anything and I didn't push her. I wished Bull was around because he always had a way with her. He'd have her baking something in the kitchen and snapping her out of her funk.

- - - - - - - -

Bull and AJ still weren't back by Tuesday night, but that was okay, since it was my coupon group. According to the experts in my group, we had group on Tuesday nights because Wednesday was the best day to go grocery shopping as that was the day the new deals started while the old deals were still on until the end of the day. Plus, the stores were restocked, so a shopper could fill their stockpile. I didn't have a stockpile, mostly because I couldn't see the sense in it, and Aunt Rose wouldn't likely give me a space to store a hundred tubes of toothpaste and fifty bottles of mustard.

This week's group was held at Vivie's house, which meant all the food was healthy. It was a bummer, because I always looked forward to Aggie's barbecue sauce and meatballs, which weren't allowed through Vivie's door. I liked carrots and hummus alright, but it couldn't compete with meatballs and sauce.

I brought a fruit tray that I paid full price for at the grocery store. I wasn't a liar, but if they asked, I'd say I bought it on sale. It was easier than having a lecture or the ladies wondering why I was in a coupon group if I insisted on paying full price for my food.

I put the fruit on the island in Vivie's kitchen next to the veggie plate, and the fat-free cheese with gluten-free cracker plate.

Then I carried my coupon binder into the dining room where the rest of the ladies were already gathered. All of them except for Vivie's sister, Tracy, who never came to group when it was at Vivie's ever since it came out that Tracy had been sleeping with Vivie's husband.

"Oh hi, Sophie. How is your aunt doing?" Aggie asked, dipping her carrot in fat-free ranch dressing. I don't know why she bothered. She might as well dip it in water.

"She's doing alright," I said, purposefully not going into detail about her funk since Carl's death. Aunt Rose wouldn't want me telling others about her business. They could learn it from someone else.

"There's a rumor that she poisoned Carl with her pie," Gwen said, sipping her wine, the only non-healthy thing Vivie allowed in her house.

"No way," Vivie chimed in. "I have no doubt that Rose would

murder Carl, but she wouldn't do it by tainting one of her prized pies."

"That's true," Lani said, as she sorted her coupons for trading.

"What? That she might have poisoned him or she wouldn't do it with a pie?" Gwen asked.

"She wouldn't poison him with a pie," Lani said.

"Where would such a rumor start?" Aggie's face pinched into indignation.

"Probably because Carolyn Jenkinson said that her uncle died similarly to Carl and his cause of death was bad moonshine," I explained as I sat next to Lani.

"Drinking bad moonshine isn't murder. It's stupidity," Aggie said shaking her head. "And Hoyt Jenkinson was about as dumb as a person could get, bless his heart."

"How do you get bad moonshine?" Gwen asked. She was always the one with the morbid fascination when the topic of death came up in the group.

"You should ask Dwayne," I said, nudging Lani next to me. "He knows all about that sort of thing."

Lani beamed. "Dwayne is working to become a detective in Jefferson Grove."

"I think he's also Sergeant Scowl's annoying sidekick," I quipped, remembering Sergeant Scowl's annoyance at Dwayne's constant interjection when Carl died.

Lani frowned. "Why would you say that?"

I realized I might have offended my best friend. "Because he clearly knew more than Sergeant Scowl about it."

She smiled. "He's studying so hard. Maybe someday when you fall over a dead body again, you can work with him."

I shook my head vehemently. "Nope. No more dead bodies for me."

"Speaking of dead bodies, have you seen Tracy?" Vivie asked, stealthily absconding with a peanut butter coupon from one of Lani's piles.

"I thought you were worried about Randy and Shelby Conners?" I said, with a nod to her hand to let her know I saw her.

Vivie rolled her eyes. "If it has boobs, I have to worry about it where Randy is concerned."

"She never comes here, you know that," Aggie said, giving up on her carrot.

Vivie shrugged and I wondered if maybe she was missing her sister.

We all started pushing our coupons for trade in the middle of the table. I was eying a two-dollars-off ibuprofen from Gwen's pile.

"Did you mean that when you said Sophie's aunt could kill someone?" Gwen asked.

"You're morbid." Vivie pursed her lips at Gwen. "But yes. Everyone knows Rose hated Carl."

Aggie shook her head as she picked up a thirty cents off coupon for ketchup. "If Rose was going to kill Carl, she'd have done it fifty years ago."

"Because he left her?" Gwen asked.

"Yes. Personally, I think it turned out for the better. Carl, for all his charm, he's a slippery one." When it came to historic gossip, Aggie was our woman. She was nearly as old as my aunt Rose, so she'd been around a long and time and seen a lot of things. Plus, as a former schoolteacher, she'd had a lot of involvement with most of Jefferson Grove's families.

"Aunt Rose always says he's a liar and cheat. Oh, and she was livid that he took her pie," I said, snatching the ibuprofen coupon and also a buy-two-get-one-free on sugar. With the holidays, Aunt Rose was doing a lot of baking.

"Dwayne went and got the pie." Lani took one of my shaving cream coupons.

I turned to look at her. "Why?" It's not like Aunt Rose wanted it back.

She shrugged. "I think he's just being proactive. Maybe it has a clue to why Carl died."

I gasped. "He probably had a heart attack. You don't think my aunt—"

Her eyes rounded and she put her hand on my shoulder as if she just realized what Dwayne's actions suggested. "No. I didn't mean that, Sophie. Really."

"Then why get the pie?" Gwen asked.

Lani bit her lip as she looked at me. She shrugged.

"Aunt Rose didn't kill him. And she didn't use any ingredients that would make him sick." I was really hurt by Dwayne's actions, but I tried not to take it out on Lani.

"Now, now," Aggie said, rising from her chair and grabbing the wine bottle on Vivie's buffet. "Dwayne is just being a go-getter. Nothing wrong with that. I'm sure he's just practicing being thorough."

I looked at Aggie. "Thorough on what? Why get the pie unless he thinks there something wrong with it?" I turned to Lani. "Which there wasn't."

"Oh Sophie, don't get all riled up," Vivie said, hogging all the produce coupons. "Dwayne is just trying to kiss up to Davis."

"He is not," Lani said, lifting her chin in indignation.

"You said yourself that he's being proactive. Why do that except to score points with the boss. Unless he really did think Rose killed Carl," Vivie said, pointedly looking back at Lani.

Lani's eyes darted to me and then back to Vivie. "He just wants to be a good detective, that's all."

"No wonder there is a rumor about Rose killing Carl, if Dwayne went and got the pie," Gwen said.

Lani's eyes filled with tears and I felt bad for her even though Gwen was right. If Dwayne went and collected the pie as evidence, it would make Rose look guilty.

"Dwayne is a good person," Lani said.

"So is Aunt Rose," I said in her defense.

There was one audible snort that I was sure came from Vivie. "Relax, Lani. Let's not have you two besties getting hot over nothing."

"That's right," Aggie agreed. "Let's talk about something else."

"So, Sophie, have you seen AJ lately?" Vivie asked in her sweet tone and prissy expression. I'd rather talk about Aunt Rose.

- - - - - - - -

The next day, was the same as always. I left Aunt Rose drinking coffee and reading an entertainment magazine as I headed to the library for work. Since it was the holiday break from school, we had many children's programs running. Today I was going to do all my programming around the Italian folklore of Befana, a good witch, who was said to fill the stockings of Italian children on January 5th and then sweep their home before leaving.

I was just telling the group of four- to six-year-olds about Befana's origin story related the birth of Jesus and the three magi, when my boss, Mrs. Wayland, interrupted me.

"Ms. Parker." She always called me that in front of the kids because in the south, children were still taught to use surnames when talking to their elders. I'd have been happy with Miss Sophie, like Bull called me, a less formal and usually accepted alternative, but Mrs. Wayland nixed that idea.

"Yes, Mrs. Wayland."

"You have an urgent phone call." She looked over at the tables where I'd set up an art craft for the children to make stockings out of felt for Befana to fill. "I'll get the children started on the activity."

The last urgent phone call I'd ever received was from my mother telling me my father and brother were arrested and she was on a flight out of the country. Needless to say, I wasn't too thrilled about having another urgent call, but I left Mrs. Wayland with the children and went into the library's back area.

"Hello?"

"Sophie? It's Lani."

Lani worked for the sheriff's department so if she was calling me this couldn't be good. Had AJ or Bull gotten into trouble repo-ing a plane, which often came close to stealing as far as I could tell? It wouldn't be the first time AJ was picked up by the cops on a repossession. No, they were out of town. If they were arrested, Lani wouldn't be the one calling me.

"Sergeant Davis is planning to go visit Rose to question her about Carl's death."

My heart skipped a beat as nerves trickled along my spine. "What? Why?"

"I think they're suspicious of her."

"She didn't do anything but witness Carl having a heart attack or something. Why would he be suspicious? About what?"

"Sophie, the medical examiner says it's homicide. Poison."

My gut clenched. "What?" I looked around the room in case anyone there could hear what was going on. Kathy Danvers, another library worker, looked up for a moment, but then went back to pasting the sleeves for book due cards into newly received books.

"They think Rose murdered Carl."

I was stunned—paralyzed. Why would Sergeant Scowl think my Aunt Rose killed Carl? Okay, so she often said she wanted him dead, but still.

"Sophie, are you there?"

"Yes, I'm just in shock. Aunt Rose wouldn't kill anyone."

"They don't have the toxicology report yet on the specific poison. They also plan to test her pie." She told me that with hesitation, probably because she knew I'd be upset that law enforcement had the pie because of her husband's overzealous desire to please his boss. She was right in that thinking.

But I couldn't worry about that. I had to figure out how to help Aunt Rose. The first task was clear. I had to go home.

I hung up with Lani and found Mrs. Wayland with the kids.

"Something's come up with Aunt Rose," I said.

"Oh? I hope it's nothing serious."

I shrugged. I wondered if Virginia had the death penalty for octogenarians. That would constitute as serious, right?

"If you need to go, you can. We're about done here," she said. I was glad I didn't have to come up with some lame reason to go home. Then again, this was Jefferson Grove. It wouldn't be long before the whole town knew that Aunt Rose was a suspect.

Lucky for me, the library was closer to Rose's house than the Sheriff's Department was. I had to drive over the speed limit and roll through a stop sign, but I pulled in the driveway before Sergeant Scowl arrived. I trotted up to the house and through the door rushing in like a crazy woman.

Aunt Rose looked up at me from her chair where she was watching one of her shows. "What has gotten into you, Sophie?"

"Lawson Davis is coming," I shut the door behind me and then looked out the window. I was just about to turn my attention back to her when I saw his sheriff's cruiser SUV pulling up in front of the house.

"What does he want?" Aunt Rose said, turning her attention back to whatever soap opera was on. I never paid attention to soap operas, but Aunt Rose had been fussing a lot lately that too many of them had been canceled.

I hurried into the living room and sat on the couch next to her chair. "It's about Carl Jackson. The medical examiner says that his death is a homicide."

Rose's expression was blank for a moment. Then her brows drew together as if she wasn't sure what that meant. "Does Lawson think I know who killed him?"

There was no way I was going to come right out and tell Aunt Rose that she was a suspect—probably his only suspect. "I'm sure he's just questioning everybody that was at the Winter Jamboree last weekend."

"Then why do you look like a rat that's just been trapped by a cat?"

I inhaled and exhaled a deep breath and rolled my shoulders because I didn't need her to be agitated more than she already would be when Sergeant Scowl reached the door. "It's just nerve-racking to be questioned," I said, by way of explanation.

Aunt Rose waved a hand. "You just tell the truth, Sophie that's all you gotta do."

I had no doubt in my mind that she was right, and that she would tell the truth. But I also knew that Rose had a way of telling the truth that could cast suspicion on her. Before I could comment, there was a knock at the door.

Aunt Rose lifted the remote and turned off the TV. "Go let them in, Sophie. Let's get this over with."

I rose from the couch and walked to the door, opening it, crossing my fingers behind my back in a silent prayer that this would go okay. What would I do if Sergeant Scowl tried to handcuff Aunt Rose and arrest her?

Chapter Five

Sergeant Scowl gave me his name-sake scowl when he saw me at the door. "Miss Parker, I was under the impression you were working." He cast a glance to Dwayne Rafferty standing next to him. That could only mean Dwayne had found out from Lani that I was supposed to be working. Dwayne looked at me and I could see that he understood that while Lani had given him information about me, she'd also given me information about him. Perhaps it was her way to make amends for the pie.

"I got the afternoon off. What can I help you gentlemen with?" I said acting like I didn't know why they were there.

"We're hoping to speak to Ms. Rose Parker about the death of Carl Jackson."

"Oh?" I arched a brow and hoped I was showing the appropriate amount of intrigue.

"He was murdered, Sophie," Dwayne blurted.

Sergeant Scowl grimaced. "The medical examiner has determined that Mr. Jackson died from some sort of poison, although we don't know what it was."

"That's awful, but I don't see how Aunt Rose plays into this."

Sergeant Scowl glared down at me. It was that look he gave me when he was telling me I know your game, you know my game, let's just cut the crap and get to talking.

Working at the library meant I had access to a lot of books about crime and law enforcement investigation. Even if we didn't have a book on it in the library, I had access to resources through interlibrary loan, or through online library databases. Because I'd been involved in two previous murder investigations, I'd used those books and I knew I was well within my right to not let Sergeant Scowl and Deputy Rafferty into the house. I even considered exercising that right because I couldn't trust Rose not to say something incriminating.

Before I could suggest that they come back later, Aunt Rose's voice bellowed across the living room. "Oh, for Pete's sake, Sophie. Let them in the door. They're never going to find who killed Carl if they can't come in and ask their questions."

I hoped that her open invitation to them would play in her favor and have them not being suspicious of her. I was pretty sure that was hopeful thinking.

I opened the door, letting the men in.

"What's this you're saying about someone killing Carl Jackson?" Aunt Rose demanded.

"That's what the ME says. Can I sit, Ms. Parker?" Sergeant Scowl asked, making me really nervous. Normally, Sergeant liked to use the bulk of his body, his bulldog face, and harsh growl to intimidate the people he questioned. He wasn't one of the dumb oaf-like Sheriff's detectives often depicted on TV. He was smart and wily, and I could only imagine that he was deciding to use a softer approach to lure out Aunt Rose's answers, instead of his usual gruff demeanor.

"Yes, yes Lawson take a seat. And tell me what's going on."

Now I wished I had mentioned to Aunt Rose that Dwayne picked up her pie at Carl's because maybe knowing that she would have the sense to be careful in choosing her words, but now it was too late for that. Then again, I was thinking like she could be guilty, and I knew she wasn't. She'd never ruin one of her pies with poison, so maybe it was a good thing that Dwayne had picked up the pie because when it was tested and found not to have poison, she'd be in the clear.

Feeling a bit more settled, I went over and sat on the couch. Aunt Rose took her seat in her chair, while Sergeant Scowl sat in the recliner that had belonged to my father before he was sent to prison. It was the only thing the family had left of his after all his assets and possessions had been sold at auction to pay legal bills, as well as some restitution to the people he robbed in his Ponzi scheme.

Sergeant Scowl cleared his throat. "The medical examiner has given us the preliminary report indicating that Mr. Carl Jackson, was poisoned.—"

"And you're here to ask me who I think did it," Aunt Rose said. She had that same expression she wore when she watched Deadly Women on IDTV. She was on the case now.

"Well, there's still more tests that need to be done, but we are talking to everybody in Mr. Jackson's life and people who were at the Winter Jamboree. We're hoping to learn who might have wanted him dead."

Aunt Rose pursed her lips. "Who didn't want Carl Jackson dead?"

I closed my eyes and prayed to God for strength.

Dwayne, standing by the fireplace behind Sergeant Scowl, said, "There are some people who think you—"

Sergeant Scowl's hand shot up in a stop sign, effectively halting Dwayne's comment. "Are you saying that there are a lot of people who didn't like Mr. Jackson enough that they would poison him?" he asked.

"There are plenty of people who didn't like Carl Jackson. How many of them would resort to murder, I don't know," Aunt Rose answered.

"What about you, Ms. Parker?" Dwayne interjected.

Sergeant Scowl glared over his shoulder at him.

"What about me?"

"Did you want him dead? Perhaps you poisoned him with your pie?"

"Deputy Lafferty—" Sergeant Scowl snapped.

"If I wanted to kill Carl, I wouldn't use poison." Aunt Rose shook her head in disgust.

I didn't want to know how she'd kill Carl. "You can't really think she killed Carl. Aunt Rose has a sharp tongue but she'd never kill anyone."

"I'm surprised at you Lawson accusing me of killing Carl. How you got to be a detective is beyond me. I swear Sophie, if you hadn't helped him, Joe Cullen and your friend Marla's murders probably would still be unsolved." Aunt Rose stared over at Sergeant Scowl and Dwayne. "If I wanted Carl dead, I'd have done it fifty years ago when I really hated him."

"You don't hate him now?" Sergeant Scowl asked.

"Now I dislike him. He's like a gnat. Irritating but small."

"Is that all?" I asked Sergeant Scowl hoping to end the interview before Aunt Rose said something that got her in trouble.

"I'd like to review your statements from the other night again," Sergeant Scowl said.

"I know the drill." The number of times I had to repeat myself in past investigation should make investigators look inept, but I'd watched enough IDTV with Aunt Rose to know it was a tactic used in case witnesses remembered something new or to catch the bad guys in a lie. I hoped he was looking at me as a witness.

His jaw tightened at my attitude, but I was tired and grumpy, and not in the mood to be questioned.

"Walk me through starting at the time you found Carl in the kitchen Saturday morning," he said to Aunt Rose.

"I was telling him I was going to call the cops for stealing my pie," Aunt Rose said. "By the way, you were late that day. I was counting on you to arrest him."

Sergeant Scowl took a breath and ignored her comment. "What was happening before that?"

"I just told you. I was looking for you to arrest him." Aunt Rose glared at him.

It occurred to me that if Carl died of poisoning, it couldn't have been Aunt Rose's pie as he'd taken it the night before.

"If Carl was poisoned, wouldn't it have happened that day?" I asked. "Even if it was the pie, someone else would have had to have tampered with it because Aunt Rose handed it over to Mrs. Conners for the contest and never handled it after that."

"Some poisons take longer to kill," Dwayne said.

Sergeant Scowls nostrils flared at Dwayne's comment but he kept his attention on Aunt Rose. "Are you saying you never touched the pie again once you gave it to Mrs. Conners?"

"That's right," Aunt Rose said with a definitive nod.

"Carl wasn't the only judge either. No one else was poisoned, so it couldn't have been Aunt Rose's pie." I hoped I was right about that and no one else had gotten sick or died.

"What about after the contest? Where do the pies go?" Sergeant Scowl asked.

I frowned. Why were they so focused on the pie?

"They're returned to the kitchen. Mrs. Conner's packs them up," Aunt Rose said.

"Does anyone help her?"

"Maybe. Alice and Carolyn were lurking about probably wanting to know why they lost the contest," Aunt Rose said.

"Mrs. Conner took Aunt Rose's pie to the kitchen for her," I said, wishing Aunt Rose would limit her commentary.

"Where were you?" Dwayne asked Aunt Rose. She glared at him, clearly not liking the way he questioned her.

She huffed out a breath. "I was looking at Betty Bealton's art with Sophie. Then I went to the kitchen to get my pie, but it was gone." She shook her head. "But that was the night before. If he was poisoned, someone must have done it that morning."

I'd already been thinking the same thing.

"It's possible he was poisoned the night before," Sergeant Scowl said, with a glance at Dwyane like he was telling him to keep quiet. "Until we know the exact poison, we won't be sure, but we're looking at all possibilities."

"It doesn't sound like it," Aunt Rose quipped. "It sounds like you think it was my pie."

The look Sergeant Scowl gave Dwayne made me wonder if they knew more than they were telling us. If that was the case, and they were asking about the pie, did that mean it had been tested already?

"Do you have any proof that there was poison in Aunt Rose's pie? Or any of the other pies?"

"Not yet," Dwayne said.

"Deputy Lafferty," Sergeant Scowl chastised.

"Not yet?" I repeated. "Is this an investigation or an interrogation?"

"Lawson—"

"Aunt Rose, don't say anything more," I snapped.

She flinched, and glared at me, but listened.

"Maybe we need a lawyer," I said, although I couldn't imagine who and how we'd pay for it. The only lawyer I knew was Becca Thoreaux, AJ's ex, and since she tried to win him back the last time that she was around him, I wasn't about to invite her back to Jefferson Grove.

"This is an investigation," Sergeant Scowl said. "We're simply working to ascertain when and how Mr. Jackson ingested the poison."

"No, you're saying it was in her pie. But it could have been in another pie," I argued.

"Or the water," Aunt Rose said.

"What water?" Sergeant Scowl asked.

"The water they drink between taste tests," she answered. "You know, to wash away the remnants of the last pie."

"He would have noticed if there was poison in the water," Dwayne said low to Sergeant Scowl like it was a secret and we wouldn't hear it.

We all glared at him.

"Probably . . ." Dwayne said with a half-shrug.

"Deputy Lafferty—"

Dwayne held up his hand. "Sorry."

Sergeant Scowl sighed and turned back to us. "Between pie tastings, he had water, is that what you're saying?"

"Yes." Aunt Rose nodded.

"Plus, there was lots of food and beverages there," I added. "He could have been poisoned by anyone of those. Or maybe at home that night. Or the next morning."

"We're looking into all possibilities." Sergeant Scowl wrote a note on his notepad. "I would like to revisit the pie though. When you returned to the kitchen last night, where was the pie?"

"It was gone," Aunt Rose snapped. "Are you listening?"

I bit my lip. I often had the same reaction when questioned by Sergeant Scowl.

"Where were you, Sophie?" Dwayne asked.

"She had to use the little girl's room," Aunt Rose answered.

Good lord, I hoped that wasn't going into a police report.

"Did you see anything, on your way from the bathroom back to the kitchen?" Sergeant Scowl asked me.

"Like Carl with the pie?" I asked, tracing my steps in my head.

He nodded. "Or anything else that might be noteworthy."

I shook my head. "No. I didn't see him or anything out of the ordinary."

Sergeant Scowl made another note. "Do you know where he took the pie from? Did he get it out of the refrigerator or was it left out?"

I didn't know the answer. I looked to Aunt Rose wondering if she knew.

"I don't know. Normally they're out waiting for us to take, but I don't know when he got it," Aunt Rose said.

"Did you see him take it?" Sergeant Scowl asked.

Aunt Rose pursed her lips. "Why would I have to see him? Who else would take it?"

Since Dwayne had picked up the pie from Carl's place, it didn't seem like they should be disputing that Carl took it.

"I believe Mrs. Connor might have seen him, right Aunt Rose? She's the one who said he took it," I offered.

"In normal circumstances, do all the pies get left out for the owners to pick up?" Sergeant Scowl asked.

"Usually. Like I said, Mrs. Conner has them packed and ready for me to bring home. Carl always steals a piece but this time, he took the whole thing," Aunt Rose's face tensed, showing she was still angry about Carl's theft of her pie. I hope it didn't read "possible murderer" to Sergeant Scowl and Dwayne.

"So, it was in a box or container?" Sergeant Scowl asked.

"It should have been," Aunt Rose said. "I never saw it because he stole it."

"Where there any other pies left with yours?" Sergeant Scowl asked.

"Well, I don't know Lawson. Probably." Aunt Rose's tone indicated that Sergeant Scowl had gotten her last nerve.

I thought back to the night but couldn't remember if the other pies were on the counter. Alice and Carolyn were still at the event, so their pies had to be around there somewhere.

"Do you know who had access to the pie?" Dwayne asked.

I shrugged. "I imagine anyone. The kitchen was open." I looked over at Aunt Rose who nodded.

"Was the kitchen off limits to anyone?" Dwayne asked. "Or could anyone go in?"

"You'll have to ask Mrs. Conner," I said. "She ran the pie contest. I don't know that she had rules about who could and couldn't be in the kitchen, but I only ever saw her and the other pie contestants and Carl."

"That would be Carolyn Jenkinson and Alice Filmore?" Sergeant Scowl asked.

"Yes."

"What about the morning he died, what did Carl say to you, Ms. Parker?" Sergeant Scowl asked.

"He said something about it snowing then he started breathing funny and fell over, just like I told you the other night. Don't you write this stuff down? On IDTV the police take notes."

Dwayne frowned but Sergeant Scowl retained a poker face. "What about you?" he said to me.

"What about me?" He wasn't asking about my trip to the bathroom, was he?

"When did you find Mr. Jackson?"

"He was already on the floor when I saw him," I answered.

"Dead?" Dwayne asked.

"I think so, but I'm not a doctor. He seemed dead," I said.

"Was anyone else in the kitchen with you?" Sergeant Scowl said.

I thought for a moment. "At that time, it was just me and Aunt Rose."

"Was there any food or drink items in the kitchen that he might have consumed?" Sergeant Scowl asked.

I looked at Aunt Rose and she glanced at me. We both shrugged.

"I don't remember seeing anything," I said. Aunt Rose nodded in agreement.

Dwayne looked like he was going to ask something else, but Sergeant Scowl stood. "Thank you, ladies. We may have more questions in the future."

I rose with them, glad to be walking them to the door.

When they'd left, I found Aunt Rose in the kitchen, yammering away. Since it was more of a rant mixed with venting, it wasn't a conversation I was required to participate in.

She reheated a pot pie she'd made the other night and we sat at the table to eat.

"Do you think they are going to arrest me?" she asked. "They think I killed Carl, don't they?"

"I think they're just getting as much information as they can from everyone who was there," I said, not wanting to admit that at least Dwayne thought she was a murderer.

"I should probably go with you the next time you visit your father and brother," she said, poking at the crust of her potpie.

"Oh?" I pulled the top off my pie piece so the chicken and vegetables could cool off a little bit.

"I'll need to learn how to live in the big house. Do you think they have bunco in prison?"

I pursed my lips together to keep from laughing because that was funny. But looking over at my aunt, her pursed lips and furrowed brow suggested she wasn't joking.

"If not, you could start it. But I wouldn't worry, Aunt Rose. You didn't kill Carl and eventually the real murderer will be found." I crossed my fingers under the table.

"Maybe you can find the killer. You're good at that."

Not really. Mostly I was lucky I hadn't been killed. But I'd poked my nose into a murder investigation for a friend, it seemed like I should do it to help my aunt.

"If Carl was poisoned, we'd have to figure out when and how."

Aunt Rose leaned forward; her soft face scrunched into a quizzical expression. "Do you think someone poisoned my pie?"

"If someone did, we need to figure out who was around it that could have slipped it in for Carl to eat."

"Who'd want to poison my pie?"

That was a good question. It seemed to me that there could have been many sources of the poison, but since Sergeant Scowl and Dwayne were so focused on the pie, I had to believe they knew something they weren't sharing with us.

The fact that no one was poisoned during the contest suggested the pie wasn't poisoned, or if it was, the toxic substance was put in later. Most pies were packed up ready to go home, which meant that if the pie was poisoned then, maybe it was meant for Aunt Rose. Or me. A chill ran down my spine. It wasn't the first time someone would have wanted me dead, but it wasn't a feeling you ever got used to.

"If the pie is the source of the poison, we need to think about all the people who were in the kitchen especially after the contest." I got up from the table and went to Aunt Rose's junk drawer in the kitchen, pulling out a pad of paper and a pen.

"What's that for?" she asked.

"To take notes."

"Right." She pointed her finger at me. "We need a big sheet of paper. We can make a murder board like they do on the TV crime shows."

Again, I held back a snicker. "For now, let's start with this." I opened the note pad to a blank page. "Let's start with Friday night. Did you see Carl in the kitchen after the contest?"

"I was talking to Verna Gordon and I saw him in the kitchen stealing my pie." Aunt Rose poked a chunk of chicken in her pot pie.

"Verna Gordon was there?" I didn't remember her on Sergeant Scowl's list or Aunt Rose mentioning that.

"She was congratulating me on winning the pie contest."

"He was in the kitchen. Where were you?" I drew a little schematic of the space with the kitchen and general layout of the activities at the event.

She huffed out a breath. "I just told you Sophie, with Verna Gordan. By the face painting. Why she lets her grandkids paint goop on their face I'll never know."

"And you saw Carl in the kitchen, stealing your pie."

She stabbed a carrot with her fork. "Yes. But by the time I got there, he was gone."

"Did you see him with the pie or just in the kitchen?" I asked.

She thought for a moment. "He was in the kitchen. But I knew he was taking my pie and I was right."

"Was there anyone else in the kitchen?" I asked.

"I didn't see anyone in the kitchen. The ladies were outside of it, though."

"Carolyn and Alice? What about Mrs. Conner?"

"She was there too."

I found it difficult to think any of them would poison Carl, but I wrote them down on our paper. I'd learned from my previous involvement in murder that killers were often the last person you'd expect.

"What about Saturday morning when you confronted him. What happened then?"

She looked up at me. "I told him he needed to keep his grubby hands off my pies."

"What did he do?"

"He gave me that phony baloney smile he gives everyone. He thinks he's charming but he's like floor wax, all shiny but watch your step. He told me it was delicious for breakfast and he looked forward to a piece when he got home."

That sounded like he ate some of the pie that morning. I wrote that down on my notes. "Then what happened?"

"I told him I hoped he choked on it."

I winced. "Then what?"

She rolled her eyes. "You're as bad as Lawson. I already told you. He started making a face like he had indigestion or some-thing. Then he started huffing and puffing like he couldn't breathe. I thought he was being stupid like he always is. Usually though he puts his hand over his heart and says I hurt him where it counts. Then he fell over. Then you walked in."

"And there was no one else in the kitchen?"

She huffed out an annoyed breath. "I told you I didn't see anyone."

"And you're sure it was your pie he took?"

"Who else's pie would it be Sophie? He always takes mine."

"Were the other pies out, or just yours? Could he have taken more than one pie?" Everyone had said he was a bit off that night so maybe he took them all.

"I don't know. I'm not sure if the other pies were there."

"He usually stole bites or a piece, right?" Why did he take the whole thing? I jotted down what I remembered along with her story. I wished I'd checked my watch then because I had no idea when all of this occurred and I suspected it would be important.

"Yes."

"Everyone knew that Carl liked to take some of your pie too, right?" I asked Aunt Rose. She was boisterous in her contempt for Carl's always taking her pie, so anyone involved in the pie contest would know about his penchant for taking some.

"Probably. Mrs. Conner did."

I looked at my notes and picture, tapping the pad with my pen. "Why don't we figure out who'd want him dead."

"Lots of people won't be grieving."

She'd said that several times which had surprised me. He'd always seemed like nice old man to me. Yes, he enjoyed poking at Aunt Rose, but I thought it was because he had a little crush on her.

"Why don't we start with people who had access to the kitchen." I made a list of people I remembered seeing in the kitchen when we dropped off Aunt Rose's pie; Mrs. Conner, Carolyn Jenkinson, and Alice Filmore.

"There weren't armed guards. Anyone could go into the kitchen." Aunt Rose turned her attention back to her dinner.

"What about Mrs. Conner. Did she have any reason to want him dead?"

Aunt Rose's face pinched up as she thought. "I don't know. She probably wished he'd stop stealing my pies because I always gave her a piece of my mind about it."

"How about Alice Filmore? He nearly always put your pie first in contests. Maybe she didn't like that." Even as I said it, I couldn't believe anyone would kill over losing a pie contest. It's not like money was involved.

"I don't know. She spends all her time out in the woods in that old cabin Tubby's family built. Why she stays there is beyond me."

I remembered running into Betty and Aunt Rose saying she had a crush on Carl.

"What about Betty? You said she liked Carl. Did he spurn her?"

"Of course, he did. But Betty couldn't hurt a fly."

Scratch that. "Do you know his grandson, Tyler?" I asked. "He was there that night."

"Fruit doesn't fall far from the tree, if you ask me. There's something rotten about that kid, as well. Oh, he hides it behind a smarmy smile like Carl, but trust me, he's a greedy cheat. I hope you're not thinking of replacing AJ with the likes of him."

I gaped. "No, why would you say that?"

"I see how you're upset that AJ missed another date. A little jealousy can go a long way, but you'd be better off to flirt with Lawson than a Jackson."

Sergeant Scowl? Eww. "How do you know about Carl's grandson?"

"Betty told me all about him. He's been going through all of Carl's things including his accounts and such. He says the family is worried about Carl mental capacity, but Carl is as sharp as a tack."

She was talking about Carl in the present tense again, but I decided not to remind her that Carl was dead. And before he was dead, he'd been acting strange.

"You know he owns nearly half the homes over in the Mayberry subdivision?" Aunt Rose said, taking a bit of her pot pie.

"I didn't," I said.

"He owned a few, but then he beat out Joe Cullen in buying the ones your dad owned when he went to prison. You know, Sophie." Aunt Rose pointed her fork at me. "Your dad might be a crook, but he took care of his properties and his tenants. Old Carl is letting those homes get run down, and he doesn't pay the people he sends out to fix things. If anyone killed him it was probably one of his renters."

I made a note to figure out who was at the event that rented from Carl, and if it was true that he wasn't caring for the properties or the tenants.

I'd learned from the two murders I'd already been embroiled in that money was often the primary motivation behind a murder. "What do you think Carl's estate is worth?"

Aunt Rose shrugged. "Couple million maybe."

A couple of million? How did a man who had a reputation for being a cheapskate have that much money?

I looked at our list. "It seems to me if we look at opportunity and motive, his grandson has the most, don't you think?"

Aunt Rose thought for a moment. "Greed. On IDTV nearly all them kill for money."

I wondered if Sergeant Scowl and Dwayne were solely focused on the pie or considering another ingestible source. "Plus, if he's staying with Carl, he'd have an easier chance to poison him. Maybe he slipped something into Carl's food or drink."

Aunt Rose stood, taking her plate to the kitchen. She left it in the sink and then went to get her purse.

"We can do the dishes later," she said.

"Where are you going?"

"To go ask Carl's grandson if he killed him." Her tone said "duh."

"I doubt he'll tell us if he did."

"Right. Killers lie." She came and sat at the table. "Should we call Lawson?"

I shook my head. "He doesn't like it when other people tell him what to do."

Aunt Rose pursed her lips at me. "How in the heck then are we going to find out who did it?"

"He's the most obvious person, but usually, the obvious one isn't the killer. You didn't kill him and there are some who will think you did. We're stuck because we don't know when or how he was poisoned, but we can try and trace his steps the night before and that morning to see who was with him and maybe what he consumed."

Aunt Rose's head bobbed up and down. "Good thinking. How do we do that?"

I looked at our list again. "We need to talk to anyone who saw him Friday night and try to find out what he ate."

"Do you think he still had my pie in his stomach?" Aunt Rose asked.

It was nauseating to think of that after eating pot pie. "Why would you ask that?"

"Because in an autopsy the medical examiner can cut open their stomachs to see what they ate. Why would they be asking about my pie unless it was still in his stomach?"

I saw my note about Carl saying he ate some of her pie for breakfast. "We need to find that out." I leaned forward. "How long does it take for something to digest, do you know?"

She shook her head. "No. Why?"

"Because if the pie would have been digested by morning, then he couldn't have been poisoned Friday night." I shook my head. "But he might have had some that morning."

"Maybe someone added the poison then."

I felt like I was going around and around. Carl was acting weird the night before, which suggested he'd been poisoned then.

"You know, in *Deadly Woman*, the killer gave the poison over time. Usually, the killer is nursing her victim of his sickness, but the whole time poisoning him," Aunt Rose said.

I found a clean spot on my paper. "We need to find out if there is a poison that can take a night before it kills someone."

"What about that bad moonshine like Carolyn said?" Aunt Rose asked.

"It seems like he'd taste that in his food or drink," I said, but still wrote it down. "What sorts of poisons do they use on your shows?"

Aunt Rose thought for a moment. "Arsenic. Strychnine. Cyanide."

I wrote them down with the intention of studying them. "Anything else?"

She shrugged. "People use all sort of things they can find around the house. Medicines. Pest control. Antifreeze."

Dwayne had mentioned antifreeze the night Carl died.

"I watched one show where someone used eyedrops," Aunt Rose finished.

I frowned. "That can kill?" How was it possible something you put in your eyes could kill you?

I finished my discussion with Aunt Rose with a promise that I'd get started on it right away by studying what I could learn about poisons on the Internet.

Chapter Six

Iwas no expert on poisonings, but based on what I learned on the Internet, I felt I could rule out arsenic and strychnine. Arsenic took longer to kill and strychnine and cyanide killed faster, plus the symptoms didn't match the drunken state Carl had been in.

The antifreeze, however, did fit. There were a variety of symptoms of antifreeze poisoning, including grogginess, slurred speech, lack of coordination, and vision problems. Untreated, it could kill in twenty-four to thirty-six ours. The one factoid on the list that caused me the most discomfort was that antifreeze had a sweet taste. Carl had said Aunt Rose's pie was too sweet. How long had it been before someone reported that to Sergeant Scowl—or maybe someone had, which was why he was so focused on the pie.

I made a plan to see Tyler the next day. Aunt Rose had a casserole of some sort in the freezer I could bring him under the guise of supporting him through his grandfather's death. It was a ruse I'd used when my friend Marla had been killed, and I wondered what it said about me to be so callous as to act compassionate while also assessing someone's capability for murder.

After work, I returned home for the casserole and was able to convince Aunt Rose not to come with me as it might be too upsetting for her. In reality, I was afraid that if Sergeant Scowl or Dwayne had tipped their hand in making Aunt Rose a suspect, Tyler might not be happy to see her.

"Are you going dressed like that?" Aunt Rose said as I prepared to leave armed with her casserole and my purse.

I looked down at my black jeans and warm gray snow boots with the fake-fur trim. Under my wool coat, I had on a V-neck sweater over a white shirt. "What's wrong with this?"

"You should dress fancy. Use your feminine wiles."

"I don't think he'll be receptive to my wiles," I said, thinking of Gwen and all the wiles she had to offer him. "Besides, he's grieving."

"Well, I guess you know best," she said in a tone that suggested she didn't believe her words.

I drove into the Mayberry section of town, built after World War II and filled with brick ranchers that all looked the same. Had things gone to plan, Aunt Rose might have ended up living in one of them with Carl. While she might be bitter, I thought her little craftsman bungalow built in the 1920's had much more character than Carl's cookie-cutter ranch style home.

The neighborhood had a significant number of rental properties, many which had been owned by my father, but sold off when he went to prison. Aunt Rose said Carl had bought some but didn't provide the same level of care for them as my father had.

The neighborhood was decked out in holiday décor. Large blow-up Santa's and snow globes, plastic reindeer, snowmen and nativity scenes filled the large lawns. Carl's house looked well-kept enough with white trim decorated and holiday lights.

I parked in front of the house noticing Carl's old Buick in the carport. I carried the casserole up to the front door knocking just below the plastic wreath.

Tyler opened the door, his brows furrowed as if he couldn't imagine someone coming to the house.

He cocked his head when he saw me. "Sophie, right?"

"Yes. You remembered. I'm so sorry for your loss, Tyler. Your grandfather was a sweet man." I handed him the casserole. "I brought you a casserole."

He took the dish and opened the door. "What's with the food?"

When I stepped in, I could see to the kitchen where on the table there were half a dozen other casserole dishes.

"It's what we do here when there is a loss."

"You feed the bereaved?" He set the dish with the others. "This is just from today. They've been showing up daily since Sunday."

It sounded lame the way he said it.

"It's one less thing for you to worry about. And I suppose it's a way for us to show our concern and caring."

He shrugged. "I was having a drink. Want one?"

"I thought your grandfather didn't drink?" I said when Tyler pulled out a bottle of bourbon.

"I bought this when I got here. He's got water and apple cider. At least that's what I think it is. It's in an old milk jug."

I nodded. "It's probably homemade by someone. I'm fine though, thank you."

I followed him back to the living area and sat on the couch, while he sat in a large recliner.

"Did you know my grandfather well?" he asked.

"Not well, I guess. He and I were always friendly though. Were you close to him?"

He shook his head. "No. He and my dad had some sort of falling out after my grandmother died so we didn't come to see him much."

"I imagine he was happy to see you, though," I said, remembering that Tyler had said he thought his parents wanted to visit Carl since he was old and might not be around much longer.

"I suppose so. I think he was annoyed that my parents planned to come. He was certain they were after his money." He shook his head. "He wasn't wrong about that. Families can be so messed up."

I nodded as I knew first-hand the truth of his statement. "Are your parents still coming?"

"My dad is planning to deal with the estate." Tyler downed his bourbon. "I'd head out of here but the cops were by earlier saying my grandfather was poisoned so I need to stick around."

I studied him and didn't notice any surprise in his expression. "You don't seem surprised by that."

"It's true what they say about small town gossip. Each casserole that has showed up came with a story about how my grandfather had done this or that that wasn't very nice. I couldn't understand why people were bringing food to me when I don't think they liked my grandfather."

"What we feel about a person doesn't factor in at all. Southern hospitality dictates that we need to feed the grieving."

He laughed. "Well, he'd like that. Free food. The guy had a ton of money, yet he'd dumpster-dive if his arthritis didn't prevent it. He took a pie from the—well I guess you know that."

I nodded wondering if he was going to change his attitude towards me when he remembered I was Aunt Rose's niece.

"What was the deal with him and your aunt anyway?" he asked.

"I don't know the details, but the rumor is that he and my great aunt were engaged fifty or sixty years ago. Then he went into the military, and when he got home a few years later, he brought your grandmother with him."

"Ouch."

Based on what I was learning about Carl, I began to think she was better off without him.

"I always thought it was cute the way he'd poke at her," I said, hoping to use this as my doorway to ask him more about his grandfather.

"Oh?"

"He was always charming and yet, would tease her."

He shook his head. "I don't want the image of my grandfather picking up a woman in my brain."

I laughed. "I suppose that would be disturbing. But you said the other night that Carl had a reputation with the ladies."

"That's according to my dad. I think that was the source of their falling out."

"Even with their estrangement, I suppose your father is sad to lose his dad. Especially by someone else's hand. I can't imagine anyone wanting to hurt Carl."

He arched a brow. "I'm told there are many people who had a beef with my grandfather."

"Not liking someone isn't the same as wanting to kill them." Aunt Rose had said something similar to Sergeant Scowl the day Carl died.

He shrugged.

"I just find it hard to think something like that would happen here," I said, even though I had two experiences of murder since returning home six months ago.

"I suppose murder happens anywhere."

"You don't seem particularly upset," I said.

He lifted his glass. "A few drinks dull the pain."

It seemed like a callous thing to say. "I remember you saying that Carl seemed drunk the other night but he wasn't a drinker."

"Maybe it was a sugar high from all the pie."

I nodded. "Normally he takes a piece home, but that night he took the whole thing."

"Yeah, and he ate more that night. And then he had a piece for breakfast." Tyler shook his head. "If he always ate like that, it was a surprise he didn't die from diabetes or heart disease."

"Did you have any pie?" I asked, thinking that if he ate a piece and didn't get sick or die, that would prove the pie wasn't poisoned.

"No. I'm not a pie eater. Besides, I don't think he'd have shared it."

"Did you talk to him Friday night after he was acting weird?"

Tyler's eyes narrowed. "What's it to you?"

I shrugged realizing I was asking twenty-questions. "Just being an arm-chair detective, I guess."

"When I got back, I headed to my room to call my parents then I went to bed."

"Was Carl's behavior still off in the morning?"

He thought for a moment. "Maybe. I didn't know him that well, you know. When I got up, he was outside with a neighbor guy fixing his car. I think that car is nearly as old as I am. I told him he should trade it in, but he was too cheap to buy a new one. Instead, he mooched free labor off his neighbor, who apparently rents from my grandfather and was telling him, not for the first time, that their heat needed fixing."

"Did Carl make arrangements to have it fixed?"

"I don't know."

I frowned. It was the middle of winter in Jefferson Grove. It wasn't a time not to have heat.

"Who was the neighbor?" I asked, thinking I might be able to help, although I wasn't sure how unless Bull new how to fix heat. He'd put a new battery in my car and he could bake. Surely a jack-of-all-trades like that could deal with a heating issue.

"Mr. Jones, or something like that. Or maybe Jones was his first name. I don't know."

I'd gone to school with a Jones Willoughby. I wondered if he lived in this neighborhood. I made a mental note to follow up on that and see if he noticed anything about Carl when fixing his car, the morning he died.

Back in my car, I jotted down a few notes and then headed home. I hadn't learned very much from Tyler and I hoped Aunt Rose wasn't too discouraged by that.

As I approached the house, I saw Bull's motorcycle parked out front. My stomach jumped in excitement as that meant AJ had to be back too. Did I miss a call or text?

I parked in the driveway and pulled my phone from my purse. There weren't any notifications. Just to be sure I clicked on my text and voicemail apps, but there was nothing from AJ. My disappointment was acute—so much so that I had tears in my eyes. I felt silly about that because the one thing I wanted to achieve when my father and brother went to prison was independence. Not just financially, but emotionally as well. I loved AJ, but I didn't want to need him for my happiness. The fact that I was on the verge of tears because he was slipping away from me suggested I was failing in my effort to not need a man.

I pulled myself together and went to the house. The scent of baking sugar and butter swirled around me as I entered.

"Hey, Miss Sophie!" Bull, dressed in a pink apron and his long biker hair pulled back in a tie, beamed at me. His tattooed arms banded around me, lifting me up and twirling me around.

I laughed despite my anger and hurt at AJ not being here with him. Then again, AJ never came here unless he was sure I was home. When we first started hanging out, I worked at the Booty Burgo, and he he'd meet me at two in the morning when my shift ended. Now that I worked at the library, on occasion he'd meet me there or I'd go to his place. I tried to convince him that Aunt Rose was okay with him, especially since he was friends with Bull, her baking buddy, but AJ still kept his distance. I needed to rethink his reasoning. Maybe he wasn't afraid of Aunt Rose but was using her as an excuse to slowly pull away from me.

"It smells like you're cooking up a storm," I said when Bull put me down.

"Christmas cookies. I'm going to teach Rose here how to decorate them using the flooding technique," Bull said.

"Seems like too much work to me for something that's just going to get ruined," Aunt Rose quipped as she pulled a tray of cookies out of the oven. Several racks of cookies sat on the counter, cooling.

"You'll love it," Bull responded. "Plus, there are cookie contests. The cooking channel has one that awards ten thousand dollars."

"Ten thousand dollars for cookies?" Aunt Rose's face squished together like she thought Bull was teasing her.

"Yes, ma'am." Bull crossed his heart. "Scout's honor."

"Were you a Boy Scout?" I asked him.

"Of course." He grinned. "Until I got kicked out."

I laughed, and then remembered AJ and how he hadn't called to let me know he was home.

"What's the matter, Miss Sophie," Bull asked frowning at me.

"Nothing." I sucked up my disappointment and put on a fake smile.

"Did you go see Tyler Jackson?" Aunt Rose said.

"I did."

"Well?" Aunt Rose demanded.

I looked at Bull, not sure I wanted to have a discussion about Carl Jackson's murder in front of him. AJ never liked it when I poked my nose into murder investigations. Then again, AJ wasn't around.

"He said he went to bed when he got home," I said.

"He could be lying," Aunt Rose said.

"Who is Tyler Jackson?" Bull asked.

"He could be. He also said that Saturday morning Carl had car trouble and a neighbor helped him. I thought I'd figure out who that neighbor is and ask him what he noticed about Carl that morning."

"Who's Carl?" Bull asked.

"Carl is dead." Aunt Rose turned back to her cookies. "I hope you figure it out, Sophie."

"I'm going back to my room."

"Yes, yes. If you want dinner there is some soup in the fridge. Betty dropped it off today. She was worried I was upset about Carl. Maybe you can bring that to Tyler and his neighbor. Betty always puts too much salt in her soup."

I turned to go up the hall when a big meaty hand came down on my shoulder. "Who is Tyler Jackson and why are you seeing him?"

Bull was a teddy bear, unless he was upset. When I turned to look at him, his dark brows were pulled together into a single line.

"That's my business, Bull," I said, pushing his hand off my shoulder. When I met him six months ago, this interaction would have scared the bejesus out of me. Now that I knew him, it just annoyed me.

"You're not dumping AJ, are you?"

I hated that the first response to that was my eyes burning as tears tried to form. I summoned anger to keep the tears at bay. "I can't dump AJ. I never see him anymore."

Bull shook his head. "Now, Miss Sophie, don't be mad at him. He's working hard."

"I know he is. He's doing his job and other people's job. What's his excuse now? I see you here, but not him."

Bull frowned. "You haven't talked to him?"

I shook my head. "The only reason I know he's home is that you are here."

His face morphed into pity, which I hated even more. "He has some things he needs to deal with."

His words were like little stabs in my heart. Whatever was going on with AJ, Bull knew about it but I didn't. I not only felt betrayed by AJ confiding in Bull, but also anger at myself for letting AJ talk me into trusting him. I'd been scared to death to fall for him. I'd been a daddy's girl all my life, always believing in him. As it turned out, he was a crook, and while I knew he loved me, it shook me to discover my father, brother, and even mother, were all not who I thought they were. I didn't want to be in a position where I had to feel the foundation of my life completely crumble from beneath me again. Yet, here I was, on shaky ground.

"I'm sure he did. He always does." Worried that I might burst into tears, I left Bull in the living room to return to my bedroom.

"He's doing it for a good reason," Bull called after me.

I closed my door to shut him out. To distract me from the pain, I researched library programming I could run in the New Year. I was taking notes on the variety of foods eaten on New Year's to bring good luck, when my phone rang.

Like a dummy, my heart flipped in anticipation of it being AJ. Then it sank when I realized that it was Lani's ringtone.

"Hi Lani."

"Hi Soph." Lani's voice was low and slightly muffled.

"Are you okay?"

"Yeah, I just can't talk for long and I don't want Dwayne to hear. Can you meet me for lunch tomorrow?"

"Sure. What's going on?"

"I might have some information for you about Carl Jackson. I assume you're helping Rose, and this might help. But I can't—" There was a knocking sound in the background. "Give me minute," Lani called. There was a pause. "I'm in the bathroom, Dwayne, who would I be talking to in here?"

I winced as I realized she was being deceptive to her husband.

"I'm back. Meet me at the diner near the library tomorrow at noon."

"I'll be there. But Lani, don't do anything that will hurt your relationship with Dwayne."

"It'll be fine, Sophie. I gotta go." She hung up the phone.

I sat on my rollaway bed, currently in the couch position, wondering what Lani knew. It was risky for her to share information with me, not just because of Dwayne, but also because she could lose her job at the sheriff's department. Whatever she knew, though, had to be important. If I was lucky, it would be something that could clear Aunt Rose's name.

Chapter Seven

My morning routine was normal enough that I could forget that Aunt Rose was a person of interest in a murder. Her spirits had been boosted by Bull's visit that included baking bourbon-soaked fruitcake. The next morning, she was still in a good mood and planning a trip to the senior center for her regular day of bunco. I wanted to question whether or not it was a good idea for her to go. The only reason I could think of was that the other seniors might accuse her of murdering Carl. Since Aunt Rose didn't seem to care what people said about her, I figured it wouldn't bother her or she'd have some sort of comeback that would shut them up.

At work, I had a preschool group story time and then I worked on organizing and shelving returns in the children's section. At lunch, I bundled up in my wool coat, heavy scarf, and hat, and walked down to the diner to meet Lani. It was at that point I began to fret over what she might tell me about Carl Jackson's murder.

When I arrived at the diner, Lani was in a back booth. It was good that she'd arrived early as the place was filling up. I had a moment to wonder if maybe discussing Carl's murder in a public place filled with locals was a good idea.

"Hey Soph," Lani greeted me.

"Hey." I slid into the booth.

"How are you doing?"

I shrugged. "I'm alright."

"Have you heard from AJ?" Lani probably hoped that reconnecting with AJ would soften the blow of whatever she had to tell me.

I shook my head. "But Bull was over last night. He cheered Aunt Rose up."

Lani frowned. "If he's back, shouldn't AJ be too?"

I picked up the plastic-coated menu with pictures of pancakes, eggs and burgers on it. "Yes. Bull said he had some things he had to deal with."

"Like what?"

I held my annoyance in check. "What news did you have for me?"

Like the good friend she was, she got the message and switched gears. She leaned closer to me, her eyes looking around as if to see if anyone would overhear us.

"Don't tell anyone I told you, but the medical examiner's office suspects ethylene glycol was used to poison Carl."

I let that settle in my brain. I knew from my research that it was antifreeze, but I wasn't sure what it meant in terms of clearing Aunt Rose.

"Was it in the pie?" I asked.

Lani shrugged. "The tests are still out, but apparently, based on the condition of the organs, the ME suspects that. How it got into his system isn't clear at this point."

Knowing the poison didn't seem to help me in this situation, I'd have to research it more to figure out if it was in other solutions and if it something that Aunt Rose would have access to.

Our waitress arrived, so we curbed the conversation until we'd ordered. I opted for grilled cheese with bacon, and fries, while Lani ordered a burger.

"I'm sorry about Dwayne," Lani said once our waitress left. "He really wants this promotion and might be a bit overzealous."

I could hardly hold it against her that her husband was a go-getter. "I understand. But you might let him know that Sergeant Scowl may not like all his eager beaverness."

Lani made a face. "I don't care if he's annoyed. I just care about you."

I smiled and reminded myself what a great friend she'd always been, especially when I returned to Jefferson Grove in the midst of my father's scandal.

At that point, we made an agreement to not talk about Dwayne, Aunt Rose, AJ, or Carl Jackson.

After lunch, I returned to the library and resumed my normal day which included more organizing and shelving, and an afternoon winter break kids' reading club. Near the end of my day, there was a lull and I was able to use one of the computers to look up ethylene glycol. According to the CDC, it was an industrial compound used in a variety of car-related products including anti-freeze and brake fluid. Aunt Rose didn't have a car, but I did, although I didn't have anti-freeze or brake fluid. I'd been relying on Bull for my car upkeep. I realized that could be a problem since Bull was Aunt Rose's friend and had ties to people in prison. I could easily see Sergeant Scowl thinking Aunt Rose asked for Bull's help in poisoning Carl.

I read on about ethylene glycol's effects which, like I read about antifreeze, initially resembled intoxication and later would cause cardiopulmonary and renal problems, and possible death . . . and it had a sweet taste. That meant it probably wasn't in his water but could certainly be in a pie. It couldn't have been in Aunt Rose's pie as others tested it and didn't get sick, although maybe they didn't ingest enough.

Then again, Carl was acting drunk according to Tyler before he took the pie home, so he wouldn't have that much either. To me, that meant there had to be another source than Aunt Rose's pie. I shook my head, as I realized I'd been considering that the poison was in her pie. That was impossible, as she wouldn't have killed him with her pie. Then again, her pie was unsupervised so maybe someone poisoned it after. This brought me back to the idea that maybe she was the target. It also meant that someone in Jefferson Grove, maybe even someone we knew well, was the murderer. I shook my head at that scary thought.

I finished my shift and started to my car, thinking about what I'd tell Aunt Rose and my next steps in proving her innocence. I remembered that Tyler had said a neighbor had assisted Carl with his car the morning he died. Car? Poison fluid from car? Could there be a connection there?

"Sophie."

My head shot up as my heart jumped in my chest. "AJ."

There was a time I'd almost expect him to waiting for me after work, but that was back when I was a wench waitress at the Booty Burgo. The last several weeks, he hadn't met me after work.

He gave me a sheepish smile as he jumped down from the back bed of his truck. Dutch, his Great Dane, scrambled up from where she lay, and stood at bed's end looking happy to see me.

AJ walked toward me with the swagger I'd first developed a crush on in high school. Even now, the woman in me couldn't help but respond to the handsome ginger-haired man with brilliant blue eyes. When he reached me, he pulled me into a hug. I allowed it more out of habit but I wouldn't say my hug back was warm. Even so, his scent and the feel of him made me yearn to give in.

"You're back," I said, with little affect as I pulled away.

"Yes. I'm sorry I missed the Winter Jamboree."

I sighed and continued to my car. "I know. You're always sorry."

His hand gently gripped my arm to stop my forward movement. "Hey. Talk to me."

I gave a derisive laugh. "Now you want to talk? Well maybe now I'm busy."

"You're not working now," he said frowning.

"That doesn't mean I don't have things to do. You're not the only one who has commitments or whatever it is you're doing."

He rolled his eyes, which I hated. It suggested I was being unreasonable.

Irked, I gathered my ire, "I know you got back yesterday. Bull was over with Aunt Rose. I'd ask you why you didn't call or come over, but I'm told you had a reason. Whatever all these reasons are, they seem to be more important than us."

"That's not true." He scrapped his hands over his face.

Hating how desperate I felt, I blurted, "I wish you'd just end it if that's what you're trying to do."

He gaped. "End it? Sophie, no. I love you." He looked away for a moment like he was gathering his thoughts. When he turned back, he said, "I love you. I'm sorry that I've been MIA so much lately. How about dinner tonight? My place. We can talk then."

"I can't. I wasn't lying when I said I had things to do."

"Your girls' group isn't tonight," he said.

"We're women, not girls, and that's not my only commitment."

He studied me for a moment. "Does it have to do with Carl Jackson's murder?"

"Maybe."

"Sophie." In that one word he was really telling me to butt out of the investigation.

"I need to get home." I moved past him to my car.

"How about tomorrow? Ah . . . wait . . . not tomorrow. How about Sunday?"

I shook my head. "Maybe you should check your calendar first."

"Don't be like this, Sophie."

I growled under my breath. I hated it when he made me out to be the unreasonable one. "Be like what, AJ? You expect me to sit around and wait for when you have time for me? I'm not—"

"No. But I think you're trying to punish me and I swear I'm not trying to avoid you. I'm doing all this for—" He stopped short.

"For what?" I arched a brow at him intrigued by his response.

He sighed. "Please. Tell me when I can see you. How about Monday if Sunday isn't good?"

He was right that we needed to get our relationship sorted and the only way to do that would be to talk.

"Monday." Maybe by then I'd have my heart more in sync with my brain.

"Great. Hey." He reached for me before I could get into my car. "I do love you." He tugged me closer. I blamed the stress of Aunt Rose's predicament for giving in and letting him hold me and not stopping him when he kissed me. This was all I wanted: a life with a job I enjoyed, friends and family, and a nice boyfriend who liked me as much as I liked him. Why was that so hard?

He pulled away and grinned like he knew his kisses were my kryptonite. "Does this mean you still love me?" His tone was teasing but I could hear the undercurrent of concern. *Good.*

"I wouldn't be so annoyed at you if I didn't love you."

"It won't be like this for much longer, Sophie. I promise." He leaned in and gave me another kiss. "I'll see you Monday." He walked back to his truck. He pet Dutch as he closed the back hatch. "Say goodbye to Sophie, Dutch."

Dutch let out a bark that I was sure echoed all the way up the hollows surrounding Jefferson Grove. She was a sweet dog, so I gave her a wave. "If you wanted to eat AJ's favorite sneakers, I'd support you in that."

Dutch let out another woof, which I took to mean, "Will do." Us women in AJ's life had to stick together.

- - - - - - - -

When I arrived home, Aunt Rose was in the kitchen frying chicken. "Dinner will be ready in ten minutes, Sophie."

"Let me wash up. I have some information for you," I said as I went to the sink to wash my hands.

"Is it about Carl?"

"Yes."

She turned off the burner as she put the last piece of chicken on a paper towel. "Did you clear me?"

I sighed. "Not yet. But I learned that the medical examiner thinks it's a poison found in antifreeze and other liquids used in cars."

"Is it in your car?"

"Probably. But I don't have any here. Bull takes care of it for me."

She nodded and pulled her potato masher out of the drawer. After draining the water from potatoes, and adding butter and milk to them, she began mashing. I'd have used an electric mixer, but maybe manually mashing them was why her arms looked so strong. She never exercised so maybe it was old fashioned living that kept her lean and trim.

"That clears me then, right?"

"I don't know. It can't hurt. But the information I found on it suggests he was poisoned the night before. It has a sweet taste so—"

She whirled around and waved the masher at me. "He said my pie was too sweet. Maybe someone poisoned it then."

"I don't think so. The other judges would have been sick too. We have no reason to believe that the poison was in your pie. But it does sound like something that could have been slipped into something he ate or drank."

She nodded. "What about his grandson?"

"It could have been him, or maybe he ate something at the jamboree. We still need to figure that out."

She went back to her potatoes, until satisfied that they were lump-free. She plopped some on two plates, along with a piece of chicken, and the requisite green veggie, tonight it was green beans.

"It sounds to me like we haven't learned anything helpful at all. Maybe you're asking the wrong questions," she said, as she peppered her potatoes.

"This sleuthing stuff is like a puzzle. We get pieces and we have to put them together."

"Right. Like Nancy Drew."

Yes, except she was fiction and the star of her own series and this was real life. "We just need to keep on it."

"Well, we need to work fast because I'm pretty sure Lawson's sidekick is chomping at the bit to put me in jail."

"I don't think that will happen," I said hoping I sounded more reassuring than I felt.

"Just in case, you need to take me with you when you visit your dad. Are you going this weekend?"

"I wasn't planning on it." I tried to get there once a month, but it depended on if the roads were safe from winter snow and ice, and what was going on in my life. Of course, now with AJ gone more, I had time.

"I need to see him soon. Can you arrange it?" she insisted.

"I can, but I really don't think you should be worried about learning to live in prison." I decided not to mention that she'd probably end up in the women's prison and not the federal one housing my father. The good news was that the women's prison was closer so it would be easier to visit her. God, was I really going to have three family members incarcerated?

"Maybe Monty will know something about that neighbor," Aunt Rose said.

She had a point. "I'll arrange for it this weekend."

That night, when I went to bed, I reflected on the strange turn my life had taken. It had been weird in June and then in September to be involved in murder, but now, to have it so close to home, was unsettling. If something happened to Aunt Rose, I'd be alone. Sure, I had Lani and my coupon group, and if AJ were here, he'd say I had him, but I didn't feel like I was tethered to anyone except Aunt Rose at the moment. I hoped that Sergeant Scowl would solve the crime soon so that life could go back to normal.

My phone pinged with a notification. I reached over to where it sat on the arm rest of the rollout bed.

I love you Warrior Princess.

AJ sure made it hard to stay mad at him. But being a warrior princess, a nickname I earned when I tried to save us from another murderer by whapping him with a frying pan, meant I could be strong against my hormones that wanted to forgive AJ for his continuous absences. I texted back.

Goodnight Flyboy

Chapter Eight

The next day was Saturday and normally I worked, but since I had put in so much time for the Winter Jamboree, I was given this weekend off. I arranged for Aunt Rose and me to see my father in prison.

Driving my 30-year-old poop brown Volvo, nicknamed the Brown Bomber, to the federal prison in Petersburg was always stressful. It was a long drive down the mountain, through the piedmont to central Virginia. Coming back was worse because it was uphill, and sometimes I wasn't sure the Brown Bomber could manage it, especially during the hot humid summers.

Today it was winter so heat wasn't a factor in my stress. Aunt Rose was. She sat next to me as I drove us east to Petersburg. At the moment, she was prattling on about Carl Jackson and how his death was going to be his last laugh at her because she was going to jail. That's why she was with me on my visit to see my father. She wanted to know what it was like to live in a prison. No matter how much I assured her that she'd be okay, she insisted Carl had died on purpose to get her.

It was the longest two and half-hour drive of my life, but finally we arrived, checked in, and were taken to the visiting room.

"When I'm in the slammer, Sophie, I don't want you worrying about me." Aunt Rose sat at the table the guard indicated to us.

"You're a strong woman, Aunt Rose."

The door opened and my father entered the room. His eyes lit up when he saw me, but immediately narrowed when he saw Aunt Rose.

He mustered a smile. "Aunt Rose, what a surprise."

"You look terrible, Monty," she said.

My father sighed. "You seem the same as always Aunt Rose." He sat across the table from us. "I didn't realize you were coming. Were you on my list?"

"You put her on the visitor list when I moved in with her," I reminded him. All visitors were required to be pre-approved. I wasn't sure exactly why he put her on the list, except maybe to make it seem like there were more people in his life than me. After all, my brother was in another unit and mother had run off. All he had left was me and Aunt Rose.

"Oh, right." His expression suggested he regretted that now. "Well, I'm so glad you made the drive. How are you both?"

"I need to know what it's like to live in the pokey." Aunt Rose was never one for small talk.

"Oh?" My father looked at me for an explanation.

"I'm a murder suspect," she blurted.

"She's a person of interest," I clarified.

"Who died?" My father leaned forward, clearly intrigued.

"That nitwit Lawson Davis thinks I killed Carl Jackson."

"Did you?" my father asked.

"No. I wanted to many times, but I didn't." Aunt Rose huffed out a breath. She was keeping a brave front, but I could see she was worried.

"Well, I wouldn't worry, Aunt Rose." My father patted her hand. "I'm sure the real killer will be found."

"Plenty of innocent people go to jail, Monty." Her clipped tone told him she didn't want her concerns to be dismissed. "You need to help me."

"What can I do?" My father looked at me with a "help me" expression in his eyes.

"You can start by telling me how to keep the cops off my back."

My father sat back, holding his hands out to the side. "I can't do that. If I knew how, I'd have done it myself. I got caught, remember?"

"You were guilty." Aunt Rose punctuated her comment with a finger point jab at him.

"I was. If you're not, you have to trust that the system will work."

Aunt Rose's eyes narrowed into little slits. It was the look that made many people, including our hulk of a friend, Bull, cower. "After all I've done for you, Montgomery Parker, this is the thanks I get?"

He rolled his eyes. "How did he die?"

"Poisoned. They think it was with my pie."

My father started to laugh, but quickly reined it in. "I think that's karma, isn't it, Aunt Rose?"

Her face squished up like she was thinking. "Yes, but I didn't poison it."

"So how did it get there?"

"We're not sure it was there," I clarified. "He was poisoned but the source of it is unknown."

"How could it get there then?" he asked.

"Well, if I knew that, I wouldn't be here, would I?" Aunt Rose gave him a hard stare like she thought he was one peanut short of a Snickers bar.

I decided it was time for me to help manage this conversation. "It couldn't have been there during the contest, since no one else was poisoned."

"Were the other pies poisoned?" my father asked.

"We don't know. They were all boxed to go home—"

"Carl stole my pie like he always does and it killed him."

My father's expression turned concerned. "Are you sure he was the target?"

"What do you mean?" Aunt Rose asked.

I shook my head hoping my father wouldn't explain what he meant. I'd already considered that she might have been the target if the poison was in her pie and didn't think she needed to.

He frowned at me and then looked at Aunt Rose. "If the pies were ready to go home and that's when the poison was added, assuming it was in the pie, maybe Carl wasn't the intended victim. Maybe you were, Rose."

"Me? Why would anyone want to kill me?" She jerked back, looking from my dad to me and back to him with an expression that suggested she was completely taken aback by the idea.

My father stared at her deadpan. I wondered if he mastered the poker face in prison or perhaps when he was swindling people out of their money.

"According to Aunt Rose, it was well known that Carl would take extra from her pie after the contest. Plus, we can't be sure that the poison wasn't there before and it was simply missed during the testing."

"That's a big risk," my father said. "The killer could have killed more people than just Carl."

"Maybe he or she wanted to kill all the judges and got unlucky . . . or . . . you know what I mean," I said realizing how morbid that thought was. "Or Carl was poisoned some other way. We don't know."

"Either way, I don't see how I can help," my father said.

Aunt Rose pursed her lips. "You're as about as useful gum on a boot heel."

"Maybe you can help us with other information," I suggested hoping to diffuse my aunt.

"Like what?" My father turned his attention to me, but he kept one eye on Aunt Rose. I couldn't blame him. She could be unpredictable. I wouldn't be surprised if by the time we left it was because we were being escorted out for bad conduct.

"You used to own investment property in the Mayberry subdivision where Carl lived."

My father nodded. "Cullen bought most of them, I think. Since he's dead, I suppose his wife owns them."

"Carl Jackson bought some and Aunt Rose says that he doesn't care for them. Some of the homes he uses as storage and others are rented, but not kept up."

"That's a shame. Those post-war homes could stand forever if taken care of. I'm not sure how I can help though."

"Do you remember any of the renters or neighbors?" I asked.

"Sure. But none that would kill."

Aunt Rose leaned forward. "Think harder, Monty. My life is on the line."

My father frowned.

"Is there someone who might commit murder if pushed too far? If Carl wasn't taking care of the homes, maybe the tenants were upset."

My father thought for a moment. "By no upkeep do you mean things like not fixing the HVAC or something? Because I suppose if you were hot in the summer or freezing in the winter, that might make someone upset, although I still don't see them becoming murderers over it."

"Do you know a neighbor of Carl's named Jones?" I asked.

"First or last name?"

"Either," I said, leaning forward.

"There are, or was when I owned homes in there, two families with the last name Jones. Old Rosco, you remember him don't you, Aunt Rose?" my father asked.

"The one who's brother poked his eye out with a stick when they were kids?"

"Yes, that's him. He has a place in there and his son's family does too."

I wrote down Rosco Jones and son. "What about first name. I went to school with Jones Willoughby."

My father shook his head. "I don't remember him living there. But his grandmother did. Maybe he moved in with her."

"Gladys Willoughby died last year," Aunt Rose said. "Rest her soul. She was the bunco champion before me."

"Maybe he inherited it," my father said. "Or maybe his mother. I think she lived there to care for her mother."

I wrote a note to find out if Jones or his mother inherited his grandmother's home. "Can you think of a reason a renter would want to kill, maybe if the home wasn't kept up? What did you to do keep up the homes?"

"I had them cleaned and repainted between each occupancy. I provided filters and made sure tenants changed them regularly to keep the HVAC running. If I got a report that something wasn't working, I'd send someone to repair it. Things like that."

"You painted every time?" I asked.

"Maybe not every time, but those homes are old. The original paint is lead-based, so I wanted to check that none of it was exposed. That's a family neighborhood and I didn't want kids to get sick."

"How is it you can be so concerned about people and turn around and rob them blind, Monty?" Aunt Rose asked.

I winced and looked at my dad. She wasn't wrong, but her bluntness could be like a sharp stick in the eye.

"I don't have a good excuse except to say I only took from people who had money and, initially, I wasn't stealing. I was really trying to create an investment group."

"Did Carl Jackson invest with you?" I asked, wondering if maybe Carl's constant poking at Aunt Rose had something to do with my dad.

"No. I never approached him though."

"Why not?" Legitimate or not, since Carl seemed to be sitting on a wealth of assets, he'd have been the perfect target for my dad.

My father looked at Aunt Rose. "Because he is . . . or was a scoundrel who hurt Aunt Rose."

"See, even you knew he was a liar and a cheat. Why wasn't he locked up?" Aunt Rose said.

- - - - - - - -

Normally on my visits with my father, I stayed for a couple of hours and then would go visit my brother, Will, who was in another unit. But with the long ride, I wanted to get Aunt Rose home at a decent time. She was feisty, but she was in her eighties, and five hours in the car along with a prison visit would tire anyone out.

As we headed west on the interstate back towards Jefferson Grove, I began to wonder if maybe my father was right. What if Carl's penchant for stealing Aunt Rose's pie wasn't well-known, as she claimed. What if the goal of the killer was for her to take the pie home?

"Aunt Rose? Do you think there's anyone who'd want to hurt you?"

"Now why would you ask a thing like that, Sophie? You're the one always getting into trouble. Maybe someone is out to get you."

"Maybe." Although if someone wanted to kill me, Aunt Rose's pie wasn't the best way to do that. They'd be better off tampering with my car. "I just think it's something to consider if we're going to clear your name."

"No one wants me dead, Sophie."

"What about Alice Filmore? You beat her again in the pie contest."

Aunt Rose made a fffttt sound. "What good is killing me if she wants to beat me? Even if I was dead, people would be comparing her pies to mine. They'd say, 'Well, ol' Alice has a fine pie, but I sure miss Rose Parker's. She knew how to make a good pie.'"

I rolled my eyes. I considered offering up Betty Bealton as a suspect because she had eyes for Carl and could have been jealous at all the attention that he gave Aunt Rose, but she'd already poo pooed the idea of Betty being a killer. My best course of action would be to drop the subject with Aunt Rose, and instead bring up the possibility that she was the target to Sergeant Scowl.

I'd just gotten Aunt Rose into the house when my phone rang with an unknown caller ID. The location said Chicago.

"Hello?" I said thinking maybe it was one of those car warrantee scam calls.

"Sophie? It's Tyler Jackson."

Surprised but intrigued, I walked to my room to take the call in private. "Yes, hi. How are you?" I winced thinking it was a dumb question considering his grandfather just died.

"Doing okay. Did you know my grandfather has two houses here that are stuffed with his junk?"

"I'd heard something to that effect. Are you having to go through it?" I was wondering if he was calling me to help him sort through Carl's hoard.

"Nah. I've called local charities. They can take what they want and the rest I'll have hauled off to the dump. Then I'll just sell it all."

I sat on my couch bed. "Are you folks helping too?"

"No. They're not coming. They've left it to me. Turns out my grandfather didn't leave dad very much."

I pulled out my murder notes. "Oh? Who did he leave his wealth to?"

"Mostly me and some to the senior center. There's a little bit for your aunt too."

That took me by surprise and then it made me nervous. It gave Aunt Rose more motive to kill him.

"But that's not why I'm calling. Will you be going to his service tomorrow?"

"His service is on Sunday?" That was a church day. Most services were held any other day but that one.

"He didn't want a service at all, but some lady named Betty insisted that there be something and suggested it be at church services tomorrow." He sounded annoyed by this.

I wondered what Betty felt Carl needed since the minister already said some words about him. "I'm usually at church on Sunday's and the potluck after."

"Potluck? God, I am in the south, aren't I?"

I bristled. "They don't have potlucks in Chicago?"

"I guess. Anyway, how about dinner tomorrow?"

I sat for a moment trying to figure out why he was asking me out. Was it a date? Was he just needing help dealing with Carl's estate?

"I found out some stuff about Carl's neighbor and wanted to pass it by someone. Maybe I should talk to the police, but I don't want to jam anyone up, you know? My sense is that this is a small town and being considered a suspect is probably not a good thing here."

I couldn't imagine it was anywhere. "No."

"I was thinking you could help me figure out if it means anything or not."

"Sure. I'd be happy to help." Plus, maybe I'd learn something to help clear Aunt Rose.

- - - - - - - -

Carl's death was still on everyone's mind at church the next day. Many people continued to be shocked, but I heard a few comments that suggested they too had been affected by Carl's miserly and in caring ways. The minister announced again that Carl's wishes were to not have a service or memorial, but he felt it was only right to have a few words about Carl since he was born and raised here—a true son of Jefferson Grove.

After church and the usual potluck, I changed into black jeans and a red sweater set that I thought made me look casual but still put together, and drove to the Jefferson Tavern, which was built just after the revolutionary war. It was the closest Jefferson Grove had to a fancy restaurant, serving "Southern Fare" such as fried chicken, stewed tomatoes, black eyed peas and cornbread.

Tyler was already at the table when I arrived nursing an ale. He did have the manners to stand up when I reached his table.

"Thanks for coming," he said, as I took off my wool coat and sat across from him.

"Sure. I imagine it's nice to get out if you're stuck inside all day."

He let out a breath. "What I wouldn't do for a nightclub about now."

"Sorry." Jefferson Grove didn't have a night life, unless one counted the Booty Burgo. It was probably why most residents between twenty-one and thirty moved out. Only when they wanted to settle down did they return. Or, in my case, when my dad went to prison and I came home to help care for Aunt Rose.

We ordered drinks and dinner, and then Tyler jumped right in. "Remember that guy I told you about that helped my grandfather when his car wouldn't start?"

I nodded. "Yes. Did you learn something?"

"Well, he came over to offer his condolences, which I thought was nice, but then the lady across the street told me that his daughter got deathly ill from lead poisoning and blamed my grandfather for it."

"What?" I thought back to my father telling me how he'd have his rentals painted out of concern for lead paint. "How is that possible?"

Tyler shrugged. "I have no idea. But she said if anyone wanted Carl dead it was him. Oh . . . and his name is Jones, first name. Jones Willoughby."

The Jones Willoughby I went to school with didn't strike me as a murderer, but if his daughter was sick and he thought Carl was to blame, maybe that would drive him to poison Carl. Plus, if he was helping Carl with the car, he'd have easy access to car fluids with the poison.

"Do you know if he offered your grandfather something to drink that morning?" I asked.

"No clue." Tyler leaned forward and looked to the right and left, as if he knew people might be listening in. He hadn't been in small town Virginia for long, but he seemed to know how gossip traveled like a virus. "The thing is, I don't know if I can believe her. I mean, maybe it's just talk, you know? Gossip based on rumor."

I nodded. "That's certainly a possibility."

"The thing is, my grandfather makes Scrooge, pre-epiphany, look like a philanthropist. The houses he uses for storage will cost a fortune to clean and update, so I wouldn't put it past him to not take care of his rental properties. I looked it up on the Internet and old homes have lead paint."

"So, the child could have gotten sick from that," I inferred.

"But would someone murder for that? Why not just sue my grandfather?"

"Some things money can't fix, maybe." If Jones' daughter was permanently hurt by Carl, that could lead to revenge which could be more powerful than money.

"Do you think I should tell the police? What would you do?"

I shifted in my seat because in the past, I'd have probably told him to let Sergeant Scowl know and he could decide if it was important. But since I was hoping to learn more to clear Aunt Rose, I said, "I know Jones a little. Why don't I talk to him? I can get a sense of if he's capable of revenge like that."

He let out a breath of relief. "I was hoping you'd say that. I don't know people and I don't need to make this town mad at me by accusing people of things, you know?"

"I know."

Our dinner came and the discussion moved on to some of the odd ball things that Carl stored in his hoarding homes.

"I think he has every receipt he's ever been given," Tyler said with a shake of his head. "And pennies. Good God, I think he could buy a house with the number of jars full of pennies I've found."

We were finishing up, when Gwen sidled up to the table. "Well, fancy seeing you two here. Together." She made a thing out of scanning the restaurant before bringing her attention back to me. "Is AJ here?"

"No. Tyler just asked for some help with his grandfather's estate," I said hoping to reassure her that this wasn't a date.

"Sophie's been great. I don't know how'd I'd get through this without her," Tyler said.

Gwen smiled, but her eyes were daggers on me. "How nice."

I stood and put my coat on. "I should get home. Thank you for dinner, Tyler."

He stood. "It was my pleasure, Sophie. Maybe we can do it again before I leave."

Crap! Gwen wasn't going to like that.

"We'll see," I said by way of an answer. "Gwen why don't you take my seat?"

"I'm meeting a friend and saw you here and just wanted to say hello," she said, her voice still sweet, but I could hear the venom behind it.

"I have to go anyway," Tyler said, tossing several bills on the table. "I'll walk you out."

Inwardly I groaned.

"See you Tuesday, Sophie," Gwen said.

As I got in my car, I considered leaving the coupon group. I had enough troubles with Vivie, I didn't need Gwen's hostility on top of it.

When I arrived home, I pushed the Gwen-Tyler issue away and wrote down what Tyler had told me about Jones and his daughter.

"Did you learn anything?" Aunt Rose asked me from the doorway of my room.

"Do you know anything about Jones Willoughby's daughter getting sick and blaming Carl?"

She thought for a moment. "You know, I think Gladys might have said something about it before she died. That poor child has some sort of developmental issue because of it."

"Did he go to court or something?" I asked.

"I don't know." Then like a light bulb going off over her head, she said, "I know there were several bake sales to raise money for her medical care a year or so ago. I'm not sure they'd have the money to sue."

"Isn't there a regulator of landlords or something?" It didn't seem right that a landlord could shirk his duties simply because someone didn't have the money to go to court.

"How would I know?" She shook her head. "Do you think he killed Carl?"

I felt like Tyler. I didn't want to make accusations about Jones, and yet, it seemed to me he had a more compelling reason to kill Carl than Aunt Rose did. Plus, he met with Carl the day he'd been poisoned and would have access to anti-freeze or other car chemicals that were suspected of killing Carl.

"I don't know."

Chapter Nine

Work was the one thing in my life that was normal: no murder, no angry jealous coupon friends, no missing boyfriend—just me, stories, and children. After my morning pre-school group, I took a break and noticed a text from AJ.

Are you still coming to dinner?

I frowned at the message as AJ rarely confirmed a date. No, he cancelled them. So why was he asking if I still planned to meet him.

Yes. Why?

A few minutes later his reply came through.

See you at my place at 7?

Why didn't he tell me why he was asking?

See you at your place at 7, I replied.

The library closed at five on Mondays, which gave me a couple of hours before I had to drive up to Jefferson Lake to AJ's house. I decided to visit the Mulberry subdivision to speak to Jones. Before I left the library, I used an old-fashioned phonebook to look up Jones' address. He wasn't just a neighbor, he lived next door to Carl. His mother was listed as living a few blocks away.

I drove over to his house, parking out front.

"Sophie Parker." Jones' smile was genuine when he saw me on his doorstep. I'd remembered that he'd always been a jovial person.

Everyone, even strangers, was a friend in his world. So, while we weren't buddies, we'd always been friendly in the classes we had together.

"Jones. Hello."

He opened the door. "What brings you here?"

I walked into a quiet home, making me wonder where his wife and child were.

"As you might have heard, I've been living with my great aunt."

He laughed. "Everyone thought you were soft in high school. But to live with old Rose Parker, you've got to have balls of steel." He motioned to his well-worn couch.

"Yes, well, as lovely as Aunt Rose can be," I said jokingly as I sat. "I've been thinking of moving out. My father used to own homes in here, and I always thought they were nice."

Jones made a face. "Are you buying or renting?"

"Renting."

He shook his head. "Maybe you should look elsewhere. Or at least makes sure who the landlord is." He pointed to the kitchen. "Do you want something to drink?"

"No thank you."

He sat in a dining room chair used as a living room chair.

"What landlords should I avoid?"

"Carl Jackson, although now that the old miser is dead, maybe his family will sell the homes or run their properties better."

"Oh?" I arched a brow, hoping I looked surprised in my intrigue. "He isn't . . . or wasn't a good landlord?"

Jones affable smile morphed into a hard grimace. "That man nearly killed my daughter. He definitely has impacted her development."

"How'd he do that?" I asked.

"He doesn't take care of his properties. Even when we need something fixed or repaired, it's always done with duct tape or some half-ass fix." He leaned forward. "Do you know that by law he's supposed to let his tenants know about lead paint in the house?"

"He didn't?"

Jones sat back. "He said it was taken care of when it wasn't. My daughter nearly died from it and he didn't care."

"If it's the law, don't you have any recourse?"

Jones laughed derisively. "I'm a mechanic in a Podunk mountain town. I don't have the money to sue him. I can't even afford the medical care and ongoing treatment my daughter needs."

I felt bad for him and could certainly understand his anger. "Surely there's some sort of tenant rights advocacy group that could help?" Maybe I could get Tyler to give him all the jars of pennies. It sounded like there were a lot of them.

He let out a breath and it was as if all the air had left him. He sagged into his chair. "I signed something saying he told me about lead paint and he says that I never told him any paint was exposed, so he's not liable."

It was hard for me to reconcile the charismatic, mischievous Carl Jackson I'd come to know for this heartless cheapskate.

"Did you tell him?"

"Of course, I did. But I didn't write it down in a formal complaint or request or whatever I need to prove my case."

"I'm so sorry Jones. I'd be really angry. Especially if I was living next door to him. I don't know how you could do that."

He shrugged. "You know me, Sophie. I try to be friends with everyone. I even fixed his car for him the other day."

"Really?" I was glad this conversation was going so easily. Or maybe I was getting better at this sleuthing business. "Why would you do that?"

"Because I'm that kind of guy. Besides the car didn't sound right. He might not care about my kid, but I'd feel bad if he died in that car when it was something I could have fixed."

That didn't sound like the words of a murderer. Then again, if he was the murderer, he'd be smart to come up with a story as he had to know that someone saw him helping Carl.

"Sounds like someone else got to him though," Jones said.

I nodded.

"I'm not a man who'd wish death on anyone, but I'm not sorry. A person can't go through life treating people like they're disposable."

I thought of Aunt Rose and how Carl had tossed her aside fifty years earlier.

"I tried to be nice to him. My Lucy would pickle vegetables or make cookies and we'd give him some. Oh, he'd smile and thank us, but when we needed something?" Jones made a slashing motion. "He cut us off like we were nothing." Jones launched up from his chair and paced, letting out a long list of curse words with an angry rant that had me wide-eyed.

Finally, he stopped and looked at me. "Sorry. It's just when I think that his negligence hurt my child . . ." He took in a breath. "I wanted him dead. There was a time when my daughter was in the hospital, I even plotted it out."

"But you didn't?"

He shook his head. "Not me."

But I had to wonder if maybe it wasn't his wife. Could she have put anti-freeze, which Jones surely had around the house if he was a mechanic, into her pickled foods?

"Where is Lucy and your daughter," I asked.

He sank back into his chair. "They're in Richmond this weekend visiting my in-laws."

"I imagine Lucy's pretty upset too."

"About Carl?" He frowned.

"I mean about Carl's neglect of your house."

Jones' lips twitched upward. "Carl angered the wrong woman that's for sure. We didn't have the money to sue him, but she constantly called the authorities about condemning the homes that he uses as storage."

That sounded more reasonable than murder.

But then he shook his head. "Of course, it never amounted to anything. If he had an extra expense, he'd either raise our rent or not fix something to offset the cost."

"Why not move?"

He looked at me. "How easy is that? All our savings has gone to medical expenses. Plus, I paid to have the place repainted to cover the lead paint. Then, to move we'd need a deposit and first month's rent. Do you think Carl was going to return our deposit on this place? Of course not. He'd find some reason to keep it."

Jones and his wife were stuck here, much like a caged animal.

They were good people, but their daughter was nearly killed and Carl was indifferent to their plight. Everyone had a breaking point, and I wondered if Jones and Lucy had hit theirs with Carl.

- - - - - - - -

When I left Jones, I headed home to check on Aunt Rose. I decided not to give her too much information about Jones. I didn't want her gossiping to her friends and then having Jones get mad at me and make other people in town leery of me if I showed up asking about Carl. Fortunately, Bull was over and they were making a yule log.

I freshened up and headed up to the Jefferson Lake. The roads were clear and the night was dark but lit by the moon. Normally, that could make the mountain drive eerie, but I was glad for the quiet calm. As I approached AJ's house, I noticed that his neighbor's home was dark. Mrs. Kaczynski watched Dutch when AJ was off on a job, but I often checked on her because she was elderly and while Dutch was a sweet dog, she was humongous and prone to jump on a person when excited. I could picture Mrs. Kaczynski stuck on the floor after being knocked over by Dutch.

With her home dark, I wondered if maybe she'd gone to visit family for the holidays. If AJ went out of town, who'd watch Dutch? I'd do it except there was no way she'd be allowed in Aunt Rose's home, and I couldn't stay at AJ's, as someone needed to keep an eye on Aunt Rose.

I parked in front of AJ's home. I got out of the car and looked out over the lake, taking in a deep breath to enjoy the clean air.

The door opened and Dutch came flying out. The first time she'd done that, I was sure she was going to eat me. Now that we were old friends, I knew she'd skid to a stop just before reaching me. She looked me in the eyes and gave a soft woof. I pet her and laughed. It was nice to have unconditional love like that.

I looked to the door. AJ leaned against the doorframe, his arms crossed, and his expression tense. My heart dropped and I wondered why we couldn't have the same unconditional love for each other that Dutch had for us.

"You made it," AJ said.

I frowned. "Of course. Why did you think I wouldn't? You're the one that cancels dates." Inwardly I winced, at my last comment. I didn't want to fight and starting my conversation with snark wasn't a good way to avoid arguing.

"No, you're the one that dates other men."

I stopped just short of the front stoop as I tried to process what he was saying. "What are you talking about?"

"You're seeing someone else."

"No, I'm not." What was he talking about? I had just been to Jones house, but he was married and that was for Aunt Rose. I had dinner with Tyler but that was for Aunt Rose too. And how would AJ even know about that? Ever since he left Jefferson Grove to join the military, he hadn't been back. Even now, living at Jefferson Lake, he went out of his way to avoid going into town and instead took care of shopping and other business when he went down the mountain.

He gaped. "I never pegged you for a liar, Sophie."

Tears sprang to my eyes, but I worked to hold on to anger. "I'm not lying, AJ. I have no clue what you're talking about."

"Your friend from the coupon group told me you were on a date with Carl Jackson's grandson. Bull confirmed that you'd been with someone else."

Gwen. I should have guessed. Although how she knew AJs number was beyond me. Then again, there was a time she set her sights on him. But Bull? He should have known better.

"It wasn't a date, AJ. It was dinner."

"What's the difference?"

I gaped at him. "A few months ago, I stood right here with you shirtless because your ex was wearing said shirt and you told me to trust you. And I did."

His jaw tightened. "Yesterday you said you wanted me to end things. Is it because you've got a new man?"

"I said that if you were trying to leave me to just get it over with."

"And I told you I loved you."

"I told you I loved you too."

"No, you didn't."

What? I scanned my brain. Surely, I told him I loved him, but I couldn't remember. "Well, I do." So there. This had to be the strangest fight we'd ever had.

"So why are you out with another man?"

"I'm going to tell you why, but I want to point out again, that I shouldn't have to. You trust me or you don't. I think that's exactly what you said to me when I found your ex here."

I paused, hoping he'd say he trusted me. Instead, he waited. In that moment, I felt like maybe this was the beginning of our end.

"You don't trust me." I looked down as I worked to accept that things were about to change. "I had dinner with—"

"Stop."

AJ stepped out of the doorway and stood in front of me. He studied me for a moment. I hoped he found whatever he was looking for.

"I trust you." He let out a low growl as he pulled me to him. I was stiff for a minute, still miffed at him. "I'm sorry."

With his words, I wrapped my arms around his waist. "I'm not a cheater."

"I know."

"No, you don't," I said, looking up into his blue eyes.

His hands cupped my cheeks. "I had a moment of insanity at the idea of you being with another man."

"Then you know how I felt when I saw you with Becca."

"How you didn't rip her hair out, I don't know."

I grinned. "It was hard."

He let out a breath and it was like he let out all his worry. "I know I've been gone a lot lately, Sophie. It won't happen much more, I promise." He took my hand and led me into the house where I could smell something delicious cooking.

"Why do you have to work so much anyway? Do you need the money? Is there something wrong with your mom or brother or sister?"

"I'm just trying to get things squared."

That made me wonder if he'd gotten into some sort of trouble. I could see Bull being a part of it.

"That Cullen repo, remember, I didn't get paid for that."

"Why? The killer was caught."

"But it's still not at the bank since there's a trial and the DEA is involved with the drug angle."

"I didn't know you were so low on funds," I said.

He shrugged. "I'm not about to be bankrupt. I just want to get my finances sorted."

I felt like he was still holding something back, but money could be an embarrassing topic. I knew firsthand having been rich while growing up and now having to hear the snickers of my parents' old friends as I handed over coupons when I grocery shopped.

"What's for dinner? I'm starving," I said, ready to change the subject. I headed to the kitchen, but he stopped me, instead, pulling me down the hall.

"It won't be ready for at least thirty minutes and I figure I need to make up to you."

A sizzle of excitement ran through me. "Oh? Do you think you can do that in thirty minutes?"

He moved quickly, scooping me up in his arms and half running to his room. "I'm gonna try."

- - - - - - - -

Forty-five minutes later, we were made up and sitting at the table having dinner. As usual, I discretely would drop a few bits of the meat on the floor for Dutch to enjoy. AJ pretended not to know, but he did. In some ways, when we were like this, it felt like we were a family but I'd always toss that thought out. I loved AJ and the fairy tale would be for us to live happily ever after, but I knew fairy tales weren't real. Even if he did propose, I didn't know how I could say yes. Who'd take care of Aunt Rose? It's not like AJ could move in with me at her place, and I couldn't imagine her moving out of her home.

"I'm sorry again, Sophie for not trusting you. I wonder why your friend made a point to tell me about it."

"Because she thought the same thing and was jealous." I shook my head and wondered how things would be with Gwen and me at the coupon group tomorrow.

AJ reached over and took my hand. "I felt like you were slipping away when I'm trying so hard to keep us together."

"You don't have to try that," I said wondering why he felt that need. "I don't like how you're gone all the time. I'm trying to be understanding."

"I know. I guess it's my own guilt."

Since he was being so honest, I figured I'd do the same. "Tyler is Carl Jackson's son. I don't know if you heard, but Carl was poisoned."

AJ nodded. "Please don't tell me you're pulling a Nancy Drew again."

"A neighbor told Tyler some things that he wasn't sure he should tell the police because maybe it was just gossip."

"So, he took you dinner?" AJ arched a brow. "I trust you Sophie, but not other men. I don't think you know your appeal."

"If you're trying to flatter me, Devlin, it's working. But I think he partly wanted out of the house. Carl was a hoarder, did you know? It's a bit creepy."

"You didn't answer about the investigating. It never goes well when you get involved."

I pulled my hand back, offended even though he was right. "Cullen and Marla's murders were solved with my help."

"And you nearly died both times."

"You nearly did too once."

He sighed. "I just worry about you, that's all. I don't think I'm being unreasonable."

"It's not unreasonable to worry. But you can't tell me what to do. Besides, it's not the same this time."

He rolled his eyes. "I've heard that before."

"I just need to make sure Aunt Rose isn't accused."

"Last time you were helping Vivie Danner to not be accused."

"Are we going to fight? I haven't seen you in a long time and I don't want to this one time I see you to become an argument."

He inhaled a deep breath, something he often did with me. I suspect it was his way of pushing aside his true feelings so that we wouldn't argue. "Just be careful."

I was going to say I was always careful, which I was, but being careful didn't always mean I was safe.

Chapter Ten

Tuesday night I headed to Aggie's house for coupon group. As I pulled past Gwen's coupe, I remembered that she'd actually called AJ to tell on me. Gwen and I weren't best buddies, but I'd have thought she'd have confronted me about dinner with Tyler. Then again, I suppose she had that night. Maybe she had a retaliatory streak.

"You didn't!" I heard Lani say as I approached the house. The door was open but the glass screen door was closed and fogged over from the warm inside air contrasting with the cold night.

"He had the right to know," Gwen's voice argued.

"I don't believe it," Vivie said. "But if she did, good for her."

"Believe what?" I opened the door and walked in knowing I was the topic of conversation. I was used to it. First it was because of my dad. Later it was because I always managed to get involved in murder.

"Gwen says you went to dinner with Tyler Jackson," Lani said. They were all sitting at the table getting their coupons ready. I didn't see Aggie, which meant she was probably in the kitchen.

"I did go to dinner, but it wasn't a date," I said, being honest as well as clarifying.

"Knowing you, you were picking his brain about Carl's death," Vivie said, absently as she scanned the coupons Lani had stacked in front of her. "You should learn to stay out of other people's business."

I gaped at Vivie's lecturing me on staying out of people's business.

Lani did a spit take of her warm cider. "You're one to talk."

Vivie look at her and blinked.

"Sophie helped you when you were accused of murder," Lani reminded her.

Vivie shrugged. "That was different." When I said it to AJ it made sense, but coming from Vivie, it didn't.

"I know what I saw," Gwen said. "You knew I was interested in him."

I set my coupon binder next to Lani, across from Vivie and Gwen.

"It was an innocent meal, Gwen. He just heard some gossip from his neighbor and wasn't sure he should tell the police."

She glared at me. "First, he could have asked me and second, he could have asked you over the phone."

"Do you know Jones Willoughby?" I arched a brow. Gwen had lived in Jefferson Grove for a few years, but she didn't grow up here. She didn't know everyone like the rest of us did.

"Jones? Really?" Lani asked.

The way Gwen huffed out her breath, I knew she didn't know Jones. "He still could have called you."

"Yes, he could have, but didn't. If you have a problem with it, talk to him. Meanwhile, you'll be glad to know that AJ and I are just fine, thank you very much."

"I still think you should have gone after Tyler," Vivie said, sipping her warm cider.

"Hey!" Gwen cried.

Vivie shrugged. "Sorry. He's too . . . short for you."

"What is all the commotion about?" Aggie said in her former teacher's voice. "Good lord, I feel like I'm back in the classroom." She entered the dining area carrying a crockpot filled with her famous meatballs. We all jumped up, even Vivie, to get a plate.

"There's no problem," I answered Aggie. "Just a misunderstanding."

"Sophie went on a date with Tyler Jackson and so Gwen told AJ," Vivie said.

We all frowned at her. Just when I thought the conversation would move on.

"Ah lordy, I *am* back in the classroom," Aggie rolled her eyes.

"It wasn't a date. Like I said, he's just dealing with Carl's passing—"

"Murder, you mean." Vivie plucked two meatballs from the Crockpot and then went to sit down. I used the ladle in the other warmer to pour myself some of Aggie's warm cider. Like Moonshine, cider was another concoction often made in this area, although most people kept it non-alcoholic. Aggie usually enhanced hers with something stronger than spices and sugar.

"How is Tyler doing?" Aggie asked.

"He's fine," Gwen said with her dark eyes on me.

"No one really thinks Jones Willoughby is involved do they?" Aggie asked sitting at the head of the table.

"I'm sure Rose is at the top of the list," Vivie quipped. When I gave her a look, she said, "What? Everyone knows she hated him."

"Aunt Rose said there are plenty of others who didn't like him," I said, trying not to sound too defensive. To help distract me, I pulled out my coupons for trading.

"That sweet old man?" Gwen said.

"Rose isn't wrong. I've heard plenty of grumbles where he's concerned," Lani said.

"Like who?" Aggie asked her.

"There are plenty of others at the senior center who agree that he cheats," Lani said and I got the feeling she was repeating information that Dwayne had learned from talking to Carl's peers. At least he was doing his job and not solely focused on Rose, unless of course he was trying to get her friends to turn on her. "Also, Alice Filmore blames Carl for Tubby's death."

Aggie made a tsk tsk sound. "I'm sure she does."

We all turned our attention from our coupons to Aggie. "Why would you say that?" I asked.

Aggie was quiet for a moment. "Well, you know I'm not one for gossip." We all nodded even though it wasn't true. Aggie was a well of information about past and present on the going-ons in Jefferson Grove. "First, his death was ruled an accident. He might have been careless because he was angry at Carl, but Carl didn't kill him."

"I heard he was smoking around his moonshine still," I said.

"Right. However, Tubby might have been simple, but he wasn't reckless. His family had been distilling moonshine for generations. He knew enough not to smoke around the still."

"So, how'd it happen?" Gwen asked, and I was glad we were on the subject of murder instead of Tyler.

Aggie shrugged and gave us a coy expression. "I don't know."

"Come on Aggie, you have a theory," Vivie said, equally intrigued.

"There's some folks who think maybe Alice had something to do with it," she said.

"That doesn't sound like Alice," Lani said.

I nodded in agreement. "She doesn't seem the type."

"And Rose does?" Aggie asked me.

"No." The truth was, I'd learned since returning home that people weren't always who I thought they were—or I was very bad at reading people. It was why I'd nearly been killed. More than once.

"Now I'm not saying Alice Filmore killed Tubby or Carl for that matter—"

"Why would she kill Carl?" I asked.

"Carl swindled both her and Tubby in a land deal," Earl said from the dining entryway.

"Now Earl, you know it's coupon night," Aggie said.

"I know. I won't bother you gals. I'm just letting you know that I'm heading over to Joe's. He has some deer meat he's selling us."

"Wear your hat. You'll catch your death of cold."

He smiled mischievously. "Yes ma'am."

"What was that about the land deal?" I asked once Earl put on his hat and coat, and went out the door.

"He had some land adjoining theirs that he sold to them," Aggie explained. "I don't know if he over charged them or maybe didn't sell them all the land rights."

"I bet that's a matter of public record," Lani said to me.

I nodded.

"Not again, Sophie," Vivie said rolling her eyes. "Maybe you should just stay out of murder investigations."

I shrugged not wanting to confirm or deny that I was involved. I didn't want to lie, but also, I didn't want to have Gwen suggest to Tyler that I was picking his brain during our so-called date—and I didn't want it to get out to Alice or anyone else that I was asking around either.

The conversation switched over to coupon exchanging. I did my best to grab all the sugar and butter coupons for Aunt Rose. She baked often but even more so when she was stressed. With Carl's death and suspicion on her, I imagined we'd be able to open a bakery, which would come in handy if we had to hire a lawyer to defend her.

The evening was coming to an end when Gwen's phone started playing *Real Good Man* by Tim McGraw. "Oh, that's Tyler," she said cutting a glance at me.

I only just barely kept myself from rolling my eyes or telling her that Tyler didn't strike me as a guy who liked country music.

"You know I try not to get in the way of you living your life, Soph, but I sort of agree with Vivie that you shouldn't get involved in Carl's murder," Lani said as she put her coat on.

"I'm not getting in Dwayne's way," I said.

"So, you are investigating?"

"I'm just making sure that Aunt Rose isn't blamed. I don't care what the tests on her pie say, she didn't poison him."

"I'll ask Aggie if I can bring some of her cider to your place," Gwen said into the phone. She was turned away from us, but the volume in her voice made it clear she wanted us, or at least me, to overhear her.

"I'll pack some up for you now," Aggie said, going into the kitchen.

Lani turned her attention back to me. "I know you're looking out for her, but I promise you, Dwayne is being very thorough."

"Much to Sergeant Scowl's dismay I bet." I zipped my binder shut and used the strap to hook it over my shoulder.

Lani laughed. "He now knows why you call him that."

"I'm sure it's just as good as what you had at the jamboree," Gwen said into the phone.

"It's better," Aggie called from the kitchen.

"Aggie does have good cider," Vivie agreed. "Of course, adding a little adult liquid to it wouldn't hurt."

"Was there adult cider at the jamboree?" I asked. "All I heard about was the adult eggnog."

"There was cider at the refreshment table with the other drinks. Dwyane brought us some."

Oh yeah. I couldn't imagine anyone offering Carl poisoned cider from the refreshment table. That was too open. Anyone would see.

I shrugged it off. "I've gotta run. See you all Tuesday."

"I'll walk out with you," Lani said.

We were out the door and away from eavesdroppers when Lani asked, "So everything is okay with AJ. I don't mean about dinner with Tyler, I mean about his being gone."

"It sounds like he needs the money. I definitely understand that."

She smiled. "I'm glad you've worked it out. AJ is good for you."

"How so?" I pulled the keys from my purse.

"He offsets all the bad from your family. He's solid."

"I suppose." I opened my car door and then turned to look at her. "Do you think I'm good for him?"

She rolled her eyes. "Yes, of course."

"How?" It seemed to me that I brought a lot more complication to his life.

"For him, you're solid too. With his siblings gone and his mom having problems, he needed someone in his life too."

"He has Dutch."

"God Sophie, sometimes you're hopeless. The man loves you. Duchess is a great dog but she's not you."

I still wasn't sure I offered as much to AJ as he did me, but I was all in to try.

- - - - - - - -

When I arrived home, Aunt Rose was watching TV but for once it wasn't one of her true crime shows. In fact, it looked like a Hallmark movie.

"Is this one of the cozy mystery movies?" I asked, as I hung my coat up in the closet.

"No. It's one of those romances."

"Really?" As a lover of fairy tales, I of course loved a great romance story, but Aunt Rose didn't have a romantic bone in her body. That wasn't just my assessment. She told me so once. She said she was glad she wasn't prone to fall for wine and roses because men just disappointed. My sense was she fell for wine and roses once and was disappointed. She was definitely a woman who wouldn't risk something like that again. In some ways it was sad because there had to be a man out there that would have made her happy. He'd have loved her pies and wouldn't cheat at bunco. It was a reminder to me that while love was a risk, when it worked, it could be quite sweet. Not a perfect happily ever after maybe, but still, something fulfilling, like what Lani and Dwayne had.

"I've just finished one and am in the middle of another. There's not enough kissing."

I held back my snort. "I didn't know you liked that sort of thing."

"I don't. But if you're going to watch a romance, there should be kissing. It's like watching a mystery without a crime."

That didn't sound like fun. "I think the point is the relationship. They overcome obstacles to find their happily ever after."

She looked at me with a smirk. "Are you telling me you and AJ don't kiss?"

Ahhh … There was no way I was going to talk about that aspect of my relationship. "I picked up several sugar and butter coupons. Plus, one for pure vanilla. I can buy you more baking ingredients tomorrow."

She turned back to the TV. "I need confectioners' sugar."

"I've got a coupon for that."

I was about to go to my room, when I remembered what Aggie suggested about Tubby's death.

"Aunt Rose, do you think someone might have killed Tubby Filmore?"

She craned her head around to look at me. "Now who would have told you that?"

"It came up at the meeting. Tubby came from a long line of moonshiners, so he wouldn't have been smoking while stilling, would he?"

She thought for a moment. "Normally, no. But Tubby started drinking his profits and wasn't always in his right mind after Carl cheated him."

"That had to make Alice mad."

Aunt Rose let out a loud laugh I'd never heard before. "Alice was madder than a box of frogs."

I once used that statement when I lived in New York and was asked how I knew if a box of frogs was mad.

"I think poor old Tubby had to live in the shed for a week."

"Do you think she could murder?" I asked.

"Who Tubby?"

"That's what was suggested. If she could kill him, she could kill Carl."

Aunt Rose was shaking her head. "Alice has a big bark, but she doesn't bite. She loved Tubby, bless her heart."

I nodded. "I'm heading to bed." But tomorrow, I'd see about talking to Alice.

- - - - - - - -

After work the next day, I walked out to find AJ sitting on the back of his truck bed with Dutch. Usually, he left Dutch with Mrs. Kaczynski if he was leaving for a repo so I was hopeful he was here simply to surprise me.

When I approached him though, he had that look on his face that said he had to tell me something and I wasn't going to like it.

He gave me a kiss and then lifted me up to sit on the back of the truck bed.

Dutch set her head on my shoulder and I gave her a scratch. "Hello Duchess." Then I turned to AJ. "You're leaving town, aren't you?"

He nodded. "Last one before Christmas, I promise. It's a big one, Soph. This plane is a six-hundred-thousand-dollar plane and Gordo is giving me half the cut."

I whistled at the price. "So that's . . . ?" I did the mental math knowing that the company he worked for received ten percent of the bank's appraisal for the plane, so if AJ was getting half of that, it was big chunk of change. "Thirty thousand?"

"Yes." His grin was so wide and happy, I couldn't help but smile with him. He looked like he'd hit the jackpot even though he'd had some good payments before. He also told me he once received nearly fifty thousand on a repo, but he's used that to help his younger brother pay for medical school.

His hands rubbed up and down my arms. "After this, I won't be volunteering for extra work. I promise."

I smiled. "You're not breaking a date, so I'm not mad. I know you have to work, AJ."

He stepped between my knees. "I know I owe you."

I looped my arms around his neck. "You do. How will you ever repay me?"

He flashed me that cocky smile that had made my insides melt since the first time I saw him at fourteen years old. I was a high school freshman and he was a senior. "Make a list."

I laughed and gave him a kiss. "Where are you going this time?"

"Louisiana. It's a float plane."

"So, you have to steal it on water?" That sounded more dangerous than taking the plane from an airport. There were gators in the water in Louisiana.

"Probably, but it will be docked. It will be okay."

"How long will you be gone?"

"I hope to be in and out tomorrow, but you know these things sometimes don't go to plan."

"Is Bull going with you?" I was pretty certain he could wrangle and alligator if needed.

He cocked his head. "Are you worried about me, Soph?"

"Of course, but at least I don't tell you to stop."

He glared at me. "I haven't told you to stop anything. At least not in a while. But I do want you to be careful. You don't have a Bull to look after you."

I thought about that for a moment. "Maybe you should lend him to me."

"You'd have to ask your aunt."

I laughed, thinking he was probably right. "When do you go?"

"Tomorrow. Tonight, I'm all yours. How about dinner? Maybe at the Jefferson Tavern."

"Why there?" I knew why of course. That's where I'd had dinner with Tyler.

"It beats the Booty Burgo."

"Jefferson Tavern it is."

He helped me down from the truck and I climbed into the cab knowing he'd drive me back here to get my car when the night was done. On the way, I called Aunt Rose to let her know I was going out to dinner and not to expect me.

"Tell me truthfully, Sophie. Are you poking your nose into Carl's business?" he asked once we were seated at the table and ordered drinks.

I shrugged. "I was hoping for a tension-free dinner."

He reached out and took my hand. "I worry about you. It's worse when I'm out of town."

"Back at you," I said.

"I'm going to take that as a yes. So, who do you think killed Carl?"

I sat back as the waiter set our wine glasses on the table. "Are you ready to order?"

"Fried chicken dinner," I said. "Baked potato and green beans."

"Me too, except I want my potatoes mashed," AJ followed. When the waiter left, he looked at me expectantly. "Carl? Murder?"

I leaned forward again, wanting to speak lowly to avoid our conversation being broadcast over the gossip grapevine.

"I don't know who killed him, but I know Aunt Rose didn't. She wouldn't."

"Are you sure about that?"

I narrowed my eyes at him. "I dare you to ask Bull that."

He shivered. "No thanks. He might rip my arms off."

I smiled. I liked feeling that Aunt Rose and I had a personal bodyguard in Bull. "I don't believe she's capable of killing, but I know for sure she'd never put poison in her pie."

"Was the pie poisoned?"

"I don't know. But it's being tested. So far, what I've been able to find out is that the M.E. is certain he was poisoned, probably with something found in car fluids, likely the night before he died." I looked around again to make sure no one was eavesdropping. "The morning he died, he got car help from Jones Willoughby, who's a mechanic."

AJ thought for a moment. "He was your year in school, right? What reason would he have to kill Carl?"

"Carl owned the property that Jones rented. Apparently, he didn't care for it and Jones' daughter got lead poisoning. Jones blames Carl for that. I need to research that more."

"Wait, you said he was poisoned the night before, but Jones helped him the morning he died."

I nodded recognizing the problem with my thinking.

"Who else is on your list?"

"Well, there's his grandson, Tyler."

AJ's eyes narrowed to slits. "I bet it's him. He wants Carl's money."

"How do you know about Carl's money?" It reminded me that I had to find out what Aunt Rose was getting from Carl.

"I don't, but murder is usually about money, right?"

Not always, but he had a point. "It's a possibility. He was staying with Carl so he had the most access to him. It's possible someone at the jamboree poisoned him too, but I can't figure out how it would have happened."

"Except your aunt's pie."

I glared him. "She didn't do it."

He took my hand and held it tight. "If there is poison in Rose's pie, have you considered that she or you were the target?"

I swallowed the gulp in my throat. "Yes. But it's risky on the murder's part."

"How is it less risky to poison Carl than you or Rose?" He shook his head like I wasn't making sense.

"Carl was known to take her pie. At least a piece of it."

"God, Sophie." He stared at me and in his eyes, I saw all he wanted to say but wouldn't, like, *stop butting into murderers' business.*

"Do you know Alice Filmore?" I asked, looking down so I didn't feel bad for making him worry.

"Sure. She grew up in the hollow." There were many hollows around here, but I knew he was referring to Cooters Hollow where he grew up. "She married Tubby Filmore. A step up, most here in Jefferson Grove would say although his place is in a hollow as well."

I frowned. "Do you really think like that?"

"Sure. You're an entire staircase up from me."

I sat back and crossed my arms over my chest, hating it when he did that. "I'm not better than you, AJ."

"You are, but not because you grew up in Monticello Heights." He sat back as our waiter brought our dinner. "Why are you asking about Alice?"

"I heard Carl duped her and Tubby on a land deal."

AJ shrugged. "I wouldn't know about that."

I scanned the area again not wanting my next question to be overheard. "Is it possible that she killed Tubby?"

AJ's eyes widened mid-bite of his mashed potatoes.

"I heard a rumor that some people think Tubby wouldn't have been smoking by the still. That Alice is the one that blew him up."

AJ sucked in a breath and let out a derisive laugh. "Right. The woman from the hollow blew up her husband." He stuffed the potatoes into his mouth.

"So that's a no. You don't think she'd do that. Because most people think Tubby was too smart to smoke around the still."

"I don't know, Sophie. Alice was a quiet spinster until she married Tubby. But I only know of her. I don't know her personally. Still, I'd question anyone who blamed someone from the hollow for anything. You know how we're treated."

"It's not like that so much anymore. Maybe the older folks are like that," I said, realizing I heard the rumor from Aggie. But while she was older, I never pegged her as discriminating against the various social economic groups.

"What do you think people say about us?" His jaw tightened; his body was tense.

"I don't care what people say."

He let out a breath and relaxed. "But people do talk."

"AJ, people who talk about me, talk about my dad and Will. Of all the scandals I'm involved in, they're the top of the list, not you. Except maybe now Aunt Rose."

"Do you care?"

"That people talk about my family?" I shrugged. "I don't love it, but it doesn't get to me like it used to. The people I care about don't hold it against me."

"I mean about what people say about you and me?"

I shook my head. I wasn't sure what people said about us, except Vivie who thought I deserved better, but not so much because he was a Devlin but because he'd stood me up.

"I don't know what people say about us. I do know that if you weren't so chicken to go out in public with me, you'd know that people don't talk about you as much as you think they do."

"What am I doing now?" he asked, miffed, holding his hands out to indicate that we were out in a restaurant.

"I mean things like the jamboree where we have to mingle with others as a couple. Maybe I'm the one who should be asking you if you're bothered by how people talk about me?"

He turned his head to the side, one of the things he did when what he really wanted to do was confront me. After a breath he looked back.

"I don't know what people say about you and me either. And I don't care. There's nothing more important than you," he blurted.

The people at the table next to us looked over.

"Why do we always fight when I'm trying to tell you I love you?" he asked.

"Maybe because you don't just say it." I sat and waited patiently.

"I love you."

I picked up my wine glass and waited for him to pick up his. I clinked mine against his. "I love you too, AJ Devlin of Cooters Hollow."

Chapter Eleven

On Thursday, I was doing a school-age group, talking about Colonial Christmases, when I saw Mrs. Conner walk in carrying a stack of books. After dumping them in the return bin, she headed to the new book section. I hoped she'd take her time, because she was an ideal person to talk about Carl and Alice.

I finished the group, cleaned up our mess, and then made my way to Mrs. Conner. "Good afternoon. Are you finding what you want?"

"Oh Sophie. How are you?" She put the new large print book from J.D. Robb back on the shelf.

"Oh, I'm okay. I'm a little worried about my aunt," I said mostly to get her attention.

"Rose? Is something wrong?" She turned her attention to me.

"Carl's death hasn't been easy."

She shook her head. "I heard the sheriff's office was questioning her. I told them I couldn't imagine Rose poisoning Carl. Personally, I think they were always flirting."

I was sure Aunt Rose didn't see it like that, but I didn't contradict Mrs. Conner. "Have they talked to you too?"

"Oh yes. I think they're talking to everyone." She went back to looking at the books on the shelf.

"I guess so. I'm told there were many people who didn't like Carl. I was surprised because he was always seemed so happy and dapper."

"Hmmm . . . well looks can be deceiving." She pulled out a reprint of an Agatha Christie book.

"So, I've heard."

"Are you getting involved again?" she asked, pushing the Christie book back to its place and instead, pulling out a new release from Joanne Fluke.

"No. My sleuthing days are over," I lied. "Although I'd sure like to clear Aunt Rose. Would you have any information that could help me?"

"No," she said, pushing the Fluke book back onto the shelf. "Some of these are so violent."

"The Agatha Christie and Joanne Fluke ones aren't," I said.

"I'm looking for a mystery with some humor. Do you have any recommendations?"

"Murder and humor?" How did one make murder funny?

"Have you read Janet Evanovich's Stephanie Plumb series. It's humorous."

"I've heard of that. Do you have her books?"

"All twenty-something of them." I led her to the fiction section where all her books were shelved. "This is the first one." I handed her *One for the Money*.

"Thank you, Sophie." She smiled at me. "I'm so glad you left the Booty Burgo and landed here."

"Me too." I wished I could think of another question to ask her that might help me, but I couldn't come up with one that didn't reveal me as a liar about my sleuthing for Aunt Rose. "Is there anything else?"

"I'm just going to look around some more."

"Okay. Let me know if have questions." I turned and started back to the front desk.

"Oh, Sophie. You know, I was thinking about any information I might have."

Yes! I plastered on an even expression to hide my hope that this was the proverbial smoking gun info. "Oh?"

"Well, this could be nothing, but Alice did try to bribe Carl before the contest."

"Really?"

Mrs. Conner waved her hand. "It was probably nothing. I mean, it's not like she hadn't tried before."

"Are you saying she bribed him to make her the winner?"

She nodded. "Yes. I suppose that's not something anyone would kill over for though, right?"

"Right." I made my brain do cartwheels to find an appropriate follow up question. I couldn't come right out and ask if she thought Alice killed Tubby. "I thought Alice didn't like Carl. That was something she and Aunt Rose agreed on."

"You're right. What Carl did to poor old Tubby. And then for him to go like he did . . ." She leaned closer to me, her eyes darting from side to side as if to make sure no one could hear us. "It wouldn't surprise me if Tubby killed himself."

Ah . . . I wasn't expecting that. "Killed himself?"

She nodded. "You know, for the insurance. He made it look like an accident, but with his death, Alice was able to get out of the financial mess Tubby put them in with his deal with Carl."

Blowing oneself up seemed like a crazy way to kill oneself, but then again, almost any other way would likely look suspicious. These days, forensic science would know if someone drove purposefully into a tree.

"Did you ever hear a rumor that Alice did it?"

Mrs. Conner's pursed her lips and looked at me with disappointment. "Don't listen to gossip, Sophie. People can be so judgmental. Alice is a fine woman. Trust me. I know. Ask your aunt. She and Alice are fierce competitors when it comes to pie, but they are kindred spirits in other ways. Both duped by Carl. Both talked about negatively in town. Both alone."

I swallowed the guilt she was making me feel.

"If I were to guess who killed Carl, I'd say his grandson. He's not as hoity-toity as he makes himself out to be."

"Oh?" Had Tyler been trying to put me off his scent by pointing the figure at Jones?

"You know I read a lot of these mysteries. Killers have to have a motive, means, and opportunity. To my mind, Tyler Jackson is the only one who has all three."

"That's a good point. I hope Sergeant Davis is looking into him."

She patted my arm. "I told him what I told you. Don't worry, Sophie. Carl's murderer will be caught and Rose will be off the hook. I'm sure of it." With a final smile, she left me to peruse the romance section. I went to the back office and pulled out my little notebook to write down everything she'd said. Reviewing it, I wasn't sure I got anything new, except Alice's penchant for trying to bribe Carl and a second opinion that Tyler had a questionable character.

I decided I'd pay him another visit, although I wasn't sure what I needed to ask him. Mrs. Conner was right that out of everyone, he had the most motive and easiest access to poisoning Carl. But I couldn't come right out and ask, "Did you poison your grandfather?"

While Aunt Rose was staying strong, I could see the cloud of suspicion that hung over her was bringing her down, so I headed home to check on her before going to see Tyler. I hoped that she wouldn't press me on my investigation. I didn't have anything to tell her except what Mrs. Conners said. I wasn't sure it was a good idea to mention Alice's attempts to bribe Carl. The fact that she never said anything about it suggested she didn't know, otherwise Alice would be part of her pie contest complaints.

As I pulled into the driveway, I noticed an old pickup truck parked in front of the house. It wasn't AJ's. Who was visiting Aunt Rose?

When I walked in, I was surprised to see Alice sitting in the living room with Aunt Rose. I knew they were friendly when not competing in pie contests, but I couldn't remember Alice ever visiting Aunt Rose.

"Alice, hi," I said as I hung my coat on the coat rack by the door.

"Hello Sophie."

"Alice brought me some of her special apple cider," Aunt Rose said, holding up a mug presumably with the warmed drink. "You could bottle and sell this."

Alice blushed. "You're too kind Rose. Or you're just trying to keep me from baking pie."

"Why bake pie when you're so much better at making apple cider."

I wondered if Alice would be offended by that comment. "Maybe I'll make an apple cider pie. With Carl gone, I might have a chance at winning." As if she realized what she was saying, Alice winced. "I apologize for my insensitivity."

Aunt Rose waved her comment away. "We all know Carl was a liar and cheat."

How strange that Carl was a liar and a cheat but wouldn't accept Alice's bribe. Was pie the one area he didn't corrupt. Or maybe he did take her bribe but didn't follow through on his side of the deal. That still seemed like a flimsy reason to kill someone.

Alice nodded. "Yes, but even so. I shouldn't speak ill of the dead."

"There's still some cider warming on the stove, Sophie if you'd like a cup," Aunt Rose said.

"I'm not here for long. I just wanted to check in before heading out," I said, sitting on the couch.

"Where are you off to? Have you and AJ made up?" Aunt Rose asked.

"I have to say, Sophie, I was surprised when I heard about you and AJ Devlin," Alice said. "I always thought he was a good boy, but of course, he's a Devlin and you . . . well. . . your family once were royalty in Jefferson Grove. I'm glad to see you don't have any prejudice against people from the hollow."

"AJ's no knight in shining armor," Aunt Rose quipped. "No man is, Sophie. You have to remember that."

Alice took offense. "Just because he's from the hollow, Rose, doesn't mean he's not good."

"Being from the Hollow has nothing to do with it," Aunt Rose responded to Alice. "Men can't be trusted. Even the good ones tell their share of lies. Sure, they might be white lies, but they're not the truth either."

Alice shrugged. "My Tubby, bless his heart, did tell his share of fibs."

"No doubt because Carl told him too," Aunt Rose said.

Alice looked down at her hands clasped in her lap. She was always prim and proper like that. I wondered if that was something she learned to do as a way of trying to be accepted in Jefferson Grove. "I blame myself for not looking out for Tubby better when dealing with Carl. Tubby had a kind and trusting heart and bought everything Carl was selling him."

"What did Carl sell Tubby?" I asked, hoping she didn't think I was being too nosy.

"Now Sophie, we don't need to ask Alice to dredge up all that history," Aunt Rose chastised me.

I sent Alice an apologetic smile, but inside I was annoyed. How could I help Aunt Rose, if I couldn't talk to the people who had motive to kill Carl or at least had information about him.

"It's no problem, Rose," Alice said, turning her attention to me. "Tubby's family owned all of the land from his farm up to the ridge of the mountain. Over the years, his family would sell a few acres. Carl knew this and approached Tubby about buying twenty-five acres that ran along the highway near Casters Road."

"Where that new townhome subdivision is?"

Alice's jaw tightened. "Yes. That was Tubby's land. Carl offered to buy it at a really good deal." She shook her head, pursing her lips. "One of those too-good-to-be-true deals."

"I told you, Alice, Carl was a liar and cheat."

"I know you did, Rose. But Tubby, he was getting on in age and wanted to make sure the land wasn't a burden to me and have some money set aside." She sniffed and pulled a tissue hidden under the sleeve of her plain brown sweater to dab her eyes. "He was a simple man, but a good one." She looked at Rose. "You know Rose. You grew up with him."

Aunt Rose gave a small nod. "Tubby's mother and mine were cousins. We didn't see each other much though except in school since he was always out on the farm. He dropped out at fourteen though to work the farm full time."

"He always thought of you as family, Rose." She laughed. "He tried to talk me out of the pie contest as he didn't want me to ruin your winning streak."

Aunt Rose stiffened, and I was sure she was thinking something like, "As if you could." Except Alice had beat my aunt one time. Had that been a successful bribe or maybe it was when Carl was trying to buy Tubby's land. Maybe he thought Tubby would be more agreeable if he judged Alice's pie as the winner.

"Anyway, Tubby of course agreed to the deal, and the paperwork was started, but then Carl dragged his feet. He started making excuses about why the transaction couldn't be completed. This went on for . . . what Rose . . . two years?"

Aunt Rose nodded.

"Anyway, the whole thing wore on Tubby and I didn't help. I told him to get out of the deal, but you know Tubby. He was a man of his word." Alice dabbed her eyes again.

"So, what happened?" I asked.

"Eventually Carl came by the house, all that charm of a snake oil salesman and told Tubby that he could finish the deal now for a much lower price, or he'd have to wait longer until Carl could sort out his assets or some story like that. I told Tubby, the land was worth more and he should find another buyer or just keep it. But by then, he was so worn out by the whole thing, he took the deal."

While that seemed underhanded, it didn't rise to the level of lying and cheating.

"The minute the ink was dry and money was transferred, Carl turned around and sold that land to the developer for twice as much as he'd originally offered."

Cripes. That did seem bad. I could understand being angry and bitter about that.

"Tubby was devastated. He never quite recovered. He lived in a haze of his feeling foolish. And it killed him. Oh, Carl didn't out right kill him, but he might as well have lit the match. Tubby was so distraught that he wasn't thinking when he lit up at the still."

"God rest his soul," Aunt Rose said.

"Guess who helped him on that deal?" Alice's sad tone morphed into anger.

"Who?"

"Tyler, his grandson. I heard a rumor you were spending time with him, trying to clear the cloud of suspicion over Rose. You be careful, Sophie. He's just like his granddaddy. Maybe even worse."

Huh. I suppose that was something I could ask Tyler about. "Several people have mentioned that Tyler was like Carl. I couldn't understand why since he's not from here, but I guess people know about his involvement in the land deal?"

Alice nodded. "You know this town. Everyone knows everyone else's business. But at the same time, you need to be careful poking into people's lives, Sophie."

"Sophie knows what she's doing," Aunt Rose said with a curt nod of surety.

"I just want to make sure that law enforcement is looking at other suspects. Aunt Rose didn't kill Carl."

"Well of course, she didn't. Have you made any progress?" Alice stuffed her tissue back into her sleeve.

I shrugged. "It's hard to know sometimes. I've been learning a lot about Tyler, and you've added to that."

"My money is on him," Aunt Rose said. "Wily runs in the Jackson family and that boy has it in spades."

"I agree." Alice nodded.

"What is his motive?" I asked.

"Money of course. Carl didn't just horde junk, he horded a fortune," Alice said.

"I wonder, though, if he was making money working with Carl on deals, why would he kill him?" I asked, thinking out loud.

"Carl probably stiffed him too," Aunt Rose said. "I don't think anyone was safe from Carl's selfish lying cheating ways."

That was one option. "There seems to be many people who had reason to want him dead."

Alice arched a brow at me. "Am I on your list, Sophie?"

I swallowed as I worked to keep my face impassive.

"Now Alice, you just heard her, she's suspicious of Tyler. And maybe Jones Willoughby, isn't that right, Sophie?"

I nodded. Was it lying if I didn't say I had Alice on my list? Granted, Tyler was higher because like Mrs. Conner said, he had all the elements of motive, means and opportunity. Alice definitely had motive, and maybe opportunity at the Winter Jamboree, but I wasn't sure about the means. Plus, that land deal was a while ago, even before Tubby died. Like Aunt Rose, if Alice wanted Carl dead, she'd have likely done it back when she learned they'd be duped, or right after Tubby died since she blamed Carl for that too.

- - - - - - - -

I excused myself to my room where I decided to call Lani about the land Carl, and apparently Tyler, had bought from Tubby. Everything I was hearing from people suggested that Tyler should be the prime suspect, but that wasn't the impression I was getting from Sergeant Scowl.

"Hey girl," she said when she picked up the phone. "What's up?"

I realized I was calling at dinner time. "Am I interrupting?"

"Nah. Dwayne is working tonight. Is everything alright?"

"Do you know anything about Tyler Jackson being a part of the deal when Carl bought Tubby's land?" I lay down on my couch bed. It was a position I had as teen and I'd talk with Lani on the phone. Back then, we talked algebra and boys, not murder.

"What? No. Really. How is that possible? He lives in Illinois. Why would he buy land in Virginia?"

"Didn't he say he was in finance or something? Maybe he helped Carl get the money? Or maybe he was investing. I don't know, but Alice Filmore said Tyler was part of the deal. You didn't know?"

"I had no idea."

"Do you think Dwayne and Sergeant Scowl know?"

She sighed and I knew it was because she didn't like being put in the middle between me and Dwayne and her job. "I don't know. Because of Rose, Dwayne has a been a bit tightlipped. He knows I tipped you off the other day."

"I'm sorry. I don't want to cause trouble in your marriage."

She made a ffffttttt sound. "He should have known better than to go charging after Rose. He's just being an eager beaver to get his promotion. But I don't think they're singularly focused on Rose, if that helps."

"So, they're considering Tyler?"

"I'm sure they are. He had the most to gain out of anyone except maybe his father, but his father isn't here."

"They're leaving all the arrangements to Tyler?"

"There are no arrangements except for that little memorial at church," Lani said in her shocked and appalled voice. "Carl is being cremated and that's that."

"Wow. I guess he didn't endear his son to him, but Tyler . . . if he did business with Carl, you'd think he'd have a funeral or bury him so people could say goodbye."

"You'd think. Listen, I know you're looking out for Rose, but I'm not sure it's wise for you to be investigating this. Dwayne and Davis are doing their jobs. They'll find the culprit."

"What if the test comes back that someone put poison in her pie? I'm not sure they'll keep an open mind." I wanted to trust the system, but I couldn't—not with Aunt Rose's life at stake.

"Just be careful. You always seem to get into trouble when you get involved in these murder investigations."

I agreed to be careful although I was careful before and still got into trouble.

"How are things with A.J." she asked.

"Good." I decided not to tell her that he had to go out of town again because she'd make that sound she did when she was feeling sorry for me. "I've got to run, Lani. Alice is here with Rose."

"I suppose they have a lot in common where Carl was concerned."

"Is Dwayne looking at her too?" I asked quickly.

"Sophie."

"Okay, okay. But I wouldn't have to investigate if you told me what was going on."

"You have to trust that they'll get to the bottom of it. They had no problem-solving crimes while you were gone. They don't need you involved now."

Her words stung a bit, even though she was right. Still, in my experience, Sergeant Scowl looked in the wrong places, too often at me or people I cared about, so I had no choice but to get involved.

I hung up and then freshened up in the bathroom before

heading back out to the living area. Alice was putting her coat on.

"Alice is just leaving," Aunt Rose said.

"I don't want to overstay especially since I just dropped in. But I wanted to give my support to you Rose. I know what people are saying and I don't believe it one bit. Carl was a snake, and I'm not sad he's gone, but I know you didn't have anything to do with it." She leaned in conspiratorially toward my aunt. "Besides, why ruin a good pie, right?"

"That's what I keep telling people! I'd never sully my pie."

I shook my head as I got my coat off the hook.

"Where are you off to, Sophie?" Aunt Rose asked.

"I thought I might go see Tyler."

Alice's eyes narrowed. "You're not stepping out on AJ, are you? He's a good hard-working boy who takes care of his mama and his brother and sister."

"She's doing what Lawson should be . . . finding the true killer," Aunt Rose said.

"Oh right. Well good. But be careful. I think he might be even worse than Carl when it comes to lying and cheating," Alice said.

"I'll be careful," I agreed, again noting that I was always was careful even when I ended up in trouble.

I drove past Carl's house where Tyler was staying to make sure Gwen's car wasn't there. The last thing I needed was her getting upset and thinking I was interested in Tyler. On the next pass, I parked in front and made my way up to the front door, realizing I hadn't come up with an excuse to be there. I couldn't just ask him if he helped Carl take advantage of Tubby over the land deal.

The door opened. Tyler's initial expression was a smile but his jaw was tight and his eyes held annoyance.

"Sophie?" His face relaxed morphing into curiosity. "What are you doing here?"

"I'm sorry to drop in unexpected, but I just wanted to check to see if you needed any help in taking care of your grandfather's things or making arrangements. We haven't heard about a funeral—"

"There won't be a funeral."

"Oh?" If Tyler was as stingy as Carl, maybe he saw a funeral as too big of expense.

"Come in. I was just pouring a glass of Scotch. Want some." He held the door open.

I walked into the house noting that nothing had changed since I'd last been there. It didn't look like Tyler was sorting or packing any of Carl's things. Then again, there were several houses full of stuff. Maybe he was starting with those.

"No Scotch for me."

"I think there's some cider from one of Carl's friends."

I wondered if that was from Alice Filmore, but then again, she and Carl weren't friends. "I don't need anything thank you." I sat on the couch as I waited for Tyler to return from the kitchen with his scotch. "Are your parents coming?"

He sat in an old recliner across from me. "No. I've been left in charge to deal with my grandfather's estate. I'm his executor."

I couldn't decide if Carl had a coldhearted family or if he'd brought their disdain for him on themselves.

"It sounds like a daunting job considering Carl seems to have a lot of assets."

Tyler shrugged. "I'm waiting for some lost heir or a legal loophole in which it turns out all his money goes to charity or something." I hadn't seen this sort of disdain toward Carl before. I wondered if this wasn't Tyler's first Scotch and perhaps the alcohol was loosening his lips.

"Would he do that?" I asked, playing dumb. "I mean, you're his family. Surely he wouldn't cheat you."

Tyler laughed. "Sure, he would. But unless he found a way to take his money to hell with him . . ." He shook his head like he'd caught himself. "Sorry. I know it's wrong to speak ill of the dead. Did you talk to that Jones guy?"

I nodded. "I don't think it was him. He was angry about Carl's neglect of the homes, but apparently their revenge was on calling the city about condemning the homes he used as storage."

Tyler snorted out a laugh, sloshing his scotch. "Sorry. I just

. . . my grandfather, for all his miserly and greedy ways, wasted a fortune by tying up those homes with his crap. As far as I can tell, there's nothing worth anything in any of them. I've decided to open them up and let people just take whatever they want. It's not worth my time to go through."

"If you need help with anything here, just let me know. I bet there are people at the senior center who'd be happy to help too."

Tyler responded with a shrug and a sip of his drink. "So, you don't think that Jones guy poisoned my grandfather?"

"I don't think so, but . . . I wasn't aware at how much animosity many held toward your grandfather. I didn't know him very well, but he always seemed charming to me."

"That was his secret. And no one was safe from him."

I frowned. "That sounds like you were a victim too."

"I could have been if I wasn't smart. I definitively learned not to partner with him on financial projects. My father warned me."

"What about the housing development?"

He arched a brow like he was surprised I knew about it. Considering how much I was playing dumb, that was an odd tidbit for me to know.

"You know about that. I suppose you would. Nothing gets past anyone in this town, does it? Yes, I partnered with him on that. We made a killing."

I winced at his choice of words as I thought of poor Tubby by his moonshine still. "Did you know that part of your killing was because Carl cheated the landowner?"

"No, but I'm not surprised. Maybe that guy killed him."

"He's already dead. Some think that Carl is to blame."

Tyler shook his head. "My grandfather was a lot of things, but not a murderer."

"It's not that. It's more like he created the situation in which Tubby ended up dead."

"Tubby?" Tyler arched a brow. "The south has some interesting names."

I didn't bother to explain that it was a nickname. "Have the investigators talked to you more?"

I watched his ice as he swirled it in his glass. "They've been by a few times, mostly to go through my grandfather's things."

"So, they've ruled you out?" I asked, deciding to be a bit more direct.

"I doubt it. You sure you don't want a drink?"

I nodded. "I'm sure. Why do you think they're still considering you?"

He lowered his drink and gave me a direct look. "What about you, Sophie? Do you think I did it? Is that why you're here?"

I swallowed, wishing I'd accepted a drink so I could hide my discomfort and give myself a moment to gather my thoughts. "You asked me to talk to Jones, remember?"

"Yes, but now you're asking about me. People in this town talk and they say you like to poke your nose into police business."

"Like I said, you asked me about Jones," I said lamely.

"I suppose I have more reason to want Carl dead."

"You had opportunity too," I pointed out before I could think better of it.

If Tyler was offended, he didn't show it. "I'd have much rather found a way to hit my grandfather where it hurt . . . his bank account."

Murder seemed like the ultimate hurt, but clearly Tyler and Carl had skewed views of life and money. I wasn't sure how to respond to that.

"Oh, I found something that you might want." Tyler stood and walked over to a secretary desk. "I was going through some boxes my grandfather had in his closet and found this."

He handed me a stack of photos. They were black and white showing a very young Carl with a pretty dark-haired woman. I studied her because there was something about her. The short dark hair, petite body, and mischievous eyes. I turned the photo over. In pen, it had the date along with the couple: Carl and Rose.

I flipped the photo over to study my aunt as she was when she was around my age. She'd been beautiful, and the glint in her eyes told me that she didn't take anyone's nonsense then either. But even someone as astute as Rose could be taken in by a handsome charming man, as Carl clearly was. They had happy smiles as they stared at each other. Carl was in a white t-shirt and jeans, wearing a chain, while Aunt Rose wore a dress and her signature pearls.

"I'm told that's your aunt." Tyler sat back in his chair picking up his drink.

"They looked so happy." I studied the photo closer. It looked like they were downtown. Behind them, was a tractor pulling a float with several smiling and waving young women. "They're at a parade." I squinted closer, curious as to what was hanging around Carl's neck. "Is that a key Carl is wearing on a chain?"

"Yeah. Mrs. Martin, the neighbor who told me who was in the picture, said that back in the day, sometimes people who were dating did that. Key to her heart or something." His tone suggested he thought the idea was stupid, but I thought it was sweet. At the same time, it broke my heart. The Aunt Rose I knew now wasn't much into sentimentality. But at one time, she'd loved Carl enough to give her the key to her home . . . to her heart.

"Your grandfather was supposed to come home to Aunt Rose, but I guess he found someone else."

"There are rumors your aunt killed my grandfather." He said it like he was testing the waters to see how I'd respond.

I tried to keep my cool. "I know, but she didn't. She wouldn't, at least not with a pie."

He laughed. "That's what one of the detectives said."

I couldn't imagine Sergeant Scowl saying that, so it had to be Dwayne. I wondered if that meant they'd taken Aunt Rose off their list of suspects.

"But to my mind, killing him with her pie would be the same as me finding a way to cheat him out of his money. The perfect revenge."

"That's not how my aunt thinks."

He shrugged. "Everyone has a breaking point, Sophie."

I studied him for a moment. "What's yours?"

He watched me over his glass as he drank the last bit of his Scotch. He didn't say anything, but his expression was coy.

I stood. "Well, I just wanted to offer assistance if you needed any in dealing with Carl's things and to let you know about Jones."

"And pick my brain too?" He rose from his chair.

"I'll show myself out," I said ignoring his accusation.

"Does that ever get you in trouble?"

"Does what?" I asked as I reached the door.

"Getting involved in police business?"

Every time, I thought. "Like you said, people in this town talk. I don't have to snoop too hard."

His grin told me he didn't buy what I was saying. "You know what they say about curiosity and the cat?"

I opened the door exiting into the cold night, although it was his tone of voice that had the shiver of fear running up my spine. "Have a good evening."

"See ya around, Sophie."

I glanced back as I hurried to my car. He stood in the doorway watching me. I gave a quick wave and got into the car, driving until I was out of his line of sight then pulling over again. I replayed my visit. I didn't get anything new, and yet there was definitely a change in Tyler. Was it because he'd had a few drinks or something else, like my showing up and asking about his business with Carl?

I pulled out my notebook and wrote down the conversation. I also hid the photographs in it. I wasn't sure if I should give them to Aunt Rose or not. Then I drove home.

When I got there, I found pine needles strewn up the walkway. Opening the door, I saw Aunt Rose and Bull in the living room.

He grinned. "Merry Christmas, Miss Sophie." He stood by a plump tree. "What do you think?"

"I told him we didn't need a tree," Aunt Rose said, although there was a gleam in her eye that told me she liked the tree. This was my first Christmas with her so I didn't know how she celebrated, except that she'd often said decorating was too much work.

He frowned. "It's Christmas Ms. Rose. Everyone needs a tree."

"It's lovely," I said. "It smells very Christmassy too."

Aunt Rose directed Bull to the attic where he found a box of ornaments. We invited him to stay, but he said he had other errands.

"Why aren't you with AJ?" I asked, trying to ignore the niggle of worry that AJ was back and didn't call me.

"He's with Patch on this one."

Bull left Aunt Rose and me to decorate the tree.

"I don't know what he was thinking?" Aunt Rose said looking at the tree like she didn't know what to do with it.

"I think it's sweet. Why don't I heat up some of the cider Alice brought and we can have some of your cookies while we decorate the tree?"

"It just seems like a lot of work—"

"It will be fun. Festive." I didn't wait for her response. I went to the kitchen to fix the cider and make a plate of cookies. I peeked out of the kitchen and was pleased to see Aunt Rose opening the box of ornaments.

- - - - - - - -

I found a streaming music list of Christmas music to play while Aunt Rose and I decorated the tree with ornaments that had to be older than my father. Then we admired our work while drinking cider and eating cookies.

"This is nice," I said, trying to hide the well of emotion that blossomed as I realized it had been a long time since I partook in Christmas rituals.

Aunt Rose yawned. "I'll admit, it was a good idea."

"It was nice of Bull to think of us," I said, sipping my cider. I felt warm and cozy. Like I wanted to curl up for a long nap.

"He's a good boy."

I snorted at the contradiction of Bull, the man built like a tank, being referred to as a boy.

"It's been a long day, Sophie. I'm heading to bed," Aunt Rose moved a bit slower than usual. I hoped it was the fatigue of the day and not her age.

"Good night." I yawned and realized I was feeling tired too. "I'll be right behind you. I'll clean up the dishes."

When I finished loading the dishwasher, I turned off the lights in the kitchen and living room and headed to bed. I sank into the covers pulling them around me sighing at how warm and content

I felt. I closed my eyes and let sleep come.

- - - - - - - -

Something was wrong. I rolled over, snuggling deeper into my blanket. I coughed, covering my head from whatever was tickling my nose. That was no good because I couldn't breathe. I pushed the blanket down. I coughed hard. I jerked awake sitting up relieved that I would be rid of the crazy dream. I inhaled a deep breath and coughed again. That wasn't clean air I took in. Was it smoke?

Oh God!

I scrambled out of bed rushing to my door. I stopped just short of grabbing the knob and opening it when my elementary school fire drill lesson flashed in my head. *If the door or doorknob is hot, don't go through it.* I tentatively pressed my hand to the door and felt warmth. I tapped my fingers on the knob and heat seared my fingers. I staggered back.

"Aunt Rose!" I yelled wondering why I didn't hear smoke alarms. Didn't Bull just check those for her a month or so ago? My brain couldn't function. I needed to do something, but what? I swung around scanning my room for clues. The window. I could go out the window. I started for it when I saw my phone on the arm rest of my hideaway bed.

I grabbed it, dialing 9-1-1. "My house is on fire." I said the words, but my throat hurt and I wasn't sure any sound came of it. Still on the phone, I opened my window, sliding it up. Fresh cold air reached my nostrils and I sucked it in. I started to climb out, but then realized I was in my pajamas with no shoes.

"Hello? Are you there?" a woman's voice came over my phone.

"I need my shoes," I said, climbing back down off my couch bed to find my shoes.

"What is your address?"

By rote, I rattled off the address. "My aunt is in her room."

"Fire trucks are on the way."

I found my red Converse sneakers, which didn't match my pink flannel jammies but the woman on the phone was telling me to get out now, so I grabbed my comforter and scrambled out the window, onto the love seat on the porch, dropping my phone as I did. I sat for a moment, taking in deep breaths. With each inhale, my brain seemed to clear.

I stood grabbing my blanket as I went to the front door. If the fire was outside my room, then going in the front door to reach Aunt Rose wasn't an option. I rushed around to the back of the house where Aunt Rose's room was.

We lived in a one-story house, but it was on a crawl, so the ground floor window was too high for me to get a good look through. I ran to the back patio, nearly tripping over a gnome to get to a resin chair. I grabbed the chair returning to Aunt Rose's window.

I stood on the chair and rapped on the window. "Aunt Rose!" I pressed my face to the glass to look in, but only saw smoke. I gripped the lower sash, pulling on it but it didn't move. The window was locked.

"Aunt Rose!" I yelled again. What should I do? I jumped down from the chair, rushing to the gnome. I went back to the window and threw the gnome as hard as I could. I knew her bed wasn't next to the window, but her room wasn't large and I hoped I didn't hurt her.

"Aunt Rose!" I called through the jagged hole in the window. "There's a fire!"

I still couldn't see her. I wrapped the blanket around my arm, and carefully reached in the window to undo the latch. I pushed it up. I lay the blanket over the sill to cover any glass and climbed in.

"Aunt Rose!" The smoke filled my lungs and burned my eyes. I felt my way to her bed. "Aunt Rose!" My hands found her on her side. I pushed at her. "Get up!"

She made a moaning sound.

"Get up Aunt Rose! The house is on fire!" I grabbed her arm, tugging harder. "We have to get out!" Aunt Rose was petite, but so was I. I didn't think I could carry her. I pulled her until she was sitting.

"Go away," she said drowsily.

"Aunt Rose, the house is on fire. Come on." I moved her until she was sitting on the side of the bed. I took a moment to catch my breath, except it was impossible. I coughed as the attempt to fill my lungs with oxygen failed.

"What's happening?" She looked at me, but her eyes were unfocused as if she was disoriented.

"We have to leave. The house is on fire." I put her arm around my shoulder and stood, hoisting her up with me and dragging her to the window. How was I going to get her through it? Especially without hurting her?

Her vanity was next to the window. I grabbed the chair and pulled it over. "You have to climb up on this and go out the window."

I tried to lift her leg because I didn't think she knew what I was saying. Maybe I should go out first and pull her through but how would I reach her?

"I'm tired Sophie," Aunt Rose said, coughing as she sat on the chair.

"We can't rest here." I tried to lift her and then carry her with me up to the window, but my legs gave out. I sank down, sitting on the chair with her on my lap. We were going to die here if I couldn't get us out. I could save myself, but how would I live with myself if I didn't try to save her too?

"Aunt Rose?" God I was so tired.

She didn't say anything.

I sat there with her. That's what I needed. I needed to rest a moment. Then I could get us out. I closed my eyes. Deep inside, a voice told me to keep moving.

"I'm so tired." Get up! "I just need a minute."

"Is there anyone in here?"

Who was that? I managed to tilt my head to look up at the window but I didn't see anyone.

"Aunt Rose, we need to get up," I said, finding strength to stand again and try to maneuver her onto the chair.

All of a sudden, she was pulled through the window like magic. I looked down at my hands wondering how I did that.

"Come on!" a muffled voice shouted. I looked toward it and saw a figure in the window. His arms reached out to me. "Can you get up to the window?"

I stood there like an idiot. I couldn't get my legs to move.

The figure came through the window, scooping me up and carrying me back to it. "Watch your head."

He put me through the window and I flailed as I was sure I was going to fall through it. But then arms on the other side grabbed me and carried me back around to the front of the house. Lights flashed—red ones, blue ones.

People surrounded me and started poking, prodding, and asking questions. A mask covered my mouth and nose, and all of a sudden, I could breathe again. With each breath, clarity began to return.

I pulled the mask away. "Where's my aunt?"

Someone put the mask back. "She's being treated. We'll be taking you and her both to the hospital."

"Will she be okay?"

I didn't get an answer. Instead, I was put into an ambulance and taken to the hospital. From the ride to being wheeled into the hospital to the nurses and doctor examining me; everything was a whirl of activity. I felt like I was falling into a vortex until finally, darkness came and I could rest.

Chapter Twelve

- -

I woke up feeling like I had sludge in my lungs and there was something tickling my nose. I lifted my hand but I didn't feel in complete command of it as I brought it to my face.

"Ah, ah, ah . . ." A woman's face appeared. "Leave that there, sweetie. You got a good dose of smoke and this will help you breathe until it's all cleared out."

I looked around noting that this wasn't my room. Smoke—she said smoke. If there was smoke there was fire. *Oh God, Aunt Rose!*

"My aunt," I said, or at least tried to say. My throat felt like it had been sandpapered.

"Your aunt is in intensive care, but doing well." The nurse handed me some water. "Drink this. It will help your throat."

I sipped from the straw. "She'll be, okay?" It was my job to look after her and it appeared that I'd failed.

"The doctor will be able to tell you more, but she's stable." The nurse prodded and poked again. "Sergeant Davis is pacing outside. Do you feel up to talking to him?"

No. Talking to him always required all my wits, and I didn't think I had a single wit left. I frowned. "Why is he here?"

"Probably because your house burnt down."

It took a moment for my synapses to connect the dots. "Someone set our house on fire?" As if my lungs needed the reminder, I began to cough. It felt like I might expel them from my chest.

She shrugged. "I can tell him to come back later. You can get more rest."

I shook my head. Even without my wits or my lungs, I needed to know if someone tried to kill me and Aunt Rose. "No. I'll talk to him."

Sergeant Scowl walked in looking gruff as usual, but also tired, and maybe concerned. "Are you up to answering some questions?"

"Did someone burn the house down?"

He gave me his signature scowl. "My questions first."

"I don't know anything. I woke up and the house was on fire." I scanned my brain to recall the night. We'd decorated the tree. Had there been something faulty with the lights? I'd turned them off, so how could they have caused a fire? In fact, everything was off, even the smoke detectors. "Why didn't our smoke detectors go off?"

"It helps to put batteries in them."

I shook my head. "I thought they also were wired for electric."

"Not necessarily in old homes like your aunt's. Even so, if there's no electricity . . ."

What did that mean? Did someone turn off the power to house—and take the batteries out? Who would do that? How would they do that?

"I don't understand." I coughed again, reaching for the tissues on the table.

"Ms. Parker . . . Sophie."

Sergeant Scowled rarely called me by my name so his use of it now got my attention.

He handed me the box of tissues. "How has your aunt been lately?"

I stared at him, not understanding the question as I took a tissue and wiped my mouth.

"Has she been agitated? Worried?"

"I guess. She knows you think she's a suspect, but other than that, she's been normal. Baking. Seeing friends. The usual."

The door opened and Dwayne walked in. "Sophie. Are you okay?"

I nodded, but Sergeant Scowl cleared his throat, bringing my attention to him again.

"We believe Carl Jackson was poisoned with something like antifreeze. Any chance your aunt had a stash of that around the house?" Sergeant Scowl asked.

"Why? She doesn't drive. I don't have any either," I said, answering the next question he'd have about my car. Bull always looked out for me in the car maintenance department. Maybe he'd stored some at the house, but I couldn't remember seeing any.

"Maybe Rose wanted to hide the evidence and take suspicion off her," Sergeant Scowl said.

This is why wits were important because I was slow to realize what he was saying. "My aunt didn't use anti-freeze to poison Carl or to burn down the house."

"Anti-freeze is water-based," Dwayne said. "That doesn't sound like a good option to start a fire."

Sergeant Scowl pursed his lips at him. "If the anti-freeze is the poison, then maybe it wasn't the starter, but the end goal was to get rid of it."

I shook my head. "Aunt Rose wouldn't burn her home down any more than she'd put poison in her pie. Especially since she got hurt too. She's eccentric, but not dangerous or suicidal. Besides, there must be many others in town who have anti-freeze and didn't like Carl. Like Jones Willoughby."

Sergeant Scowl's thick salt-and-pepper brow arched. "Playing Nancy Drew again?"

I pled the fifth by keeping my mouth shut.

"Actually, anti-freeze is flammable," Dwayne said looking at his phone. "But we should talk with the arson investigator to see if that was used."

Sergeant Scowl took a long breath, probably to calm down. "Did you know that Rose was in Carl's will. Maybe she got tired of waiting."

"That's ridiculous."

"Did you know about the will?" he asked again.

"Only when Tyler mentioned it. I don't know if Aunt Rose knows. She hasn't mentioned it. She would have told me if a lawyer had come by, which makes me wonder if Carl's family is fighting it. How much did he leave her?"

Dwayne coughed and Sergeant Scowl looked down for a moment. "Four hundred, twenty-three dollars and sixty-seven cents."

"You're joking." I looked at both men in disbelief. "You think Aunt Rose killed Carl for less than five hundred dollars."

"Apparently, it's what he owed her from wagers playing bunco," Dwayne said. "What is bunco?"

"It's a dice game." I glared at them both. I wasn't sure what was stranger; that they thought Aunt Rose killed Carl for bunco payment of a bunco debt or that Carl left her money to cover his debt. Was he still teasing her from the grave or just being a jerk?

"So, Ms. Parker, who do you think set your house on fire?" Sergeant Scowl asked, thankfully moving on from Carl's will. I hoped that meant he knew how ridiculous that idea was.

"Please tell me you have other people on your list for Carl's murder."

Dwayne nodded as he put his phone away. "Sure, we do—"

"Deputy Lafferty."

Dwayne jerked to attention at Sergeant Scowl's barking of his name. "Sir."

"Why don't you go check on Ms. Rose Parker. See if and when we might be able to talk with her."

"She's in intensive care—" Dwayne stopped short when Sergeant Scowl's eyes narrowed into tiny, slits. "I'll go check, sir."

"Let Lani know I'm okay, will you, Dwyane?" I said as he pulled the door open.

"Sure thing, Soph."

"So, who have you been agitating lately?" Sergeant Scowl asked.

I cleared my throat of the gunk living in it, then said, "Well, if you must know, Tyler Jackson would be at the top of my list. I don't know why he's not at the top of yours. He was staying with Carl so he could have poisoned his food and drink. He and his parents weren't on great terms with Carl, and they're about to inherit a fortune in real estate. Plus, he made a comment about what happens to curious cats."

Sergeant Scowls brow rose. "Curious cats?"

"Yes, you know. Curiosity killed the cat. Except he said something like 'you know what happens to curious cats.'"

"When?"

"Earlier tonight . . . or . . ." What time was it anyway? The clock on the wall indicated it was seven in the morning. "Last night."

"What did you talk about with Tyler Jackson?"

"He said he heard rumors about Jones Willoughby—"

"Who you've just accused as well."

I shook my head. "I don't really think he did it. But he did work on Carl's car and would have anti-freeze. That was my point. You have plenty of other people to suspect instead of harassing my aunt."

"Why would Tyler be talking to you about Jones?" Sergeant Scowl pulled his pen and notepad from his pocket.

"Actually, he called me and invited me to dinner. He said he heard the rumors about Jones, but not being from town, wasn't sure it was something he should tell you about." I bit my lip as I considered that. "Maybe Tyler did that as a way to take suspicion off of him."

"What do you mean?"

"He doesn't come right out and blame someone because, how could he? He doesn't live here and know all the players. But he's smart. He hears a rumor and then contacts me like he's not sure if it means anything. He solicits support from others in town." I thought of the time he was spending with Gwen, who was accusing my aunt.

"Like you?"

I nodded. "He's casually seeing a local woman as well. He's like Carl in some ways. Charming, but underneath there is a smarminess. I never saw it in Carl but—"

"You saw it in his grandson."

"Last night, he wasn't outwardly threatening. That's what made it so creepy. He knew I sometimes poked around and figured out I was poking around with him too."

"And you think that maybe he set your aunt's house on fire." He shook his head like my father used to do when he thought I was being foolish. "All the more reason to stay out of my way."

Instinct had me wanting to contradict him, except he was right.

"So, how would he have gotten into your aunt's home and disabled the smoke detectors?"

I shrugged. "I don't know. Maybe he snuck in. We were sleeping."

"We'll need to see if we can determine if there was any forced entry. Who has a key to the house?"

Did Bull? I knew AJ didn't because I figured Aunt Rose wouldn't like it and AJ was leery of my aunt. "Maybe Betty Bealton or Tilly Watson. They're Aunt Rose's friends at the senior center." An idea came to me. "Maybe Carl had one."

"Why would your aunt give her nemesis a key to her home?"

"Maybe he had it from when they dated a long time ago. Or maybe he got it from Betty Bealton. Aunt Rose said she was sweet on Carl."

I expected Sergeant Scowl to dismiss this, but he scribbled on his notepad. "Has anyone else been to the house lately?"

"You and Dwayne. Bull—"

"Bull?"

"He's her baking buddy. He wouldn't hurt her. And Alice Filmore came by." I opted not to tell him how she thought he wasn't doing a good job on this investigation. "She brought us some of her cider and offered emotional support to my aunt. She knows Aunt Rose didn't kill Carl."

"How would she know that?"

It was my turn to scowl. "Because Aunt Rose wouldn't do that. She might have a sharp tongue and no tolerance of nonsense, but she's not a killer. I know it. Alice knows. Anyone who knows my aunt, knows it."

Sergeant Scowl gave me a hard glare and I had a feeling he had more bad news for me. But I had questions of my own because as my head cleared some and I had a moment to reflect, I wound back around to the idea that maybe Carl wasn't the intended victim.

"What if Carl's murder was an accident?" I asked.

He inhaled a breath and crossed his arms waiting for me to continue. It made me wonder if he'd already been considering that.

"What if the pie was intended for my aunt, and that failed, and this fire is a second attempt."

"Alright. You tell me, who wants your aunt dead?" he asked.

Cripes. I had no idea. My aunt was a difficult woman, but she wasn't someone people wanted to kill. She didn't lie or cheat or steal. She spent her days watching soap operas or ID TV, and a few days a week at the senior center playing bunco. Once a week or so, she'd bake with Bull. Many people were recipients of her baked goods as she often gave them to neighbors or took them to the senior center.

"I don't know. I can't imagine anyone would want her dead."

"What are the odds someone was targeting you?"

Hadn't we been through this before and he dismissed it? "The fire was a good try, but not the pie."

"You don't eat pie?"

"I do sometimes, but I eat the stuff she saves at home. Anything that is in a contest or taken to the senior center I don't eat."

He gave me another one of his long stares. "I know I'm wasting my breath here, but you really do need to stay out this."

"I can't let you put Aunt Rose in jail for a murder she didn't commit."

He shook his head. "When have I failed to get the bad guy?"

I wanted to point out that usually when he got the bad guy, I'd beat him to it. But then he'd probably point out how he always showed up just in time to save my life.

The door opened and the nurse entered. "She needs rest, Lawson."

"Get well, Sophie," he said, but I heard, "get ready, because I'll be back."

I was amazingly exhausted after Sergeant Scowl left, so I took the nurses advice and slept. When I woke, my lunch was sitting on a tray near the bed, and Lani was in a chair reading an entertainment magazine.

"How long have you been there?" I asked.

She set her magazine down and rose from the chair. "Long enough to know which celebrities are breaking up, making up, and accidentally pregnant. How do you feel?"

"Like I was in a fire." My lungs still felt like they had a layer soot running up my esophagus to my nasal sinuses.

"God Soph, how do you get in such trouble?"

"It seems to find me," I said. "Have you heard anything about Aunt Rose?"

"They won't tell me anything. I even tried to be an official of the sheriff's department. Dwayne told me she was in stable condition though, so that is a good sign." She pulled the over table across my bed. "I told them to leave your lunch. It's a sandwich and chips."

I pulled the cover off. My stomach growled, as it registered that I was hungry. And thirsty. "Can you pour me some water?" The lunch had milk, but I was worried it was too thick for a palette that was already filled with mucus.

"Yeah sure. Have you called AJ?" Lani filled the glass with water from the pitcher.

"Oh God. I haven't. He's going to be so mad. I told him that last time I'd been nearly killed that I'd call if anyone tried to murder me again."

She shook her head as she handed me the water. "Do you hear yourself?" She took out her phone from her pocket. "Here, I assume yours is charred."

"No. I know I had it with me when escaped." Then again, maybe I dropped it when I tried to save Rose. "I don't know where it is."

"Well, we'll get you a new one along with all the other new things you're going to have to get. I hope Rose was adequately insured."

My heart sank. "Is it all gone?" I didn't have much stuff to lose, but Rose had a lifetime in that house.

"It's pretty much gutted. I'm so sorry."

"Do you suppose any of our stuff survived?"

"If it did, it's water-logged and will forever smell like smoke. The good news is, you can go shopping for new clothes." Lani gave me her version of the silver lining expression.

I scoffed. "Where will I put them? I have no place to live."

"I bet AJ will have something to say about that, but if not, you can come stay with me and Dwayne."

"Neither AJ nor Dwayne, nor you for that matter, will want to put up with Aunt Rose."

"I suspect she'll be here for a bit longer and maybe at a rehabilitation place."

That didn't sound like stable condition to me.

"Don't worry about all that now. You and Rose will be taken care of. It's one of the perks of living in a town where everyone knows your business. They also will help you."

I set the phone down, not quite ready to call AJ. I wanted to sound stronger so he didn't worry. This job was important and I didn't want to muck it up for him.

"Gwen might not help, but then again, she's not originally from here," she finished.

"Yeah, well, Tyler as it turns out, is a little scary. As a matter of fact, I think he burnt the house down." I picked up the sandwich and took a bite. I wasn't sure if it was stale or my mouth was dry, but I was hungry so I chewed and managed to swallow it down.

"What? How did he get in?" Lani asked, stealing a chip from my bag.

"I don't know. But I'm pretty sure he was threatening me when I left his house the other night."

Lani sighed. "You really should let Sergeant Davis handle this."

Speaking of Sergeant Scowl. "Shouldn't you be at work? What day is it?" Maybe I was out longer than I thought.

"It's Friday. I took the day off and called the library to let them know you'd be out a few days."

I groaned. "They'll fire me now for sure. I'm too much trouble."

"Mrs. Wayland was fine. Concerned, but fine." Lani picked up her phone.

"What are you doing?"

"I'm calling AJ."

I tried to grab it back. "You'll freak him out and I don't want that."

She rolled her eyes. "Would you want to know if AJ was in the hospital?"

"Yes but . . ."

She dialed the phone, making me wonder how she had his number. Knowing the two of them, it was just for situations like this.

She handed the phone to me. "He'll be less mad if he hears it from you instead of me."

I took the phone.

"Hey, this is AJ. You know what to do."

"It's voice mail." How did I possibly leave a voice mail about being in the hospital? "Hi AJ. I hope you're having success taking the airplane."

Lani did an even bigger eye roll and threatened to take the phone.

"Ah . . . I'm okay but . . . well . . . Aunt Rose's house burnt down. But I'm fine. Lani says I can stay with her until I figure out my next step. Ah . . . Rose is okay too . . . ah . . . I think. Anyway, don't worry. I'll see you when you finish your job. Ah . . . bye." Feeling like a dork, I poked the off button and handed it back to Lani. "Happy?"

She laughed. "He's on the next plane home for sure."

Chapter Thirteen

When I finished lunch, the doctor came into my room to check on me. Apparently, he was satisfied with my progress and said he'd discharge me that day. I learned the last time that I was in the hospital that getting discharged was pretty much an all-day process. The good news for me was that it gave me time to find a place to stay. Of course, once Lani returned from making a call to Dwayne, it took her two seconds to tell me she was making him set up the guest room for me.

"Can I see my aunt before I go," I asked the doctor.

"You can see her, but you won't be able to talk to her. She's still unconscious."

My heart stuttered in my chest. "Will she be alright?"

"Her vitals are stable. We need to wait to see if there are any long-term effects."

That wasn't a yes or a no, but I took it as a positive sign.

It was nearly dinnertime when Lani loaded me into her car to take me to her townhome.

"I want to see the house," I said, hoping my voice sounded strong even though I wasn't sure I was ready to see the devastation.

"It's nearly dark, Sophie. And . . . it's too soon."

I frowned at her. "I'm not weak."

"I know, but give it day." She pulled out into the city traffic. "In the back seat, I got you a toothbrush and few other items. I have some clothes at home you can borrow until we can go shopping."

It took me a minute to understand what she was telling me. The magnitude of the fire hit me then.

"It's all gone." My voice quivered and I had to concede that I wasn't strong, or at least not ready to see the total devastation of my and Aunt Rose's house.

Lani gave me a quick glance. "At least you and Rose are okay. That's what matters most."

She was right. And of course, I didn't have too much stuff. The only thing that I truly valued was the book of fairy tales AJ had given me on my eighteenth birthday. Aunt Rose lost way more than I did. It was all gone. Another wave of panic tumbled through me.

"Oh God, what are we going to do?" I pressed my hands over my face as the tears came despite my wishing they wouldn't.

Lani pulled to the side of the road. "Sophie." She put her arm around me as best she could since we were buckled into the car. "It will be okay. You're strong on your own, but you're not alone. You have people who'll help you. You've got me, AJ, the girls in coupon group, and so many others in town."

"Will they want to help us if they think Aunt Rose killed Carl?" I sniffed.

"First, no one really believes that. Second, the fact that someone burnt your house down suggests someone else killed Carl and, for some reason, is after you or Rose, or both."

"Both?" I looked at her.

"Or maybe they just wanted to get Rose and Carl. I don't know, Sophie. You'd probably know more than me. The point is, you'll be fine. I'm sure Rose has insurance. In the meantime, you know Jefferson Grove. People will help. And if I have to put Rose in the spare room with you, I'll do it."

My lips twitched upward. "She's not easy to live with."

"I know it, but I'll do it anyway." She gave me a squeeze. "Let's go home. Dwayne is making chili and corn bread."

"Sounds delicious."

"Rose can make pies, my Dwayne can make chili," Lani said putting the car in gear to finish the drive to her home.

- - - - - - - -

We arrived at Lani's townhome and Dwayne opened the door before we reached the top step of the stoop.

"Chili's ready." He leaned over to give Lani a kiss.

"I'm going to take Sophie up to the guestroom," she told him.

"I'll serve up the grub."

As I passed him, I remembered how a few months ago he worried I was brining danger to his doorstep. That time, someone had shot at me. Burning Aunt Rose's down seemed comparable to that.

"I hope it's not a problem for me to stay," I said, wanting him to know that I understood if he had concerns.

"It's not a problem, and if it was, it wouldn't matter anyway," he said, with a glance toward Lani.

"That's right. Besides, you're a big bad sheriff's deputy. Surely you can protect us." She batted her eyes at him.

He put his hands on his hips and adopted a Superman stance.

"Swoon. My hero." Lani grinned at him.

I laughed. "I'm feeling like a third wheel."

"Nonsense. Come on, let me show you your room and I put a few items of clothes out for you if you'd like to change." Lani continued up the stairs.

"Don't take too long," Dwayne called up. "The chili is perfect. The cornbread is done. I'll start without you two if I have to."

I didn't want to ruin Dwayne's dinner so I cleaned up by washing my face and then headed downstairs.

"Does Lawson have any more information on who started the fire?" Lani asked Dwayne once we were seated and served.

Dwayne looked at his wife and then me. "I'm not supposed to talk shop with civilians."

"Sophie isn't a civilian, she's a victim. Surely there's something you can tell us." Lani did that smile she used to get what she wanted from Dwayne.

He looked at each of us again. "I don't know about the fire. But . . ."

"But what?" Lani insisted.

"We did hear that Carl died of ethanol glycol poisoning." Dwayne kept his gaze on me, which made me uncomfortable.

"What is that?" Lani asked, like she didn't know.

"Antifreeze."

Lani grinned. "Just like you suspected. You'll be a detective in no time."

"Investigator," he corrected.

"Investigator Lafferty. It has a nice ring, doesn't it, Sophie?"

"Yes, it does," I said even though I was still unsettled by Dwayne's announcement. I didn't want to ruin dinner, but I had to know what that meant for Aunt Rose. "My aunt doesn't drive, Dwayne. She wouldn't have antifreeze."

He shrugged. "You have a car."

"Yeah, but I don't have antifreeze either. Bull takes care of that for me."

"A man who has a criminal history."

Oh crap. Did I just throw Bull under the bus? "Not for poisoning or murder." At least I hoped not.

"Small traces were found in the pie too," he said, crumbling his corn bread into his chili.

The proverbial other shoe dropped. It was more like a Doc Marten boot, hitting with a loud thud.

"Lawson can't really believe Rose killed Carl. Besides, someone tried to kill her. Surely that proves someone else is behind all this," Lani said.

"I think it would be enough to arrest Rose." Dwyane's brows drew down, like he was sorry he had to say that.

"That's crazy." Lani shook her head as she blew on her spoonful of chili.

"The M.E. said he would have had to consume a good amount of the antifreeze the night before. Unless it was concentrated in the pieces he ate, there wasn't enough in the pie. It seems likely there was another source as well."

"Other judges ate the pie so it had to have been put there later, not when Rose baked it." I grabbed onto this tidbit knowing it was the one thing that would save Aunt Rose.

Dwayne shifted. "Do you want to know my theory? It's just a theory. Conjecture really."

"I do." Lani looked at me.

I nodded. "Sure." I hoped he wasn't going to be told that he believed Aunt Rose killed Carl and then burned our house down.

He leaned forward with his forearms on the table like he was telling us a secret. "My research suggests that to kill a human as quickly as Carl died, he'd have to have consumed several ounces of antifreeze."

"Wouldn't he have tasted it?" Lani asked, leaning toward him. I leaned forward just like Lani and Dwayne did, rapt at his news.

"It's said to taste sweet. Maybe it was mixed with something," he said.

Carl's comment about Aunt Rose's pie being too sweet came back to me, but I didn't reshare it. "There was eggnog and cider at the jamboree," I offered instead.

He nodded. "Hot chocolate, too. Not water, but something that is already sweet."

I tried to think back on the beverages offered at the jamboree. It was pretty much a serve-oneself type of set up.

"Anyone could have spiked the drinks," I said.

"Except then many people would be poisoned. Only Carl was. I think someone offered him the drink." Dwayne said.

I leaned back in my chair, taking in Dwayne's theory.

"And there's one more thing. A few months ago, Carl got a letter threatening his life." Dwane added a curt nod like it was the smoking gun.

"What?" both Lani and I exclaimed.

Dwayne nodded. "Mrs. Willoughby."

"Jones Willoughby's wife? She couldn't have done it. She was out of town," I said, though maybe that wasn't true. Maybe Jones had lied to me.

Dwayne frowned. "How do you know?"

I shrugged. "You know . . ."

He shook his head. "Yeah, I know. That could be why your house is dust."

"Dwayne!" Lani glared he him.

He flinched. "Sorry, Sophie. Anyway, it wasn't the wife. It was his mother. She was angry that her granddaughter was nearly killed. Possibly suffering lifelong injuries from lead poisoning."

"Who'd have thought Carl would be such a miser to let his tenants suffer?" Lani shook her head.

That didn't make sense to me. Would Carl have handed the threatening letter to the authorities? "If Carl reported it then—"

"He didn't. His grandson found the letter."

I stiffened. "Is it legit?"

Dwayne's brows furrowed. "Why wouldn't it be?"

"I don't trust Tyler. There's something . . . smarmy about him. He didn't threaten me outright, but it felt like a threat when I left his place last night."

"Do you think he burnt your house down?" Lani asked.

"He's top of my list. Plus, he'd have access to antifreeze. Jones could have left it there since he'd been helping Carl with his car."

"Or his mother got hold of it," Dwayne said.

"Both these theories should clear Aunt Rose," I said. "You won't find antifreeze at the house . . . which I know Scowl was looking for."

"Why do you call him that?" Dwayne asked.

"Because he's always scowling."

"I don't want you to take this the wrong way, Sophie, but your aunt being in the hospital is why he's not moving forward at this time with charges against her. Yes, many people had motive and opportunity, but the only food item that has the poison that killed Carl was in your aunt's pie. He took it home, something she knew he'd do—"

I bristled. "No, he usually stole a piece. He didn't normally take the whole pie. And, others ate it. How could she have--"

"She had access to the kitchen and by your own admission, you weren't with her all the time."

I growled in frustration. I replayed everything I knew so far. One thing that stuck out was why Carl had changed from taking a piece to walking off with the whole pie? Was it because he'd already been poisoned and acting drunk, like Tyler said? Or did someone encourage him to take the pie?

"Dwayne, have you and Scowl considered that maybe my aunt is being set up? Everyone knew she didn't like him. You said yourself there wasn't enough poison in the pie to kill him. So maybe someone offered him the drink, spiked my aunt's pie and then encouraged him to take it home?"

"Like who?" Lani asked.

"I don't know. The only people going in and out of the kitchen were Mrs. Conners, Mrs. Filmore, Mrs. Jenkins and I suppose the judges like Carl."

"And your aunt."

"It's not like it's off limits. Anyone could have gone in," Lani said. "Even Tyler or Mrs. Willoughby."

"I agree that there are many scenarios, but in the end, Rose has the most motive and opportunity," Dwayne said.

I looked him in the eyes. "Well, then you need to look harder, because I know her, and she's not a murderer.

- - - - - - - -

Lani and I did the dishes and then I called the hospital to see if there was any news on Aunt Rose. She wasn't conscious, but she wasn't worse.

I watched a romcom movie with Lani but by nine, I was exhausted. I excused myself, heading to bed. I took a shower, as I could still smell smoke on me. I put on a pair of Lani's flannel pajamas and climbed into bed.

As tired as I was, I couldn't sleep. Every noise in the house had me in a panic wondering if someone was inside setting fire to the house.

When I'd finally fallen asleep, Lani poked at me. "Sophie."

"Wait," I said like a high schooler not wanting to get up for school.

"Get up. It's nearly eleven."

Really? I only just fell asleep. "Why?"

"You have a visitor." Lani sat on the edge of the bed. "I have dark coffee brewed just like you like it."

"Is it Sergeant Scowl, because I don't want to see him."

"No. I think you want to see this person. I know he's dying to see you."

My eyes popped open. "AJ?"

Lani smiled. "Bingo. Here's a robe. I can't hold him back much longer so he's going to have to see you with bedhead and fuzzy teeth in old flannel pajamas."

"No way. No fuzzy teeth." I leapt from the bed, and went into the guest bathroom, using the toothbrush she'd left for me last night. I ran my fingers through my short curls. There was little I could do about them without a shower. But at least I had minty fresh breath.

I walked down the stairs and could hear Dwayne and Lani talking to AJ.

I reached the bottom of the creaking stairs. AJ's head turned and, in a flash, he had me wrapped up in his arms.

"God, Sophie. You've taken another ten years of my life."

"Sorry." My voice was muffled against his chest. "How you'd you know where to find me? I don't have a phone."

"I called the phone you called me from last night. Lani's. I'm sorry I didn't pick up. God when I got your message. . . I came home as fast as I could."

I tilted my head up. "Did you get your plane?"

"Patch is getting it." He pressed his palms to my cheeks and kissed my forehead. "Why do you insist on scaring me?"

"It's not on purpose." I felt bad that I'd scared him and he'd come home before completing his job.

"How's your Aunt?" he asked.

"I called over this morning," Lani said, handing me a cup of coffee. "I pretended I was calling on official sheriff's office duty. There's no change, honey, but they still feel the prognosis is good."

"At least there's that." I shook my head. "I don't know what we're going to do. Where will we go?"

AJ's expression was hard.

"What?" God, what did I do now?

"You can stay with me."

I wanted to say yes, except. . . "I can't leave Aunt Rose."

He dropped his forehead against mine. I thought I was going to get a lecture about living my own life. "Right now, she's in the hospital. Besides, I think I have a solution."

"What?"

"I'd rather show it to you."

I looked down at the flannel pajamas. "I'm not dressed." My eyes burned as I was reminded that I'd lost everything: my clothes, my books, my coupons. It didn't sound like much, but now that it was all gone, and I had nothing, I felt untethered and so sad.

"I have some you can wear," Lani said. "Drink your coffee, Sophie. Give yourself some liquid mojo and then you can tackle the day."

I drank coffee and had toast, then I showered, and dressed in the jeans and sweater Lani leant me. AJ bundled me into his truck and we headed toward town.

"I want to see the house." Today I felt a little bit steadier. More than that, I needed to see the house. Was it as bad as I thought?

He looked at me with the same expression Lani had last night when I asked the same thing—like it would break me to see the house.

"I need to see it, AJ. Please."

His jaw tensed, but he nodded.

A few minutes later we pulled up to the house or more accurately where the house once stood. For a moment, I could only stare out the window not believing what I was seeing. It looked like it had been bombed, incinerated.

"How could all that be reduced to this? Nothing?" I whispered as the sight stole my breath.

"Let's go home Sophie. You don't need to see this now."

I opened the door of the truck, absolutely needing to see it. AJ cursed under his breath, but his door opened and he came to stand with me.

"She grew up here. My dad used to tell me stories about his grandparents in this house." I took in the sight. All the memories that were gone with all her stuff.

I looked up and down the street, relieved that no one else's homes were hurt, but surprised by how quiet and empty it was.

"Where is everyone?" I asked.

"It's almost Christmas, Sophie. I'm sure they're shopping or something. Let me take you home."

I started across the lawn, which was now covered in ash.

"Sophie, it's not safe." AJ tugged at my hand.

"I need to see."

"See what?" He walked with me until I reached the edge of what had been my room.

See what, was right. It wasn't like I had a lot of stuff. When I'd returned to Jefferson Grove six months ago, I had two suitcases and that was pretty much it. The only thing I'd kept had been a gift from AJ.

I turned to him. He brushed a stray curl from my brow.

"The book is gone." My heart ached at that.

His ginger brows furrowed. "What book?"

"The book of fairy tales that you gave me on my eighteenth birthday."

"You still have that?" He shook his head in disbelief.

"Yes. I treasure it. I told you I had a crush on you then."

His smile was bittersweet. "Now you have me. I'll buy you another—"

"It's not that. It's a piece of me, you . . . us . . . my life before . . ." I shook my head not sure what I was saying or feeling.

"I'm sorry." He pulled me close and held me.

Not wanting to be so maudlin, I looked up into his handsome face. "The wench uniform is gone."

He smiled sweetly, and as if he understood that I was trying to lighten the moment, he said, "Now that is a tragedy." He kissed me on the nose.

"I want to go to the hospital."

At least he didn't try to talk me out that.

Chapter Fourteen

- - - - - - - - - - - - - - - - - - - -

AJ parked in the hospital lot, and he held my hand as we walked into the hospital. We took the elevator up to Aunt Rose's floor. As the doors opened, we heard a commotion.

"Sir. You have to go," a man insisted.

"I'm not going anywhere until I hear about Ms. Rose."

I recognized that voice. "Oh my, God. Bull."

Bull looked over the heads of the two scrawny security guys attempting to get him to leave.

"Miss Sophie." He used his hands to part the two men, making his way to me. He pulled me into a bear hug. "AJ told me you were okay, but I'm glad to see it for myself."

"What are you doing here?" I asked.

"Someone tried to hurt you and Ms. Rose, so I'm here to stand guard. Those two won't cut it," he said with a nod to the security men.

"You can't loiter," one said.

Bull gave him his scary face. "I'm not loitering. I'm doing what you're doing. Protecting Ms. Rose."

"You can't do that here—"

"I can, I will." Bull crossed his arms over his chest daring them to do something. The two men looked at each other clearly knowing they were no match for Bull.

"Bull is my . . . cousin," I said, thinking fast. "He's very close to Aunt Rose. There must be something we can do. Can we see her?"

"You'll have to talk to the nursing staff. But you can't simply stay all the time," one of the guards said.

"Why not?" Bull asked.

"It's just . . . not done . . ."

Bull glared at the men. "Show me where it says I can't stay to protect Ms. Rose. Someone burnt her house down while she was in it."

"Can you call whoever we'd need to talk to?" I asked them.

They seemed relieved to have a new command to follow.

"I'm bringing Sophie up to my place," AJ told Bull.

Bull nodded. "Good thinking. Are they after you, Miss Sophie?"

"I don't know."

"Have you been poking your nose in something you shouldn't?" he asked.

"No." I glared at him.

"Yes, she has, but I think her sleuthing days are about done."

I swiveled my head to AJ.

He lifted his hands in surrender when he saw my glare directed at him. "At least for today."

We were able to make peace with the hospital which allowed Bull to stay during normal visiting hours.

I was disappointed that I couldn't see Aunt Rose but was relieved to speak directly to her doctor who felt fairly positive about her prognosis.

AJ drove us home and Dutch greeted me as I walked in. "Why is she home alone?" Usually, she was next door if AJ was gone for any length of time.

"Mrs. Kaczynski moved into an assisted living home. That's another reason why I was busy. She had a lot of stuff to go through." AJ opened the door and let Dutch out to run and do his potty business.

"Is she okay?" I hadn't heard any rumors but then again, I'd been preoccupied with keeping Aunt Rose out of jail.

"She's fine for a woman who is nearly ninety." He grabbed a key from a hook next to the door. "Come with me." He held out his hand.

"Where are we going?"

"It's a surprise." He flashed me that smile that made me forget my troubles for the moment.

I took his hand as he led me across his driveway and to Mrs. Kaczynski's house. He unlocked the door and stepped inside, pulling me in with him.

"What's—" I stopped as I saw the house was empty. It was small like AJ's but quaint like Aunt Rose's.

"It has a new coat of paint throughout and she's willing to put in new carpet," he said.

"That's nice." But what did that have to do with me?

He laughed. "Sophie. She's selling it. Rose needs a home. You often told me you couldn't stay the night because you had to be home to help her. This house is the answer."

I was stunned at first. I'd been too overwhelmed by the fire and losing everything, that I couldn't think about finding a new home. And yet, here it was, as long as I could get Aunt Rose out here to live at the lake. It was farther away from town and the Senior Center so she'd probably fuss. But AJ was right in that it would make it easier for me to be with him.

AJ took my hand and brought me to the kitchen. "Can't you see her and Bull making pies or cookies in here?"

I laughed as I took in the country style kitchen. It was small, but big enough for my aunt and Bull. "Yes."

He pulled me to the bedrooms. "There are three rooms, which means you'd have a little more room than in the old house."

I looked into each room.

"Perfect, huh?"

"I bet a lot of people will want this place and I don't know that Aunt Rose and I can deal with insurance fast enough to buy it."

"Sophie." He put his hands on my shoulders giving me a gentle shake. "You're killing my buzz. I'm sure if I talk to Mrs. Kaczynski, she'll let you rent until you can buy it."

"I don't know how much it is. Probably more than—"

"Stop. I can make this work. Honestly."

I wrapped my arms around him. "I don't know what I'd do without you."

"You'd persevere. You always do." He kissed the top of my head and then led me back to his house where he made me dinner and when it was time to go to bed, he tucked me close to him. I felt safe and secure for the first time in a long time.

Waking up next to AJ was a dangerous thing. He was warm and safe, something a girl could get used to. I couldn't afford to have that happen. My stay here was temporary until I could find myself and Aunt Rose a new home. I was sure there were places available, such as Mrs. Kaczynski's, but Aunt Rose could be a stickler about some things, and I didn't imagine it would be easy to find a place she felt comfortable in.

I rose from bed and went into AJ's bathroom, feeling awkward about using his shower, but I needed to clean up. After I washed, I dressed in the clothes Lani lent me and made a mental note to add clothes shopping to my list of to-dos today, which also included checking on Aunt Rose, contacting the insurance company, with fingers crossed it would talk to me, touch base with my boss, and, of course, figuring out a living situation.

When I was dressed, I returned to the room. The bed was empty. The smell of coffee wafting up the hall told me AJ was up. I made my way to the living area, hearing voices as I neared it. I listened for who might be here this early.

"You need to go easy on her Sergeant. She's tough, but everyone needs time when they've been knocked down as much as Sophie has lately."

"Ms. Parker will get back up. Carl Jackson won't."

Oh God, not Sergeant Scowl?

I hurried to the living area. "Does this mean you're not trying to find out who burnt Aunt Rose's home down?" I said, tersely, incensed at him. Not that I didn't think Carl's murder should be pushed aside, but to come to me about Carl's murder when my great aunt was in the hospital after someone torched her house was too much.

Sergeant Scowl stood near the door suggesting AJ hadn't invited him in to sit. Dutch sat at his side, like she too wanted to protect me.

"We have another investigator on that," Sergeant Scowl said, unaffected by my attitude, or AJ and Dutch's attempt to block him.

"Who? Why isn't he here?" I demanded.

AJ reluctantly opened the door. Dutch came to sit next to me.

"I want to review the night of the jamboree with you." Sergeant Scowl entered the living area.

I felt like I was channeling my inner Aunt Rose. I was tired of all this nonsense. "Oh, for heaven's sake. What do you think will be different? I told you everything I know or saw. And I'm not going to help you to arrest my aunt."

Scowl was unaffected by my outburst. "Did your aunt offer Carl anything to drink?"

I laughed derisively. "My aunt wouldn't offer Carl anything except a snarky quip. You know, she was right about him and everyone dismissed her."

Sergeant Scowl's eyes narrowed. "What do you mean?"

"She was always saying that he was a liar and a cheat, and he was. Have you looked into any of the people he hurt? The people he cheated? The ones he physically hurt? The Joneses? The Fillmores? His tenants? The people at the senior center? His grandson? My aunt is an elderly woman who relies on me to get anywhere or do anything, and I can tell you, she didn't like Carl but she didn't kill him. When you find who did, maybe you'll also find the guy who burnt our house down, have you considered that? Maybe whoever had it out for Carl had it out for my aunt too. Now if you don't mind, I'm going to the hospital to visit my aunt." I looked for my purse before I remembered I didn't have one. I didn't have a car either. I swiveled around to AJ. "What happened to my car?"

"Bull has it." He looked at me when he spoke the words, but his gaze lifted to Sergeant Scowl as if he didn't want him messing with Bull.

"Did you see anyone offering Carl something to drink?" Sergeant Scowl asked apparently stuck on Carl's drinking habits that night. But then I remembered that Dwayne had said, it was more likely that he'd drunk the poison than ate it.

"No. Ask Alice Filmore, Carolyn Jenkins or Mrs. Conner. They spent more time in the kitchen than me or Aunt Rose did."

"I'm talking to everyone. Right now, I'm talking to you." He sounded like a high school teacher reprimanding a student. "I want to ask you about a so-called friend of your aunt's, Cornelius Grimes."

"I have no idea who that is," I snapped.

AJ cleared his throat. "That's Bull."

"I beg your pardon?" Sergeant Scowl growled at AJ.

"That's his nickname. Bull," AJ clarified.

Bull's name was Cornelius?

"He's very fond of my aunt," I added.

Sergeant Scowl stared at me for a long time. I understood his confusion. It was odd enough for an elderly woman to be friends with a man fifty years her junior who looked like he just graduated from biker gang school—even odder still, because it was my aunt, and she didn't like many people.

"He has a record," Sergeant Scowl said.

"He was a bouncer," AJ said, stepping in to defend his friend.

"He's a gentle giant, really. He and my aunt enjoy baking."

Sergeant Scowl's bushy brows furrowed. "I find that hard to believe."

I shrugged. "You can ask her when she wakes up."

"If you're thinking he killed Carl for her, he didn't," AJ pipped up.

"And you know that how?"

"He was with me, on a repo, when Carl died."

Sergeant Scowl's shoulders dropped. I guess he thought he had his man, and now we burst his bubble. "Is there anyone else who can verify that?" he asked.

"Our boss, Gordo." AJ got his wallet off the table next to the door. He took out a business card and handed it to Sergeant Scowl.

"Do you know where I can find this Bull?"

"If he's not holding vigil with Rose Parker, he's probably at home. He lives down the mountain in McMinnieville."

Sergeant Scowl jotted notes in his notepad and then let himself out. *Good riddance.*

His visit forced me to add something to my list of to-dos; visit Mrs. Jones. I wanted to stay out of the way of the investigation, but if sergeant Scowl was still pointing a figure at my aunt, I had to do something.

But first, I needed coffee.

AJ came into the kitchen as I took my first sip of the dark brew. He had a grin on his face.

"What?" I asked, not sure I wanted to be patronized.

"You sure told him."

"Yeah, well, I'm not in the mood for him this morning."

"How about me?" AJ came to me, taking my mug and putting it on the counter. He wrapped his arms around me. "Are you in the mood for me?"

"I've got things to do." Even so, I sank into his body, soaking in his strength.

"Can I help? I don't have anything on my schedule."

"Maybe." I could use his support visiting my aunt and dealing with some of the aftermath of the fire, but I didn't think he'd be okay with my visiting Mrs. Jones.

"Let me make you breakfast and we can plan the day." He kissed me on the nose and then handed me my coffee. "Sit. Do you want eggs or pancakes? Or both?"

"Pancakes." I took my coffee and sat at the table. A few minutes later, AJ had pancakes with a copious amount of syrup on a plate he set in front of me. He got his plate and sat with me. It was all very homey.

I'd finished off my coffee and was halfway through my pancakes when there was a knock came on the door.

"Are you expecting someone?" I asked.

AJ shook his head. "No. Maybe it's Bull. Normally he just walks in, but since you're here, maybe he's afraid to walk into something." He winked and then went to the door. "Dwayne."

I turned in my chair to see Dwayne entering AJ's place. "AJ. Hi Sophie."

I rose and went to the living area. "Is Lani okay?"

"Yeah, yeah. I'm here on official sheriff's office business."

"Sergeant Davis just left," AJ told him.

"I'm here about the fire."

My brows rose. "Are you an investigator now?"

"Not yet. But with the holidays we're short-staffed so I've been assigned to look into the fire."

I was glad he was assigned and yet, by putting Dwayne on it, was the sheriff's department indicating it wasn't important enough for a full-fledged investigator?

"Have a seat. Want some coffee?" AJ offered him.

"Nah man, I'm good." Dwayne sat in a chair and AJ and I sat on the couch. "I want to review your statement about the fire."

Of course, he did. Why did people who made statements to the police always have to repeat themselves.

"What do you want to know?" I asked.

"Did you hear anything before the fire? Anyone in the house." He had his official notepad at the ready.

"No."

"Nothing? You said the smoke detectors didn't go off, right?"

"Right."

"Where were they located?"

I thought for a moment. "There was one at the end of the hall, outside Rose's and my bedrooms. We're across the hall from each other. There was one in the kitchen for sure and maybe the living room. I can't remember."

"Did you check them regularly?" he asked.

"Bull checked them a few weeks ago. He said they were fine."

Dwayne looked at me and then AJ. "Any chance Bull had a beef—"

"No!" AJ tensed. "Bull would crawl over broken glass for Rose and Sophie."

Dwayne nodded and took notes, but I wasn't sure he was convinced of Bull's innocence. "So, how'd you know about the fire?"

"The smoke woke me . . . I guess."

"What did you do?"

"I was going out to get Rose, but my doorknob was hot. So, I climbed out my window and went out back. I broke her window and climbed in. The fire department showed up and helped us both out."

AJ looked at me frowning. "You went back in the house?"

I nodded. "I couldn't get her and me both out. By then the smoke was choking me and . . ." I didn't think it was a good idea to mention that I thought Rose and I would die with her in my lap at the window.

"Did you see anybody when you got out of your window?" Dwayne asked.

I thought again but shook my head. "I wasn't looking, but I didn't notice anything."

Dwayne wrote in his notepad again. "What about that day? What did you do?"

"I worked at the library until four-thirty or so. I came home and spent some time with Rose. Then I went to Tyler Jackson's house."

"What?" AJ asked, giving me an incredulous look.

I ignored him knowing he was going to be annoyed at me. "He gave me a picture he found of Rose and Carl when they were young." It was sad that Carl had been too much of a jerk to love Rose. "He didn't like that I was nosing around. He didn't threaten me outright, but it felt like it when I left."

"What did he say?" AJ asked.

Dwayne cleared his throat. "I'd like to ask the questions."

"Then ask." AJ stared at me intently.

"What did Tyler Jackson say that you felt was threatening?" Dwayne asked.

"He called me out on my snooping, asking if it ever got me in trouble. Then he made a comment about curiosity killing the cat."

AJ let out a loud huff and I was sure he was going to be upset when Dwayne left.

"So, your theory is Tyler Jackson broke into your aunt's house, disabled the fire detectors, and set the house on fire?" Dwayne asked.

I nodded.

"How did he get in?"

"I don't know. I'm hoping you'll find out," I said. "I think the fire and Carl's death are related. Tyler has to be at the top of the list. He spent the most time with Carl."

Dwayne looked through his notes. "Did you speak to anyone else that day?"

I thought back. "Alice Filmore was visiting Aunt Rose when I got home from work. Later Bull stopped by to bring us a Christmas tree." I hoped Dwyane wouldn't try to blame Bull again.

"When you got home from Tyler's what did you do?"

"Like I said, Bull showed up, leaving us a tree. Rose was looking a bit down, so I suggested we have some holiday treats and decorate the tree. It was a nice evening."

"Anything out of the ordinary?"

"The tree decorating, but it's the holidays. We were both pretty tired when we finished so we went to bed, until the smoke woke me up."

"Did you go to bed earlier than usual?"

"What does that matter?" AJ asked.

Dwyane shrugged. "It might not matter at all. I'm just trying to figure out what the arsonist would be doing. Does he know your schedule? Was he watching?"

"We might have retired a bit earlier than usual. We were pretty tired. I was asleep the minute my head hit the pillow."

Dwayne reviewed his notes and then stood.

"That's it?" I didn't feel like anything came of this interview.

"That's it for now. I'll be in touch. And Sophie, try to stay out of trouble."

"I'll second that." AJ sent me a pointed stare.

I waited until Dwayne left to say, "We've had this discussion a million times, AJ. I don't think the end result will be any different this time."

"Tell me that you're done with this now."

"Right now. Yes, because I have to check on Aunt Rose, get new clothes for both of us, see if I can talk to the insurance company, and check with my boss. But later, I might want to talk to Mrs. Willoughby."

He rolled his eyes. "Why?"

"Because she sent a letter to Carl threatening to kill him."

AJ frowned. "Why?"

"Because he didn't take care of the homes and her grandchild got lead poisoning. I guess it was bad."

He put his hands on his hips as he studied me. "So now you think Mrs. Willoughby killed Carl and burnt your house down."

"No." I shook my head. "The note from Mrs. Willoughby was given to Dwayne by Tyler."

"So, you think Tyler forged—"

"I think the note is real, but I also think that Tyler is doing whatever he can to put the blame on others. He tried to blame Jones Willoughby earlier."

AJ shook his head and went to the kitchen.

"What?" I said following him.

"I don't see how Tyler could get into your home."

"Maybe the door was unlocked."

"Doubtful, but if that's the case, how would he know it was unlocked?" AJ brought up a good point. "He'd need a key, Sophie. Where would he have that, unless Carl had horded it."

I whapped my hand on my forehead. "That's it!"

"That's what?"

"The picture? In the picture, Carl has a key hanging by a chain around his neck. Tyler said that the person who told him the woman in the picture was Rose, explained that she'd given him the key just before he left for the military. They were sitting outside, like at a parade or outdoor event. It was a symbol. Like a key to her heart. But she hasn't moved. She's lived in that house since she was a kid."

AJ cocked his head to the side like he was conceding. "It's still a bit out there. I mean, what are we talking about? Fifty years or more. Maybe we should tell Dwayne."

"Dwayne is working on the fire—"

"And you said they were related."

I sank down into a chair as I realized I'd left the photo and my notebook behind in the fire. "The photo is gone. It was in the house. I have no proof."

AJ thought for a moment. "Was it the Dogwood Parade?" That was the longest running event in Jefferson Grove.

I nodded. "Maybe."

"I wonder if it was covered in the paper back then just like it is now," he said.

I grinned. "I can check the archives at the library when I see my boss."

"I'm curious after all this, why do we need to talk to Mrs. Willoughby?"

We? Was he going to join me? "I just want to know more about what happened when she sent the letter and her impressions of Tyler."

He started to laugh.

"What's so funny?" I asked, feeling like I wasn't just missing the punchline, but that I was the punchline.

"You are amazing."

"That's not funny. Why are you laughing?"

"You make me happy, Sophie. That's all." He stopped any comment I might have by kissing me.

Once dressed, AJ helped me into his truck and we drove to the hospital.

We arrived to good news. Aunt Rose woke up.

"She's groggy and a bit grumpy," the nurse told us.

"Sounds like she's well on the way to recovery," AJ quipped.

"Can I see her?" I asked, needing to look her in the eyes.

"Only for a minute. She's still weak."

AJ waited for me while I was led to Aunt Rose's bedside. She was closer to ninety than eighty, but her personality was always so strong and large, it was easy to forget how old she was. Seeing her in the bed looking pale and frail broke my heart. But at least she was alive.

I slipped my hand under hers but didn't hold it, too afraid it might hurt her. "Aunt Rose?"

Her eyes fluttered open. "Is that you Sophie?"

"Yes ma'am. How are you feeling?"

"Like someone roasted my lungs on a spit."

I remembered feeling like that when I woke too. "That will get better."

"What day is it? I have bunco—"

"There's no bunco today. Right now, you need to focus on getting your strength back."

She looked so small laying there. "Who burned my house down, Sophie?"

"I don't know."

She sighed. "Is it all gone?"

I nodded and rubbed my thumb over her hand. "But don't worry. I'm finding us a place to go when you're better."

She turned her head away from me. "You might as well just put me in a home, Sophie. What's the difference now?"

My instinct was to try boost her morale, but I knew it wouldn't help. A blow like this, wasn't something a pep talk could fix.

I leaned over and kissed her hand. "I'm going to let you rest now, okay. I'll be by later."

"You can't waste your time with me."

I ignored that comment, and instead said, "You rest."

It broke my heart to think this fire had extinguished her fight. I hoped that she would find her inner strength to be the feisty, often difficult woman she'd been before the fire.

Chapter Fifteen

Satisfied that Aunt Rose would pull through, I asked AJ to drive me to Mrs. Willoughby's house. He lent me borrow his phone to call Aunt Rose's homeowners insurance person on the way, but I had to leave a message.

Mrs. Willoughby lived in the same neighborhood as Carl and her son, but a few blocks over. Like most other houses in this area, she had a red brick rancher with white trim. Thank goodness the homes had large numbers posted on them as it would be hard to tell one from the other.

AJ parked along the curb and we walked up to the door. I knocked on the door, and a robust woman with rosy cheeks, and bright red hair that could only come from a bottle of home-hair dye answered the door.

"Mrs. Willoughby?" I asked.

"Yes." She looked from me to AJ then frowned. "You're not going to try and convert me, are you? I'm already a good Christian."

"No ma'am. I'm Sophie Parker and this AJ Devlin."

"Devlin?"

Next to me, AJ stiffened. Devlins didn't have a good reputation in Jefferson Grove, even though it had been years since any of his kinfolk had caused trouble in town.

"Yes ma'am," he replied.

"Any relation to Sally Devlin?"

AJ looked at me wide-eyed clearly surprised that she wasn't saying something negative about his family.

"Probably," he said. "I have a distant cousin Sally over in Hawthorn Hollow."

"That's her. I always get my huckleberries from her for canning. But I'm sure that's not why you're here."

"No ma'am. I was hoping to ask you about Carl Jackson," I said.

Her jovial face morphed into distaste. "I don't want to speak ill of the dead, but he was a very bad man. He nearly killed my granddaughter. Simply to save a few bucks. Meanwhile, he has several hoarder houses that I bet will be condemned." She opened the door. "Come in. I have some coffee I just brewed if you'd like a cup."

"Thank you," I said following her inside.

"She's going to be mad when you ask her about the letter," AJ whispered.

I waved off his comment. She might be mad, but I was also pretty sure she wasn't the killer. She had no reason to burn my house down. No. In my mind, this had Tyler Jackson written all over it.

In many ways, her home felt like Aunt Rose's; it hadn't changed since she'd moved in. In this case, I think Mrs. Willoughby moved into it in the 1970's. Gold and olive green were the primary color schemes.

We sat at a table that looked nearly identical to the one in Aunt Rose's kitchen. Emotion took me by surprise at the memory. That table was now melted Formica.

AJ's hand rubbed my back. "Are you okay?"

I put on a smile. "Yes."

"So, what do you want to know about Carl?" Mrs. Willoughby put two mugs, both with "World Best Grandma" on the table in front of AJ and me. "Wait . . . Parker. Are you related to Rose Parker?"

"Yes ma'am. She's my great aunt."

"Oh lordy. I heard about her home. Such a shame. That house was in the Parker family forever. I know because my family has lived in the area about as long. Is she okay?"

"Yes. I talked with her this morning."

"Good. Boy, I bet she'd have some choice words about Carl." She went back to her coffee pot and poured herself a cup.

I nodded. "Yes. She always called him a liar and cheat."

She sat at the table with us. "She was being nice. I hear the police think she did him in with a pie. I don't buy it. Eating pie is a too nice of way for him to go."

AJ's brows shot up nearly to his hairline. I realized he wasn't used to the types of true attitudes one could get when sleuthing.

"She didn't poison him, but someone did," I confirmed.

Mrs. Willoughby smirked. "The sheriff's investigator was out talking with my son, Jones. Jones couldn't hurt a fly. As a matter of fact, he tried to help Carl. He tried to get me to be nice to him too, but there was no changing that man."

"Did the sheriffs' investigator talk to you too?" I asked.

She made a fffttt sound. "Yes. They got ahold of a letter I wrote to Carl. They say I threatened him. I had every right to threaten that man. He was a menace."

"Did you threaten him?" I sipped my coffee, trying not to wince at the bitter yet watery flavor.

"Darn right I did, but not to kill him. I planned to take him to court. I was working with his other tenants and a one of those free lawyers to do a group lawsuit. To Carl, one little complaint from a family was nothing, but united, we could cost him a pretty penny, and we all know that pennies are what he cared about most."

"Do you know how the police knew about your threat?" I asked.

She made another distasteful face. "I'm sure his grandson found the letter and turned it in. He's been finding all sorts of reasons to point the finger at a Willoughby."

I nodded. "Did he come talk to you first?"

She shook her head. "Nah." She frowned. "Have you heard something else? Sergeant Davis wasn't very forthcoming about whether he believed me, but I didn't kill Carl. I didn't even see him at the Winter Jamboree."

"I don't suppose you commiserated about him with anyone else at the jamboree?" I asked.

She thought for a moment. "I don't think so. There were plenty of people there who were victims of Carl. But it wasn't just his cheating people that galled everyone. It was his attitude when you confronted him. He looked like a gentle old man, but when you called him out, he was truly evil. He blamed Jones for his daughter's illness. Like a toddler should know how to avoid lead paint."

She shook her head, turning away when tears filled her eyes. I suppose it would be emotionally frustrating when a child was being hurt and the man who could fix it was too miserly to do so.

She sniffed and turned back to us. "Your father hurt a lot of people too,"

I winced not knowing she realized who I was.

"But he was mighty sorry about it. I think the poor guy got upside down in the money and couldn't get it right. But Carl, he stole for stealing sake."

"Did you give my father money?" I asked, thinking I'd need to apologize on his behalf.

"No. But I know plenty who did. Your father should have known better, but like I said, I don't think he initially set out to steal."

Did intention matter? Maybe. People were still angry at my father, but no one killed him. Carl didn't just cheat people, but apparently, he had no remorse at doing it.

"Thank you, Mrs. Willoughby." I rose and AJ stood with me.

"So, it's true? You're an amateur sleuth?" she asked, taking a quick sip of her coffee and then rising from her chair.

"No. She's not." AJ said pointedly.

"Not really. But I want to help my aunt."

She followed us to the door. "Well, if I can be any more help, you let me know."

"I will. Thank you again for the coffee."

"It was my pleasure. And say hello to Sally if you see her," she said to AJ.

"I will."

Once in the truck, AJ asked, "So, what's next?"

"I need to get new clothes for me and Aunt Rose."

AJ swallowed the look of horror.

I laughed. "Don't worry. I'm not dragging you to the mall."

"You need to go to a mall? Don't they have clothes here in Jefferson Grove?" He turned on the engine and drove us out of the subdivision.

"I'm going with Lani. A girls' day out. You don't mind, do you?"

"Nah. I have a few things I need to take care of."

"How do I get my car from Bull?" I asked. I wondered if it had damage from the fire.

"He's giving it thorough check. Can Lani drive?" AJ turned onto the main thoroughfare that took us to the center of town.

"Yes. I just didn't want to rely on you for transportation."

He grinned. "Just call me Jeeves."

AJ drove me to Lani's house and we went in her little hatchback down the mountain to Charlottesville.

"So . . . you and AJ . . . living together now?" she asked before I even had my seat belt on.

"Not exactly. He did say Mrs. Kaczynski had moved out and maybe we could buy it. I don't know until I can talk to the insurance person, if they'll talk to me. They might only talk to Aunt Rose."

"So, you'd be his neighbor?" She shook her head.

"What?"

"Is your resistance really because of Rose or because of you? I mean, Rose did alright for herself living alone for a long time."

"My dad visited her every day. Did I mention she sleepwalks sometimes? He asked me to care for her."

"And you have. You also needed a place to stay, but now you don't at AJ's. And maybe it's time for Rose to go somewhere she can play bunco 24-7."

I shook my head. "First AJ didn't ask me to live with him."

She gave me a pursed lip stare.

"And I can't just abandon Aunt Rose to a home. What about her baking? That's her passion. No. I can't leave her. And AJ's gone a lot anyway. We're good." But even as I said, it I wondered how long AJ would put up with my situation with Aunt Rose—plus, it was nice spending the night with him.

"I'm just saying maybe you're blaming her when it's you. And I don't blame you for being afraid—"

"Afraid of what?" Annoyance flared in my tone.

"How many times have you been to my place worried it was over between you two? How often is it usually because you're over-thinking things or are afraid to trust?"

"When did you get a psychology degree?" I huffed and looked out the side window.

"I know you, Sophie. I don't need a degree. I'm just saying, don't let your fears hold you back if the opportunity to move forward with him comes."

"You know we've only been dating six months." Jeez. She and Dwayne dated for five years. Of course, four of those years they'd been in high school, but still.

"Yeah, but you've had the hots for him since you were sixteen."

Sometimes having a best friend since high school was a drag when she could use the past against me.

Shopping, however, was fun—mostly. I had the stash of money I'd saved from what Marla my coupon mentor had left me, but I didn't want to waste it on clothes when I might need it for a home and furniture. So, I focused on the necessities: bras, underwear, socks and stockings—a pair of jeans and slacks for me, and a couple of dark slacks for Aunt Rose. I got us each a few shirts, two sweaters and new coats. Since Christmas was coming, I splurged for a new pearl necklace for Aunt Rose. It could be one thing that was normal. I bought Dutch a giant bone to gnaw on, but struggled with what to get AJ. Ultimately, I splurged on a soft leather bomber jacket fit for a pilot. I bought Bull the perfect apron, with bikers and donuts on it.

We stopped at a local bagel shop for a sandwich before heading back up the mountain and down the valley to Jefferson Grove. So, she didn't have to drive up to the lake, AJ agreed to pick me up again at her place.

"Do you think you'll be at the coupon group on Tuesday?" she asked as she pulled into her townhouse community.

Maybe it was time to give up coupon collecting. I wasn't good at it anyway. "All my coupons are dust and the meeting is two days before Christmas."

"So, you'll get more coupons. You can go through community boxes at the library."

The community boxes were where people could put the coupons they didn't want, which meant most were not good.

"All those are ones you've all given away," I said. "No one will want to trade."

"Not all of them are from us. Besides, it's more than just coupons. We're your girls. I know Aggie will want to see you and support you. Plus, she always has a nice holiday spread."

"Do you realize that nearly everyone in that group doesn't like me? Tracy is mad because I told Vivie about her and Randy. Gwen is mad because she thinks I want Tyler."

"Vivie likes you." Lani pointed out.

I pursed my lips. "You and I both know that could end any minute."

"You have me and Aggie. And Gwen will get over it, especially if your theory is right and Tyler is a murderer."

She was probably right. Doing something normal, like going to coupon group might be helpful. Wasn't that why I bought a few Christmas presents—so that something could be normal in all this chaos?

At the same time, I couldn't waste time on coupons when my priority was to find a home and get it furnished enough that when Aunt Rose was released, she'd be comfortable, not happy. I had no doubt whatever I found she'd fuss about, but I'd understand. I'd be grumpy too if eighty years of my life was gone.

Lani pulled into a parking spot in front of her townhome. I exited her car and looked for AJ. His trucked pulled into her section just as I reached her trunk to get my items.

Dutch's head hung out the window which had to make for a cold drive, but she looked perfectly content. Her head bobbed up and down when she saw me.

AJ jumped out of his truck and trotted over to me. "Did you ladies have fun?"

"It would be more fun under another circumstance, but it was nice to hang," I said, tilting my head to him as he gave me a kiss on the cheek.

"Do you have plans for Christmas?" Lani asked AJ. "You and Sophie are both invited to Christmas dinner. And Rose too if she's home by then. It's at Dwayne's mom's place but she's got lots of room and always has enough food to feed an army."

"I hadn't really thought that far ahead." I handed a couple of bags to AJ to put in his truck. I kept his and Dutch's presents with me.

"Me neither," AJ said but there was something about his tone that gave me a niggle of suspicion. Like maybe he had plans but didn't want to say anything.

"Let me know if you want to come." Lani closed the trunk.

I said my goodbyes to Lani, thanking her for her help and support today. I climbed into AJ's truck. Dutch sat in the back seat, her head resting on the shoulder of my seat.

AJ started the truck and began the drive back to his place.

"Are you sure you don't have Christmas plans? Are your brother and sister coming into town? I know your mom would love to see you all together," I asked him. I'd finally officially met AJ's mother a few months back. She seemed quite normal to me, but she suffered from some sort of early dementia that had her living in an assisted living community.

AJ gripped the steering wheel and was quiet for a minute. The longer the quiet drew out, the more my gut clenched in concern.

"I've got an opportunity to do another repo."

My stomach sank. He was going to leave now? "I thought you wouldn't have more for a little bit after the last one." I hoped my voice didn't sound disappointed or hurt.

"I wouldn't have, but I didn't complete the last repo." He glanced at me and I knew he meant that he'd come home early because of the fire.

I sat for a moment trying to figure out if my feelings of abandonment were unreasonable or not. "Does that mean you'll be gone for Christmas?"

"I think we can be back by then if all goes well. It's in Iowa. But Bull will be here. It's Patch's repo and he's invited me to help since I gave him the last one."

"I see."

He glanced at me like he was trying to figure out my mood. "You can stay at my place. In fact, I'm hoping you will watch Dutch."

At hearing her name, Dutch lifted her snout and head-butted AJ. He laughed and reached back to pat her nose.

"Yes, of course I'll watch Dutch. But I'll be isolated out there—"

"Bull will have your car to you tomorrow. It's just for a couple of days."

If I had a nickel for every time AJ told me "it was just for a couple of days," I could buy Aunt Rose and me a home.

"Are you angry?" he asked.

"I'm . . . I'm scared."

"What?" He slowed and then stopped at the stop sign. He turned to me. "What are you afraid of?"

"I'm not sure. I just lost my home. Aunt Rose is still in the hospital. I feel a little untethered."

He watched me, his fingers tugging at the ends of my hair. "Then I won't go. I shouldn't have even considered it."

Now I did feel like I was being unreasonable. This was his livelihood. I had a place to stay. I'd have my car. I was a capable woman. Wasn't I always telling him how strong and independent I was when he'd try to take over for me?

"No. You go. I know you need the money."

"I need you more. And I think you need me, although I know you wouldn't want to admit that."

A beep came from the car that pulled up behind us. AJ resumed driving.

"That's not completely true. And you've done a lot for me so this is something I can do for you. I'll be okay with Dutch. Plus, I think I'll be mostly dealing with finding a place for me and Aunt Rose and visiting her."

His jaw tightened and I swore I could feel the tug of war in him.

"It's okay AJ. Really."

"If I do this one, Sophie, I can be done until after New Year's."

It must be a fancy plane. "Then go." I smiled, although based on AJ's reaction I wasn't sure it was convincing.

Chapter Sixteen

Bull arrived the next morning with my car and AJ drove him back to their boss' office. They took Dutch with them as Bull said he could watch her during the day so I could go to work. When they left, I drove to visit Aunt Rose at the hospital. She was still despondent, but the doctor told me she'd likely be able to come home on Wednesday. That didn't give me much time to find us a place.

I went to work and had to wing it with my programming since the lessons had all gone up in flames. Still the kids seemed to enjoy themselves.

After work, I visited Aunt Rose again. This time she had a little more vim and vigor to her attitude. *Good.* She'd need that as we navigated life for the next few weeks.

I drove up to AJ's place wondering when Bull was going to bring Dutch by. As I passed Mrs. Kaczynski's house, there was a moving van in front. My heart sank as a part of me hoped that Aunt Rose and I could get the house.

I parked in front of AJ's. It was dark out and I'd forgotten to turn the porch light on. As I tentatively made my way toward the porch, I heard Dutch's tell-tale paws galloping toward me, but couldn't see her. I stood still hoping she wouldn't run me over. She nudged me with her head.

"Hi Duchess. How are you?" I looked around for Bull, but didn't see him or a vehicle he would have come in. "Bull didn't just leave you alone, did he?"

"I didn't. I wouldn't." Bull's voice came from over by the moving truck. "Come over here, Miss Sophie."

I walked around my car and over to Mrs. Kaczynski's house. I guess he was roped into helping the new tenants.

He stood in the doorway with a big grin. "Welcome home Miss Sophie."

I laughed. "You do know that AJ's house is over there?" I pointed.

"Yes, I do. Do you know that your house is right here?"

I gaped. "What?"

He let out a loud happy laugh. "I sure wish AJ were here to see your face. He wanted to, Miss Sophie. You have to believe that."

"I don't know what you're talking about." I couldn't compute what he was saying.

"This is your house. AJ arranged with Mrs. Kaczynski for you to stay here."

My heart beat a million miles a minute. I thought I knew what he was saying, but it was too crazy, I must be misunderstanding.

"He's doing a lease purchase or something. That will make him your landlord until you decide to buy or maybe you'll want to move on."

"What is AJ going to do with two homes?" God, he'd never be home now. He'd have to repo a plane every week.

"It's an investment. Real estate is always a good investment. Now come on. Come see your new digs." He took my arm and tugged me inside.

I gasped when I entered the home. I expected empty space, but it had everything a home would need. "Where did all this furniture come from?"

"Here and there. It's a bit mismatched, but you and Ms. Rose can put your own little touches to it. And look here," he said leading me to the kitchen. "All new baking items. I think that will cheer Ms. Rose up, don't you think?"

"Did you do all this? You and AJ?"

"It's all AJ's idea. I just helped execute it. Plus, a little help from other friends."

Emotion welled like a tidal wave and I started balling.

"Aw . . . don't cry Miss Sophie." Bull's meaty hand pulled me in for a hug.

"I'm just so grateful and overwhelmed," I said muffled against his burly chest.

"You're not alone. AJ wanted me to be sure to tell you that. You've got him and me."

Dutch nudged me in the back. Bull laughed. "And Dutch. And Ms. Rose. It's all going to be alright."

For the first time since the fire, I believed that Bull was right. He led me through the house. We had all the requisite furniture; a couch and chair, kitchen table and chairs, and pots, pans, plates and everything a kitchen needed so we could cook and feed ourselves. The bedrooms had beds, dressers and even side tables.

"Oh, and one more thing," Bull said heading to the front door. "You wait here."

He left and few minutes later walked in with a Christmas tree. "This one is fake, I'm sorry to say. But it's already got lights." He set up in the living room and plugged it in. "It's pretty just like that, don't you think?"

A new wave of happy gratitude tears welled up.

"Now, all you have to decide is if you'll stay here or at AJs tonight." He leaned forward conspiratorially. "Personally, I think AJ would rather you stay at his place, but this is your place and Ms. Rose's."

I was torn for a moment, but then the decision was obvious. "I'll stay at AJ's until Aunt Rose comes home on Wednesday. She and I can move in together."

Bull grinned. "That's sure nice, Miss Sophie. I hope Ms. Rose will like it here. I suspect it will be a change, but she's a strong woman."

"Yes. She is."

"Well, I've got to run. Let me just show you the locks and the security." He motioned me to a box by the door.

"Security?"

Bull smirked. "AJ has become a worrywart. Anyway, it's all straight forward."

He showed me the security unit and then handed me a phone. "You can control it from this."

"A phone too?"

"That kid is in love with you Miss Sophie. It killed him to fly off today, but . . . well . . ."

"I know he needs the money. Especially if he's buying another house." I shook my head. I loved him for his generosity but this was too much. I'd have to talk to Aunt Rose as soon as possible about the insurance on the house so he didn't have to bury himself in debt.

"I'm heading out. I'll walk you back over to AJ's." Bull locked up the house and left me and Dutch at AJ's.

That night I lay in AJs bed, and since he was gone, I let Dutch sleep on his side of the bed. I thought about how six months ago I'd returned home broke, my family reputation in tatters, with only what I could fit in a suitcase. The only job I could get was at pirate-themed sports bar as a wench waitress, and I had to learn to clip coupons to afford to live.

Now, I felt richer than when I grew up in my wealthy family. Home or no home, I had Aunt Rose, and AJ and Bull. I had Lani. I had a job that I loved. And while I still needed coupons, I had a group of friends to help me learn the ropes of discount shopping.

The only thing that hung like a lead weight was Sergeant Scowl's continued suspicion of Aunt Rose. I hoped he didn't plan to arrest her when she was released from the hospital. Now that I had some semblance of order back in my life, I'd make sure that Aunt Rose's name was cleared of Carl's murder.

The next morning, I met Bull in town and he took charge of Dutch so I could visit Aunt Rose and then go to work. Aunt Rose's strength was up, but she was despondent again. I asked the nurse if anyone had come to visit her. She said a scary biker guy had, which I took to be Bull. Betty Bealton, Tilly Watson, and Alice Filmore had stopped in as well. But none of them had been allowed to see her.

"Is there any way you can make that happen? I think it would help her a lot to have visitors."

"I'll talk to the doctor," the nurse assured me.

I arrived at work a little early which gave me time to put together my children's unit for the day. The last one until New Year's. New Year's had many rituals around good luck such as breaking a plate or eating twelve grapes at midnight. I figured the safest project for kids was to have them make a New Year's good luck charm. I had them write a goal or resolution that I put in a jar, promising to save it until next year when we could see who'd achieved their goals. Mine was pretty simple: Appreciate what I had. I didn't know how to measure it, so maybe it was more of an aspiration than a goal.

The library closed early and would be closed starting Christmas Eve through the weekend. Once we had the library empty and cleaned, Mrs. Wayland called us all to the back staff area. It was decorated in Christmas colors and holiday music filled the air. All the fake packages that had been under the Christmas tree were now in a stack behind Mrs. Wayland. I'd forgotten that we were having a holiday party. I was supposed to bring some of Aunt Rose's special gingerbread cookies.

Mrs. Wayland rapped a knife on a glass to get all our attention. Everyone who worked today stayed and few of the staff and volunteers who'd been off showed up as well.

"Merry Christmas everyone. I know you're eager to finish your last-minute holiday duties, but this year especially I appreciate you all coming in." She looked me. "Sophie, honey, can you come here?"

Nerves tingled in my gut though I couldn't say why. She wasn't going to fire me in front of everyone at Christmas, was she? I wouldn't blame her. In the six months I'd been here, I'd been in lots of trouble that the library was probably tired of having to put up with. I walked up to her and she took my hand.

"You're quite a little trooper Sophie. Here you are, hardly less than a week after losing everything."

I felt self-conscious. Everyone knew what happened, but still. I didn't like being the center of attention for having the bad luck to have my house burn down.

"We all agreed. We exchanged our Secret Santa gifts and instead, bought items for you and Rose."

Just like last night when Bull brought me to Mrs. Kaczynski's house and told me it was for me and Aunt Rose, emotion welled. I kept myself from bawling, but the tears did fall.

"Thank you." I managed.

"I understand you've secured a place to stay," she said.

I nodded, wondering how she knew.

"Your boyfriend AJ also said that his friend would be by to pick these up and take them to your new place."

She'd been talking to AJ? She knew who Bull was? "Bull?"

"It's a fitting name," she said. "We also arranged for Christmas dinner to be brought to you."

"That's so . . . thank you. I'm overwhelmed by your generosity." Especially since my father had hurt some of these people. The fact that they didn't hold it against me was amazing.

"It's not just us. A few of Rose's friends are chipping in. Betty Bealton is making the turkey and stuffing."

Aunt Rose always said Betty's turkey was dry, but I'd eat it. I felt sure Aunt Rose would too.

"Mrs. Conner, Mrs. Watson, and Mrs. Filmore are all contributing as well."

I sniffed. "Thank you. Thank you so much."

"Now. Let's have our holiday party. We've got cookies from Mrs. Conner and apple cider from Mrs. Filmore."

After that, it was a party. We ate, drank, and chatted. For the first time I finally felt like I was home. Even more so than when I grew up here.

"How is Rose doing?" Mrs. Wayland asked after a few people had left and things were calming down.

"She's going to be fine physically, but I think it's taking a toll on her mentally."

"And is she still worried about Sergeant Davis' focus on her?"

"I don't know about that. I don't bring it up. I know I'm nervous.

She can be surly, but she's no murderer. And there are plenty of other suspects."

Mrs. Wayland's brow arched. "Are you sleuthing again?"

"I'm trying to protect my aunt." I sipped my cider noting it seemed to have more cinnamon than usual. It was still good. Alice was often futzing with her recipe. She and Tubby had done the same with their moonshine when they were illegally making and selling it. Their huckleberry moonshine was very popular for a while.

"That always seems to get you in trouble."

"Yeah well . . ." My new phone beeped. I looked at it and saw a text from Lani.

Are you coming tonight?

"Oh, I forgot."

"What's that?" Mrs. Wayland asked, grabbing another cookie even though two cookies ago she said it would be her last one. Mrs. Conner's cookies were edible, but they weren't Aunt Rose's. I suspect Mrs. Conner ran the baking contests because she loved baking but wasn't very good at it.

"The coupon group."

"You should go, Sophie. I know your friends will want to see that you're okay and being with them will help you begin to be okay."

She was right. I texted that I'd try to be there.

The text after that was from Bull saying he was at the library. The three of us loaded up the packages into his truck.

"Thank you, Mrs. Wayland. I can't tell you how grateful I am."

"It's the holidays' Sophie. It's all about giving." She waved to me and Bull as she left.

"I have coupon group tonight," I said looking at my watch and trying to decide if I could get up to AJs to unload the packages and back to town.

"I can take these up, but you need to keep Dutch. Once I leave these at AJ, where I'm going, Dutch can't go."

I arched a brow. "Where are you going?"

His cheeks reddened. "It's a nice fancy gentleman's club. Duchess can't see something like that. AJ would kill me."

I laughed. "You're the best, Bull."

He grinned. "There's nothing I wouldn't do for you and Ms. Rose."

Dutch hopped out of Bull's truck and managed to get into my station wagon. She was so big though, she had to lay down in the back. She propped her head over the back seat.

"We're going to coupon group," I told her, knowing Aggie and the gang probably wouldn't let me stay, but that was okay. Mostly I wanted to say hello—and be with my tribe.

The group was at Aggie's again as she liked to host the one closest to Christmas. I parked behind Lani's car and opened the back hatch to let Dutch out.

I looked her in the eyes. "I need you to behave. Can you do that?"

Her tail wagged and she appeared excited about our adventure. I took that as a yes.

I walked up to Aggie's door and knocked. Her husband Earl opened the door.

He smiled and then his eyes widened. "Great day, what is that you brought? Is it one of those miniature ponies?"

"No. It's a dog. She's AJ's great Dane. He's out of town. I know you might not want her in the house, but maybe we can put her in your mudroom so she's not cold."

He opened the door. "Come on in. I want to get a closer look at this dog."

I stepped in and Dutch followed me. When I stopped, she sat her butt down.

"Good lord, what is that?" Aggie said as she came into the living room.

"This is AJ's great Dane," Earl said. "You know, Miss Sophie, if your car broke down, I bet you could ride her home."

I laughed. "I probably could."

"Oh my God, you brought a dog?" Vivie's tone was horrified.

"We can put her in the mudroom," I said.

Dutch lay down on the floor and looked up at me with eyes that I was sure said, "Don't put me in the mudroom. I'll be good."

"Now look at that, Aggie. I don't think she needs to be put in the mud room. Not if she's docile," Earl said bending over as best he could to pet Dutch on the head. When he finished, Dutch put her hand on his foot. "Look at that. He likes me." He grinned showing his pearly whites, fitting for a retired dentist.

"Dutch is a she," I corrected him. "It's short for Duchess."

"I think Dutch is a reincarnation of a person," Lani said. "She's too well behaved to be a real dog."

"You believe in reincarnation?" Vivie gaped at Lani like she was off her rocker.

"When I come back, I wouldn't mind being a giant dog," Earl said.

"You certainly eat enough for one," Aggie quipped. "I have no problem with her staying in the house as long as she doesn't get into anything. But first." Aggie made her way to me. "Let me give you a hug, Sophie. Great day, the trouble that seems to find you."

"I was sure sad to hear about Ms. Rose's house," Earl added. "How is she?"

"Yes, how is she?" Aggie asked.

"She'll be fine. It's a blow but she's a strong woman."

"And have you found a new place to live?" Vivie asked.

I nodded. "Yes. Mrs. Kaczynski is selling her place. We'll be there."

"You're like a cat with nine lives." Aggie shook her head. "You keep landing on your feet."

That made me think of Tyler warning me about cats with curiosity. I hoped the conversation of Carl's murder didn't come up as I didn't want to have to share my theory front of Gwen that Tyler could be the murderer. Of course, I didn't see Gwen. I guess she hadn't arrived yet.

As much as I was enjoying seeing them, I decided that I couldn't stay. I'd likely cause problems with Gwen and Dutch needed to stretch her legs, which she could only really do at AJ's. Plus, Aunt Rose would be coming home tomorrow. I had things I needed to do to get ready.

"I can't stay. I just wanted to say hello and let you know I was okay."

"Why do you have to go?" Lani frowned at me.

"For one, I should get Dutch home and two, Aunt Rose is coming home tomorrow afternoon." Assuming Sergeant Scowl didn't arrest her.

"Oh, that's wonderful, Sophie. Do you need anything? I've got a lasagna in the freezer. You take it." Aggie didn't wait for my response. She left the group heading to the kitchen.

Grocery shopping was on my list for tomorrow, which would be expensive since I didn't have any coupons. "That would be wonderful, if it's not too much trouble." I called after her.

"Pah! It's no trouble." She responded.

"Where's AJ?" Vivie asked. "Did he abandon you again? Right before Christmas." Her face showed concern, her tone was snarky.

"It was a last-minute job," I said.

"Sophie is staying with him." Lani waggled her eyebrows.

"Staying or living?" Vivie asked.

I rolled my eyes. Sometimes I wondered if anyone ever really grew out of the high school mentality.

"You should make that boy give you a ring before you give him too much of you, Sophie," Earl said.

"Stop being so old fashioned, Earl." Aggie arrived back with a potluck carrying bag. "There's lasagna and I threw in a few other things you might need. I suspect you'll need to go to the grocery. Do you need any coupons?"

"Did anything survive the fire?" Vivie asked.

I shook my head. "No. It's all gone."

"Come on girls, let's see if we can't give Sophie a few coupons. I've got toothpaste, shampoo, and cereal," Aggie said as she went back to the dining room where the coupon exchange occurred.

"I've got some feminine hygiene and condiments," Lani said.

"I gave you ton of coupons a few months ago, Sophie." Vivie clearly had no interest in giving up her coupon booty.

"You did, Vivie." I didn't need coupons from her anyway.

"Viviane Danner." Aggie chastised. "I'm sure you have a couple of coupons you could spare to help Sophie and Rose out."

Vivie pursed her lips but did what Aggie guilted her to do. She handed over a couple of coupons for batteries, shaving cream, and fiber laxatives.

I thanked them and headed to the door.

"I know it's the holidays Sophie, but if you need anything, you just call, you hear?"

"Thank you, Aggie."

Dutch and I left and made our way to the Brown Bomber. I'd just let him in the back when Gwen's car pulled up on the other side of the street. I shut the hatch and went to the driver's side of my car.

"Is it true you're telling people that Tyler killed his own grandfather," Gwen charged at me.

It was true, but I couldn't think of who I said it to that it would get back to Gwen.

"You're just jealous. He didn't fall for your perky, country, innocence and now you're getting back at him." She towered over me, her dark hair tipped in red blew out of her face, giving her a harsher appearance than usual.

"Do you know that you sound like Vivie now?" She might be a foot taller than me, but I wasn't scared of her.

She jerked back. "Now I know why Vivie doesn't like you."

I sighed. "Gwen, I have no interest in Tyler. I never did." I held my hands up in surrender. "He's all yours. If you want him."

"Why wouldn't I want him?" she sniffed.

Even taking out the idea that he could be a murderer and an arsonist, there was the fact he was probably more like Carl than he let on. He was definitely part of the swindle that led to Tubby Filmore's death. But I didn't say any of it.

"No reason. I've got to go. Have fun tonight." I got into the car and headed home.

- - - - - - -

The next morning, I woke early, letting Dutch out to do her business, and then I got ready for the day. I called the hospital about Aunt Rose's discharge and was told it would be later in the day, as they'd indicated before. I went next door to check the house and make a list of everything I needed to get at the store. I called the power and phone company about changing the services over to my name. I called the cable company to switch Aunt Rose's service to here.

I checked the master bedroom that would be Aunt Rose's. I decided I should get her some flowers or something to spruce it up.

Dutch started barking which was unusual. I found her looking out the front window. Following her gaze, I saw Sergeant Scowl's SUV parked in front of AJ's house.

"Come on, Dutch." I left the new house and walked over to AJs.

Sergeant Scowl's brows drew together. "Are you living with Mrs. Kaczynski?"

"She moved. This is where Aunt Rose and I are going to live. Have you found Carl's killer?"

He gave his signature scowl stare. "I'm going to need to talk to your aunt again."

I put my hands on my hips. "Do you really think she killed Carl. Really?"

He sighed. "It doesn't matter what I think. Only what the evidence suggests."

"Suggests?" I shook my head. "I could suggest that chocolate is better than peanut butter, but that's not a fact. It's not the truth. If it looks like Aunt Rose did it, then someone set her up because she wouldn't even know how." I wasn't sure that was true. She did watch a lot of ID TV, but all those people were caught, which would be a good deterrent.

"Who would set her up?"

"Someone who wanted Carl dead and knew she'd be a good suspect. Maybe they didn't like her either. It's even possible that he wasn't the intended victim. Someone did burn our house down. Please tell me you've considered all that."

He gave one curt nod. "We're looking at all of it. But like I said, the evidence is against Rose."

"You know, for that to be true, then someone else burnt our house down. Are you saying they're unrelated?"

He crossed his arms over his chest. "I have no reason to think they are related. There's nothing that ties one to the other."

"Except my aunt."

Sergeant Scowl had gotten under my skin more than once since moving back home, but now, I was incensed.

He let out a breath and released his arms. "I understand that you have your own theories, but I need proof. If you have information that leads me to a new direction, I'll follow it up. But right now, what I've got is Rose Parker's long vocal dislike of Carl, the poison in the pie—"

"Except the M.E. says—"

"He likely drank it, too, but she could have given him the drink."

I frowned. "Could have isn't proof. You just said you need proof."

"I'm sorry Sophie."

There he went again, using my name—acting like he was sorry.

"Are you really going to arrest an eighty-five-year-old woman who's home just burnt down on Christmas Eve? Really?"

He flinched, and for once I thought maybe he might have a teeny tiny beating heart. "That's not determined yet. I need to speak with her."

"Not without a lawyer," I snapped.

"Ms. Parker can decide for herself if she needs a lawyer."

I jammed my fist into my hip. "Why are you here then? She's not here."

He sighed. "I'm here because I don't want to arrest an eighty-five-year-old woman who's home just burnt down on Christmas Eve and I know you've been poking around. Do you have something that will help?"

Aunt Rose was in dire straits if I was her last hope because Sergeant Scowl didn't have anything to suggest a different killer.

Chapter Seventeen

When Sergeant Scowl left, I wasn't sure what to do. I couldn't let him arrest or even threaten to arrest Aunt Rose. I needed to get something that would clear her, but what? The only ally she seemed to have who was around the night of the jamboree was Alice. Maybe she could remember something that would help my aunt.

I really should have been preparing the house for Aunt Rose's arrival, but what good would that do if she couldn't come home, so instead I drove to the other side of town and up into the hollows to visit Alice.

The hollows were densely wooded. The roads through them were narrow and curvy. When the area was settled, these features were highly valued by the people who wanted to live free and unencumbered by social rules and laws. This was especially true during prohibition when these hollows produced more illegal liquor than a modern-day distillery.

Today, the environment still worked for people who liked to be left alone, but it also isolated them. Alice and Tubby Filmore were two people who liked to be away from social norms. I suspect his unfortunate loss of money from Carl's scheme reinforced his desire to avoid the town folk.

Getting to Alice's house required driving deep into one of the many hollows and then getting off the main road onto a dirt road that traversed a gulch. I wondered if she ever worried about being swept off the road in a heavy rain or sliding off in sleet or snow.

The road went right to her house. Her car was out front and my only choice was to park in the road or around the other side of her shed. I hoped no bears were there.

The home was a rustic cabin that was tidy, yet tired looking. I walked up onto the porch and knocked on the door.

"Who is it?" Alice's voice wasn't welcoming and I imagined she had her shot gun pointed at me on the other side of the door.

I looked up and saw a security camera. I waved. "It's Sophie Parker, Ms. Filmore. I'm sorry to just drop in—"

The door swung open. "Sophie. Please come in." She set her gun next to the door. "You can never be too sure out here, you know?"

I nodded. Her living area was decorated in country kitsch, with lots of patchwork designs. The home smelled like meat in a slow cooker.

"What can I do for you? Is Rose alright?" she asked looking out the door like she was making sure the coast was clear, and then shut it.

"Yes. She's coming home later today unless Sergeant Scowl arrests her."

She shook her head with a tsk tsk. "It's a crime that he's focused on her."

"That's why I'm here. I'm hoping maybe you can remember something about that night that will help me convince him that she didn't kill Carl."

"I haven't remembered anything new, but have a seat and we can chat. Maybe you'll jog something loose. Would you like some pie? I know it's not like Rose's but—"

"I'm fine, thank you. I don't want to intrude more than necessary."

"How about some cider? I just have some warming now."

I got the feeling she really wanted me to have something to eat or drink, so I accepted her offer of cider. I wondered if she was lonely way out here. I could spare a little time if it would cheer her up.

She brought me mug of cider. I sipped and made an mmm sound. "It tastes like fall."

She smiled. "Thank you."

I licked my lips. "Are you experimenting with the flavors?"

She looked at me in a mix of confusion and perhaps offense. "Why?"

"This tastes more like what you gave me and Aunt Rose, but I just had some of your cider at the library, and it was a little different."

She waved a hand. "Sometimes I mix a little more cinnamon or other ingredients. Is it okay?"

"Oh yes. I didn't mean to imply it wasn't. I like that you have different nuanced flavors."

She laughed. "That's me. A cider connoisseur." She sat in her rocking chair with her own mug. "So, you're wanting me to remember the night of the jamboree." She squished her face and looked up as she thought. "I don't remember anything new."

"Carl taking Rose's whole pie was different."

She looked to her right and left as if she wanted to make sure no one could hear her, which was weird because we were alone in her house in the middle of a hollow where no one could hear anything.

She leaned toward me like she was telling me a secret. "Maybe I should have said something, but when Carl came into the kitchen to sneak his piece of Rose's pie, he was acting . . . strange."

"Like he was drunk?" That was one of the effects of the poison.

She nodded. "Yes. Mrs. Conner was not happy about that. You know she's a teetotaler."

That wasn't a word I heard much anymore except from the older folks. I think Aunt Rose called Carl one.

"Anyway, Carl seemed to have trouble with the knife to cut a piece, and so she said, 'Oh for heaven's sake Carl, just take the pie. I'll deal with Rose.'"

"She told him to take the pie?" I thought about that. Had Mrs. Conner's poisoned it? In retrospect, she was the most obvious suspect. She had the most contact with the pie. But why? As far as I could tell, she had no reason to want Carl dead.

Alice sat back in her chair. "Now I'm not saying she poisoned the pie, but it looks bad, doesn't it?"

I nodded wondering why this was a secret.

"I can't imagine her killing anyone can you? That's why I didn't say anything, but if you think it will help Rose . . . maybe I should come forward."

"It might." Although I hated getting Mrs. Conner in trouble especially if she was innocent.

"I'll call Lawson after Christmas," Alice said with conviction.

I grimaced, hoping Aunt Rose wasn't going to spend Christmas in the pokey, as she called it.

"Don't you worry, Sophie. Lawson won't put her in jail for Christmas. The optics of that would have the senior center running him out of town."

She was probably right. And it was clear he didn't want to put her in jail on Christmas either.

"Do you remember seeing Carl drink anything?" I asked, remembering that a beverage was the most likely source of the amount of poison needed to kill him.

She thought for a moment. "Well, there was the water during the contest."

"It wouldn't be that." I shook my head.

"It wouldn't be what?" she asked. "What does his having a drink have to do with anything?"

"I learned that there wasn't enough poison in the pie to cause Carl's death. So, the idea is he drank it sometime that night."

She pursed her lips. "Probably that grandson of his wanting his inheritance now."

I nodded. Why wouldn't Sergeant Scowl put him in the pokey for Christmas? Even so. What if I was wrong?

"So, you didn't see anyone offer him something to drink?"

"I know there was some enhanced eggnog served in one of the rooms outside of the main hall. I saw Rose there."

Rose and Earl had been keen on finding the spiked eggnog that night, but again, she wouldn't have poisoned him. Earl and Aggie were there. They'd have seen it—plus, Carl was over by the pie contest table—and he wasn't a drinker.

"Aunt Rose said he never drank. So, it had to be something else."

Alice shrugged. "I don't know. Drink your cider Sophie before it gets cold."

"Oh right." I leaned back to ponder what I knew and didn't know as I sipped the cider. I let out a breath feeling so tired. I wondered if that was a residual affect from the fire.

Alice stood. "I need to go check on my dinner. It's a pork roast. It's been cooking all day."

"Yes, of course. I should go."

"No. Not yet. Let me think for a moment. Maybe something will come to me. You could stay for dinner. I haven't had a dinner guest in a long time."

I wanted to go, but she'd been helpful and she was going to be alone on Christmas. It was the least I could do. In fact, maybe I'd invite her to Christmas with me and Rose. I realized that I hadn't heard from AJ. Would he be home tonight? Tomorrow was Christmas. *Focus on one thing, Soph.*

While Alice was checking her pork roast, I pulled out my phone and texted Sergeant Scowl telling him about what Alice said about Mrs. Conner. I found it hard to believe Mrs. Conner was a murderer, but maybe it would be enough to get Aunt Rose off the hook, at least today and tomorrow.

Alice returned with a kettle. "Can I warm up your cider?"

"Ah, yes please." I held out my mug which she refilled.

"Have you ever thought about moving closer to town?" I asked.

"Why would I?" She carried the kettle back to the kitchen and returned with her own mug refilled.

"You're so isolated out here." I cupped my mug, letting it warm my hands.

"I can take care of myself just fine," she smiled, but I heard annoyance in her voice.

"I didn't mean that. I just meant in terms of seeing friends."

She sat in her chair. "Oh, I suppose that would be nice, but I couldn't leave this place. This was Tubby's, you know. He's buried here. No, I couldn't leave him."

Although it was commonplace to bury people on their property in the old days, that wasn't normal now. Perhaps there was some grandfathered clause that allowed it on Tubby's family's property. Many older homes had family cemeteries where generations of people were buried.

I yawned and decided I'd stay a few more minutes and then leave. I didn't want to traverse the road when I was tired. In fact, maybe I'd splash some water on my face.

"Do you mind if I use your restroom?" I asked.

"Of course. It's the first door on the right."

I stood and took a minute to get my bearings. I wondered if there was more than cinnamon in the cider. The Filmore's had a long history of moonshine making after all.

I went into the bathroom, turning on the water splashing some on my face. I looked at myself in the mirror. My eyes appeared dull and my lids drooped some. But that was to be expected considering all I'd been through the last few days.

I walked out of the bathroom, turning right instead of left by accident and going down the hall. When I realized my mistake, I turned around, and was distracted by the photos hanging on the wall. Most were of Alice. There were a couple from when she won the pie contest. In several she was holding up jugs of moonshine, like they'd just brewed a new batch. I could see why didn't want to leave. She clearly was attached to this place. Except . . . I moved from picture to picture and there was one thing missing: Tubby. Why didn't she have any pictures of him? *Weird.*

I made my way back to the living area. Alice wasn't there, so I hunted her down in the kitchen. She was pouring the cider from kettle down the sink. Weird, although maybe it wasn't as good reheated.

My stomach growled at the delicious scent of her roast in the slow cooker. I looked over toward it sitting on the counter next to the stove. I went over to inspect it. I wondered what spices she used for the rub. I picked up the bottle next to it to read what it was she'd used. I had to squint my eyes as the print blurred. Diaz . . . Diazepam.

I frowned. What spice was that? I shook my head. I felt like I had cotton in my brain.

"Ah . . . Sophie . . . you should haven't have come in here."

"Why?" I turned but while my shoulders moved, my feet stayed in place. I was falling but I couldn't get my body to react.

As I went down, I looked over at Alice. "You?"

I hit the floor. I'm sure I hit hard, but I couldn't feel anything. I could barely see.

She huffed out a breath as she leaned over me. "Why couldn't you have left well enough alone?"

"Did you poison me?" At least that was what I wanted to ask. My mouth didn't seem to be working.

"Come on. Let's get you in your car so you can drive home."

"I can't drive." What I heard was, "I iiii cc . . .drv . . ."

"I can't have you falling asleep forever here. People might get suspicious."

"Why?"

She squatted down and put her hands under my arms, lifting me until I was sitting. My body felt like a giant limp noodle.

"Oh dear. I should have let you leave earlier. How are we going to get you to your car?"

"Why?" I asked again.

"Why do you need to get in to your car? So, you can drive off the road and have a terrible tragic accident."

"Why?" I tried to shake my head to clear the fog, but it was seeped into every crevice of my brain. I was going to die. I probably should have been more scared than I was, but I was too tired. "I need sleep."

"You'll be sleeping forever soon. Goodness. Why couldn't you have just died with Rose in the fire?"

"You?"

"Of course, me."

"Why?" *Did I ask that already?*

"If things had gone as planned, Rose would already be in jail for murder. It wasn't Mrs. Conner who gave him the pie, it was me. And to answer your question, I gave Carl a glass of cider filled with antifreeze.

I was trying to sweet talk him into swinging the contest so I'd win, that way when Rose lost it would have given her even more motive to poison him. He didn't take the bribe, but he did drink the cider. It was the best cider he ever had. He told me it was too bad I couldn't bake a pie as good as my cider. I got the last judgement on him."

"He was bad to you and Tubby." I got why she'd want to kill Carl but why me and Aunt Rose?

She dragged me along the kitchen floor. "Tubby." Her tone was filled with disgust. "Idiot man. Killing him with his beloved still was the best thing I could have done for him."

My brain wasn't working very well, but still well enough to know that I was going to die. Did I think that already?

"And Rose . . . that old bitty. My pies were every bit as good if not better, but Carl was sweet on her. God knows why. Then again, he was a terrible person. Maybe they were meant to be."

"Rose isn't terrible."

"Kill two birds with one stone. Carl dead and Rose in jail. That was the plan."

"You burnt my house down." I tried to twist to look her in the face so she could see how angry I was. She jerked me straight again and continued to drag me to the door.

"I couldn't have you and Rose snooping about. It wasn't hard. Once the cider put you to sleep all I had to do was go through the backdoor that I unlocked earlier when I was there, disable the alarms and set the fire."

"How . . . the alarms?"

"I got a chair," she said it with a tone that sounded like "duh". "You two were out like a light. I took out the batteries, put the chair back, set the fire and waited for you to die of smoke inhalation or burning. No one would know you'd taken sleeping pills. Or if they did, they'd think it was the stress you and Rose were under about Carl's murder and her being a suspect. This time I'm not making a mistake. Although perhaps I've given you too much. Really Sophie, you need to stand up."

"My legs don't work." How come what I was saying wasn't coming out right? I sounded like the teacher in a Peanuts cartoon.

A ringing sound went off and Alice dropped me.

"Who could that be?" She left me and walked over to look at small box on her wall.

I flopped back. My head landed with a bang, but I didn't feel it. That couldn't be a good sign.

"It's a sheriff's deputy." Alice ran back to me. "Get up, Sophie."

"Can't I just sleep here?"

"I've got a nice bed upstairs. But you have to stand up." She grabbed me under the arms again and jerked me up. Somehow, I got my feet under me, but they didn't work very well. She half dragged me to the stairs. "There's a bed up there. You can sleep as long as you want."

I fell forward, but my hands were there. Like magic.

"Crawl up, Sophie."

I did what she asked, but I felt like I was moving through marshmallows. Eventually I reached the top and she pulled me into the first room. With a final hoist she pushed me on the bed.

I sank back, grateful for the soft mattress. I closed my eyes.

"That's right, Sophie. Go to sleep. I'll deal with your body later."

"Thank you." Somewhere in the back of my mind that didn't sound right. My body?

I lay half wanting sleep to come and half terrified that it would. Something was wrong.

A clomping sound emanated from outside the window. Then there was a knock.

"Sergeant Davis. What a surprise," Alice said cheerfully.

I know him.

"I'm sorry to bother you Ms. Filmore, but I had a couple of questions about Carl Jackson's murder," he said.

"You know I'll always help the sheriff's department although I'm surprised that you're here. It's Christmas Eve."

"I know and I'm sorry about that. But this is important. I need to talk with you."

"Of course, come in," Alice said. "Can I get you something to drink?"

"No," I mumbled. Don't have something to drink.

"No ma'am. I'm fine."

"Well, what brings you here?" Alice asked.

"I wanted to see if you remembered anything about the night of the jamboree."

"I see. You haven't by chance been talking to Sophie Parker, have you?"

"Is there something?" he pushed.

"Maybe she texted you? She was here earlier you know and I told her that I did remember something. I was going to call you after Christmas."

"I'm here now, so you can tell me know."

"Yes, of course." Alice proceeded to tell him about how Carl was acting strange and so Mrs. Conner told him to take the pie. Except that wasn't right? Didn't she just tell me that she was the one who told him to take the pie?

My brain felt like it was fighting with itself. Don't sleep. Don't sleep.

"Are you saying you think Mrs. Conner poisoned the pie?" he asked.

That's Sergeant Scowl, I finally realized.

"Oh, I couldn't say. But she did have the most access to it."

"Did she serve him anything to drink as well?"

"I suppose it's possible. Mrs. Conner is very friendly that way."

I rolled over falling off the bed, landing on my shoulder. Luckily that didn't hurt either. If I lived, I'd probably be battered and bruised.

"What was that?" he asked.

"Oh. I have a cat. He's fat and frequently knocks things over. I'll check on it later."

"I guess I'll leave you to your Christmas Eve. Thank you for your time," Sergeant Scowl said.

"Not a problem, Lawson. I hope you have a lovely holiday."

The door opened. Adrenaline shot through me as I realized this was it. If I didn't let him know I was here, I was dead for sure. Perhaps I was already dead. Carl was dead after drinking the cider the night of the jamboree even though his death hadn't come until the next day. Was I going to have a whole night of this disorientation too before I complained about seeing snow and with a final gasp keeled over? Except no . . . that was antifreeze that killed Carl. Alice gave me diazepam. I didn't feel drunk. I felt so, so tired.

I dragged myself to the window. I hoisted myself up until my forearms rested on the sill. I used my forehead to bang on the window. Another possible bruise if I lived.

"That's not a cat," he said.

Thank God.

"Oh . . . whoa Ms. Filmore. What's going on? Put the gun down."

"I'm sorry Lawson, but I can't do that."

Oh no. She had her gun on him. I lost my strength and slid like slime down the wall. I had to do something. My head felt like Westley's in the *Princess Bride* before the magic medicine fixed him. It was a lead weight. I turned to look for anything I could use to help him or me. There was nothing I could reach. I turned to the left toward the bed. On a short bedside table was an alarm clock.

I flung my arm and did my best to grip it. I twisted my body, and fell onto my back facing the window. I gripped the clock in both hands and threw it as hard as I could and prayed.

A bang and then the sound of broken glass filled the room.

"What the—"

There was a scuffle and a gun shot. I squeezed my eyes shut worried that I'd just had Sergeant Scowl killed. I would be joining him soon in heaven and I was sure he'd have a few choice words for me.

I lay on the floor and waited for my fate. I wished I could talk to AJ again and tell him that I loved him. And hug Aunt Rose to tell her she was the strongest person I knew. I would have liked to have seen my brother and father one more time. And Bull . . . I'd have done anything to see him and Aunt Rose cooking in the new kitchen.

Footsteps sounded up the stairs.

I closed my eyes. If I fell asleep now, I wouldn't feel anything, right?

"Sophie? Oh Jesus, Sophie."

That wasn't Alice.

Strong arms lifted me. I had a sense of déjà vu. I lifted my lids, which was no easy feat since they were made of lead. But yes, I'd been here before. Sergeant Scowl had saved me, carried me, like this once already.

"What did she do to you? Poison?" he asked.

I nodded my head, it flopped side to side. He carried me down the stairs.

"Kitchen."

"What's in the kitchen?" He carried me in there and I pointed toward the slow cooker. Somehow, he managed to find the pills and pick them. "She gave you these?"

My head flopped forward, my chin hitting my chest.

"Let's get you to a hospital."

"Alice?"

"She's cuffed in the car." He rushed out, and put me in the passenger seat. He put my seatbelt over me and then shut the door. I leaned my head against the window, liking the cool glass on my temple.

"Sleep Sophie," Alice said from the back.

"Don't listen to her, Sophie." Sergeant Scowl poked a button and my window went down. My head fell onto the door frame.

"Alice, another word like that it will be used against you. I've already Mirandized you."

The SUV roared to life and Sergeant Scowl drove. When we got to the main road, sirens came on. The wind blew in my face as he drove down the mountain. It sort of felt like flying. I closed my eyes, wanting to savor that feeling.

"Sophie! Don't go to sleep."

I didn't want to sleep and yet I did. Pretty soon, sleep won out.

Chapter Eighteen

My eyes fluttered open, or at least I think they did. Darkness surrounded me. Was I dead? If so, where was the white light? I heard snoring. Did God snore—or the devil?

"Hello?" My voice was weak and scratchy.

There was a shuffle. "Sophie?"

A low light came on next to my bed illuminating a bulldog-faced man.

"Sergeant Scowl?"

He smiled. "Yes. It's Sergeant Scowl."

"Are we dead?"

"No. You're going to be fine."

If that was the case, why was he here and not AJ or Aunt Rose?

"What happened?"

"Once again, you solved the mystery but nearly died. I wish you'd stop doing that," he said.

"Sorry."

He let out a long breath almost like he'd been holding it in for a long time. "Alice Filmore killed Carl Jackson."

Somewhere in my scattered thoughts I think she told me that.

"She tried to kill you and your aunt in the fire."

"She gave us spiked cider," I said as that memory filtered up into my consciousness.

"She tried to overdose you on a sedative. Luckily, I got you here in time. You're going to be fine."

"You're not arresting Aunt Rose?"

He shook his head. "No. I'd been trying to decide if I should arrest her as she left the hospital or wait. I didn't think she was a flight risk, but then I remembered your mother."

My mother had taken off to parts unknown once it was clear my father was going to jail. "She didn't do it. Aunt Rose I mean."

"I got your text. You know when I came to you this morning to ask what you knew, I wasn't telling you to go out and get information. But after I got your text and knowing you have a propensity to find the right answers, I visited Alice to hear her account about Mrs. Conner."

I had a vague memory of being stuck in a room and hearing him and Alice talking. "How'd you know I was there?"

He laughed. "You don't remember? You made a noise upstairs. At that, Alice pulled her shotgun on me and then a clock radio came through the window. Damn near hit me, but it distracted Alice long enough for me to disarm her. I cuffed her and put her in the SUV and then went looking for you."

I smiled but since I felt loopy, it was probably a dopey looking smile. "You always show up on time."

"I wish you'd stop testing that theory. How do you feel?"

"Like I was nearly burned a few days ago and then drugged today."

He smiled. "Well, Merry Christmas, Sophie. You have your life and your health. Now get some rest."

"What about Aunt Rose? I was supposed to bring her home. Who has her?" I gripped the sheet to get out of bed.

He pushed it back. "She's fine." He nodded to the other side of the room. I followed his gaze. In the next bed, Aunt Rose slept. My heart filled with such warmth and happiness to see her there.

"You both will be released tomorrow morning. I'll be happy to drive you both home if you need it."

I wished AJ was there. "Can you call Bull?"

"Bull?"

"Cornelius? He'll take care of us."

He nodded. "I'll call him first thing in the morning. Right now, you and Rose need your rest."

"I will wake up, right?" Exhaustion pulled at me to sleep, but I didn't want to succumb if there was still a chance Alice's drugs would kill me.

He laughed softly. "You'll live to be in the way of my job again."

I closed my eyes and this time sleep didn't scare me.

- - - - - - - -

The next morning, a loud crash woke me, followed by Aunt Rose's voice. "You can't keep me in this bed, Doreen."

I opened my eye to find a nurse, Doreen, trying to get Aunt Rose back in her bed.

"Ms. Parker, let us help you. We don't want you falling and needing you to stay longer."

It sounded like Aunt Rose had overstayed her welcome. The kerfuffle with her ended abruptly when Bull came barging in.

"Miss Sophie, Ms. Rose."

"Sir you can't—" She stopped when Bull picked up Aunt Rose and put her back in bed.

"What are you doing?" Aunt Rose fussed at him. "I need to check on Sophie."

"I'm fine," I said. Love filled my chest to see them both. If only AJ was here too.

"The two of you are going to be the death of me," Bull said, letting out an exasperated breath, which sounded closer to a snort, sort of like a Bull.

"When can we blow this place?" Aunt Rose said.

"I'm going to do the best I can to have your discharge papers ready ASAP." Doreen came over to me. She poked and prodded. "Everything looks okay." She did a couple of tests, that apparently, I passed. "I'll go let the doctor know you two are ready to go."

"I hope so. It's Christmas. Merry Christmas, Ms. Rose and Miss Sophie." Bull pulled out two packages from the bag he carried.

"What's this?" I asked.

"Something to get you both home in."

"We're not going to fit on your motorcycle," Aunt Rose told him.

"I brought a car, Ms. Rose."

"Car. Where's my car?" How was it possible I kept losing my car this week?

"I told Sergeant Davis I'd take care of it. You know Sophie, you shouldn't park your car out of sight when you visit homicidal maniacs."

I smirked, but then I smiled because I was happy to be alive even if I was also sad that AJ wasn't here.

"Have you talked to AJ?"

Bull rolled his eyes. "I suspect he'll never leave town again. He and Patch got the plane, and had landed in Richmond when I got the call from the sheriff investigator about you being almost drugged to death and now here in the hospital. He and Patch are driving back to the office and then he'll head here. I told him to meet us at the house. We've got you a new home, Ms. Rose. Did Miss Sophie tell you?"

"What if I don't like this house?" Aunt Rose harumphed.

"Then you'll find a new one. Now open your presents." Bull motioned with his hand toward the gifts.

I tore the paper and pulled out a green sweat suit with a reindeer on it. I laughed and looked over at Aunt Rose. She had a red sweat suit with Santa on it.

"We're going to look ridiculous, but thank you anyway, Bull," Aunt Rose said.

- - - - - - - -

Our discharges took an hour, which was shorter than most hospital discharges I'd experienced but longer than I'd wanted. Bull helped us in his car, me in the back and Aunt Rose upfront.

Then he drove us out of town and up to the lake. It snowed lightly last night, just enough to dust the trees and ground.

"Can we see the house?" Aunt Rose asked.

"It's Christmas, Ms. Rose. Let's go another time." Bull reached over and patted her knee. I was glad Bull said it as I thought she'd be more likely to listen to him.

When we exited the main road onto the lake road, I could feel the tension rise in Aunt Rose. She'd lived her whole life in town, so heading into the country would be hard for her.

"Oh lordy," she said when the road changed from paved to gravel.

"Don't you worry, Ms. Rose. You're gonna like this place. I just know it." Bull glanced at her with a big smile. I had a feeling he was willing her to have a good attitude.

When we pulled up to the house, I was disappointed not to see AJ's truck. That's when I wondered about Dutch.

"Where's Dutch?" AJ would never forgive me if something happened to her.

"Who's Dutch?" Aunt Rose asked.

"Dutch is fine. She's inside AJ's place," Bull said. "I had her last night when you didn't come home. I knew you had to be in some sort of trouble." He gave me a pursed lip shake of his head. "I left her here this morning. Now. Shall we see your new place?"

"Might as well," Aunt Rose grumbled. I wished she'd be more excited but I knew her well enough to know that she was afraid. Change was never easy.

Bull helped us both out and with Aunt Rose's arm in his, he escorted her to the door. He unlocked it and pushed it open.

"Welcome home, Ms. Rose."

Aunt Rose stepped inside and I held my breath for her response. "You did all this?"

"Well, AJ arranged it and I helped get it delivered and set up," he said.

Aunt Rose looked at us and I saw tears in her eye. She quickly turned away. "I want to see my room."

Bull grinned at me but was more serious when he turned back to her. "Right this way."

I followed them. Aunt Rose wandered around the room. The moment drew out and finally, she said, "I think this will be fine."

"You haven't even seen the kitchen yet," Bull said. "You might want to reserve judgement until then."

I snickered.

We made our way to the kitchen.

"Is that a new mixer?" Aunt Rose asked as she went straight to the pretty pastel pink mixing machine.

"Yes. It's all new. And we've even got ingredients to bake. If you're up to it," Bull said.

Her eyes narrowed. "Don't you have family that you need to be with?"

"Yes, I do." He looked between me and Aunt Rose. I knew Bull had a mother, but she lived in Florida, so I guess we were his family.

"There's lasagna in the freezer from Aggie. And a few extra things," I said.

Bull's eyes narrowed. "It's Christmas. We're having the fixings."

We didn't have the fixings. Mrs. Wayland had said dinner would be brought to us, but I hadn't heard from her. I had my new phone as thankfully, Sergeant Scowl had collected my purse from Alice's house. I pulled out my phone, but didn't see any texts or messages.

"Did you talk to Mrs. Wayland?" I asked Bull.

"Don't you worry about anything, Miss Sophie. It's all good. Now, first, we need to make dessert. We can make pumpkin or apple pie. Or cookies."

"Pumpkin pie," Aunt Rose said, rubbing a hand over the new mixer.

I left them to bake. I checked the tree and found a few more presents than what had been under there from the library party. Bull clearly had been by earlier or maybe last night.

I checked for texts or messages from AJ, but there wasn't any from him either. I tried not to be disappointed, but it was hard.

"I'm going to get Dutch," I said, leaving the house and going next door. When I opened the door, Dutch was waiting for me with her version of a hug. To think, not so long ago, I'd been afraid she'd eat me.

"Merry Christmas, Dutch." I scratched her head. "I have a present for you. Come on." I wasn't sure how Aunt Rose would deal with Dutch, but they'd have to meet eventually since we were neighbors.

When Dutch got outside, she ran around a bit and then trotted up to me as I headed back to my and Aunt Rose's house.

"We're back."

Dutch saw Bull and rushed to him.

"Great day in the morning . . . what it that?" Aunt Rose screeched.

"This is Dutch, Ms. Rose. She's AJ's dog. Isn't she a beauty?"

"That can't be a dog. Surely it's too big." Aunt Rose's eyes narrowed as she studied Dutch, that is until Dutch walked over to her, backing her into the corner of the counter. As if she knew Aunt Rose's fear, Dutch dropped to a sit and simply stared at her.

"What's she doing?" Aunt Rose's eyes darted between Bull and Dutch.

"She's making friends, Ms. Rose," Bull said. "You can pat her on the head."

"She won't eat me?"

I snorted.

"Don't laugh at me Sophie Parker," Aunt Rose snapped.

"I'm not laughing at you. I'm laughing because I thought the same thing when I met her. She is really sweet. Mrs. Kaczynski used to watch her when AJ was out town."

Aunt Rose tentatively reached out her hand and patted Dutch on the head. Dutch's head bobbed up and down and then she lay on the ground.

"What is she doing now?"

"She likes you," Bull said. "But she's in the way. We've got baking to finish."

I called Dutch to come with me into the living room. I was tired and thought I'd rest a bit. I wasn't sure how Bull was going to pull off a full Christmas dinner but I wouldn't worry about it.

I lay on the couch and Dutch lay on the floor with her head on the couch next to me.

I don't know how long I was there when the door bust open. For a minute, I worried that Alice wasn't our murder and instead the real murderer showed up.

"Sophie!" The next minute, arms were around me and I was held tightly.

"AJ?"

"Who else would it be holding you like this?" he murmured into my hair.

"Just you."

He leaned back and looked at me like he was inventorying me to make sure I was okay. "I'm sorry I wasn't here."

"You were working." I leaned into him again because he smelled good and made me feel safe.

"I wanted to be home two days ago, but—"

"You're here now." I looked up at him. "Merry Christmas."

"Merry Christmas, baby." His lips touched mine. His kiss was soft and gentle, and any residual effects of Alice and the drugs dissipated because he was here.

"None of that nonsense," Aunt Rose chastised.

AJ pulled away and stood. "Ms. Parker. Merry Christmas."

"Merry Christmas AJ. I understand I have you to thank for getting me and Sophie a home."

"I hope you like it. Of course, you can make any changes you want."

AJ's expression was apprehensive as Aunt Rose walked over to him. She reached up and held his face. "You're a good boy, for a Devlin."

He smiled. "Thank you."

He let out a relieved breath when she turned and went back to the kitchen.

"You don't need to be with your family?" I asked.

"My brother and sister aren't here, and my mother has a new beau at the home. She's spending it with him."

"Did you bring the dinner?" Bull said appearing from the kitchen.

AJ nodded. "I picked it up from Mrs. Wayland and it's in the car."

"I'll help you bring it in," I said.

Dutch was up bouncing around us as we walked outside. When we got to AJ's car, he pulled me to him again and this time, his kiss packed a bigger punch.

"Please stop scaring me like this, Sophie," he murmured against my cheek.

"Okay."

He lifted his head and looked at me. "Okay? Are you sure?"

"It's not like I go looking for trouble."

He kissed my nose. "No. Trouble likes to find you."

Somehow, AJ got his hands on all the Christmas fixins; turkey and stuffing, potatoes, green beans, biscuits, and cranberry sauce.

That evening, we feasted; me, Aunt Rose, Bull and AJ. We weren't a traditional family, and yet, it felt like family.

After dinner, we opened presents.

Aunt Rose cried when she opened the pearls. "My pearls had been my mothers," she said, and I wondered if maybe this wasn't a good present. "Thank you, Sophie. I will treasure them."

AJ strutted around in his new bomber jacket. Bull did the same in his biker donut apron. Bull had bought Aunt Rose a similar apron, with biking grannies on it. AJ gave her a jewelry box to hold the pearls I'd bought her.

"I'm sorry, boys, that I don't have anything for you" she said.

"That pie was enough," AJ said. "It's not every day you get to eat a Rose Parker pie."

She smiled so bright. That alone made my day.

AJ gave me a new beautiful fairy tale book and Bull gave me a pretty scarf with famous books on it, like *Pride and Prejudice* and *Jane Eyre*.

The presents from the library staff contained household items like dish towels, cooking utensils, and other items that under normal circumstances would seem boring, but for us, they were invaluable.

When we finished, we had hot chocolate, vowing to never have cider again.

"You missed a present," AJ said, nodding to the tree.

"Did I?" It was hard to tell because there was so much wrapping paper.

AJ grabbed a small square box from underneath the back of the tree and handed it to me. I looked for a tag, but there was none.

"I wonder who it's for?"

"I wonder," Bull quipped.

I looked at him, feeling like I was missing the joke.

"Why don't you just open it," AJ suggested.

Why not? I pulled the ribbon off and opened the box. Inside was a velvet jewelry box. I dumped it out, and felt the slide of anticipation run up my spine.

I looked at AJ. He bit his lip. "Open it."

I flipped the lid open. Inside a plump pinkish stone sat in a rose gold setting decorated with small diamonds, and filigree vines and flowers that made me think of a fairy tale.

I gasped and looked at AJ.

He swallowed and got on one knee.

"Oh my," Aunt Rose said.

I bit my lip trying not to cry and also not to say yes before I was sure what this was.

"I love you, Sophie." AJ took the ring from the box. "I picked this because it made me think of you. Of how you love true love and fairy tales. Of how loyal you are to those you love. Of how dainty yet fierce you are. I'm no prince charming—"

"You're mine."

He grinned at me. "Then will you marry me?"

"Yes." Finally. I threw my arms around him.

He laughed and Bull and Aunt Rose clapped.

"That deserves champagne." Bull rose from his chair.

"Do we have champagne?" Aunt Rose asked.

"Of course," Bull said heading to the kitchen.

"You've been holding out Bull. Is there bourbon in that cupboard too?"

"Why Ms. Rose, you don't think I would forget your bourbon do you?"

While Bull and Aunt Rose were busy in the kitchen, all my focus and love was on AJ.

He slipped the ring on my finger. "This isn't a diamond except for these little stones. This pink one is morganite. It seemed like something a fairytale warrior princess would wear."

"I love it. I love you, Flyboy." I wrapped my arms around him again.

"Merry Christmas, Sophie."

- - - - - - - -

Later that night, after Aunt Rose went to bed and Bull and Dutch crashed in the guest room, AJ and I walked back to his house.

"Do you think you can make it through the rest of the year without getting involved in murder or almost getting killed?" He held my hand as we crossed the space between our two homes.

"What's that? A week? Hopefully."

When we got to his door, he scooped me up and carried me inside. "I'm going to like having you as a neighbor. Even better, when you're my wife."

"It turned out well that Aunt Rose is next door," I said.

"I worried you would never marry me if she wasn't."

I studied him. "Did you think of having her there even before our house burnt down?"

He nodded. "Yes. When Mrs. Kaczynski told me that she planned to sell the house and move, the first thing I thought of was having you and Rose up here, although I wasn't sure I'd succeed. Rose's house has been in the family for generations. I hate that you lost everything, but I can't deny being glad things worked out."

"Me too." It was a reminder of what was important. Rose and I lost a lot of stuff, but tonight we had everything we needed in AJ and Bull.

He carried me to his room.

I thought about all the money he had to have spent to put a down payment on the house and buy this ring. "Is that why you were working so much? To buy a ring and house?"

"A little. Mostly, I wanted to be financially sound and settled before I proposed."

"Why didn't you tell me?" I asked as he lay me on his bed.

"Because proposals are supposed to be surprises."

I looped my arms around his neck. "I'm sorry I doubted you."

"I hope you never doubt me again."

I stared up into his blue eyes and ran my fingers through his auburn hair. "This fairy tale is so much better than the books."

He waggled his brows. "We're only just getting started.

Jenna Harte loves to write about crime and passion. She is the author of the Sophie Parker Coupon Mystery series featuring a fairy tale loving, coupon clipping sleuth. She also writes the Valentine Mysteries, the first of which, Deadly Valentine, reached the quarter-finals in Amazon's Breakthrough Novel Award in 2013. Along with mystery, she also writes romance with three books in her Southern Heat series.

She's a member of Sisters in Crime and the Virginia Writers Club. When she's not telling stories, she works by day as a ghost-writer and online entrepreneur. In her free time, she loves coffee, chocolate, books, and YouTube. She is an empty-nester living in central Virginia with her husband and a geriatric cat.